Four Days' Wonder

A. A. Milne

This edition published in 2023 by Farrago,
an imprint of Duckworth Books Ltd
1 Golden Court, Richmond, TW9 1EU, United Kingdom

www.farragobooks.com

First published in 1933 by Methuen & Co. Ltd.

A catalogue record for this book is available from the British Library.

Print ISBN: 978-1-78842-455-4
eISBN: 978-1-78842-456-1

Cover design and illustration by Emanuel Santos

Have you read them all?

Treat yourself to the Marvellous Milne series –

The Complete Short Stories
The first complete collection of A.A. Milne's short stories for grownups

Mr Pim
One of Milne's most popular works – a warm, funny, comedy
of manners with a happy ending

Two People
Reminiscent of Evelyn Waugh, this gentle novel considers how a relationship can work when those concerned have less in common than
they once thought.

Turn to the end of this book for a full list of the series.

TUESDAY

Chapter One

Return of Aunt Jane

I

When, on a fine June morning not so long ago, Jenny Windell let herself in with her latch-key at Auburn Lodge, and, humming dreamily to herself, drifted upstairs to the drawing-room, she was surprised to see the body of her Aunt Jane lying on a rug by the open door. It had been known for years, of course, that Aunt Jane would come to a bad end. Not only was her black hair cropped short like a boy's, but she smoked cigarettes out of a long red holder, and knew the Sitwells. Moreover, she acted on Sundays in plays which either meant nothing at all, which was silly, or meant what you thought they did, which was hardly possible. And it was said that she—but of course that wasn't true. After all, her father had served his King in India and the Windells had always been gentlefolk.

It was not surprising, then, that Aunt Jane should have been cut short like this; nor was it surprising that Jenny should drift upstairs and find a body in the drawing-room. Jenny was a well-read girl, and knew that people were continually drifting upstairs and finding bodies in the drawing-room. Only last night Michael Alloway, a barrister by profession, had found the body of a well-dressed woman on his hearthrug, with a note by its side which said 'A K 17 L P K 29 Friday'. What it meant Jenny would not know until to-night. Flitting from shop window to shop window this morning, or counter to counter, she had let her mind wander over the possibilities of adventure for herself in this romantic setting, so much more easily to be called up, when one was in fact in the Brompton Road, than the saddle-bows of an Arab sheikh. The body ... the handsome young detective ... the Old Bailey ... Jenny Windell in the box: Dramatic Evidence. (*Oh, good morning! No, I'm just looking round, thank you very much.*)

No, the surprising thing was that Aunt Jane should be at Auburn Lodge at all. She had not been near them for—let me see, Jenny, it must be nearly eight years. Happy years, had thought to herself Aunt Caroline (the Good One), for it was so much better that Jane should not come near Jenny. Being what she was, she would be bad for Jenny; put all the wrong ideas into her head. It was a great mercy that Jane had left Auburn Lodge for ever eight years ago.

And now Jane had come back to Auburn Lodge ... had met Jenny again after eight years ... was going to be very bad for Jenny, and put *all* the wrong ideas into her head.

II

'Oh!' said Jenny. And then 'Well!' And then, in surprise, 'Why, it's Aunt Jane!'

Even after eight years she never had a doubt. The sleek, black head, the absurd gipsy earrings, the ridiculously shaved eyebrows over the Chinese eyes, the sulky, over-red mouth, the notorious cigarette-holder, now lying broken on the floor, all these had been shared so long and so generously with those who read their peerage in the Sunday Papers, that any woman of them would have said at once: 'Why, it's Jane Latour!' The Sunday Papers did not come up to the drawing-room of Auburn Lodge;

not the 'Sunday Papers'. Mr. Garvin of the *Observer* came up because he was patriotic, and really doing his best for England; but that was different. It was more a National Organ. For the real Sunday Papers one had to go down to the kitchen ... and wait for Cook to say 'There's another little bit about yer aunt, Miss Jenny. I cut it out for you.' And from Cook's little bits, and from the illustrated papers over which her fair head drooped for the hairdresser, and from the childish memories of eight years ago, Jenny had now in her mind as complete a picture of her Aunt Jane as any niece could wish.

It was a picture which, to Jenny, had all the attraction and repulsion of her first, and last, cocktail. That had been called a White Lady, which was something nobody would dream of calling Aunt Jane. Aunt Jane was a Red-and-black Lady. In as far as she was a well-known actress, one could say carelessly: 'Oh, yes, that's my aunt,' and wait for the envious 'Really?' In as far as she was notorious in other ways, one could say hurriedly: 'Well, actually she *is* a sort of relation, but—' and wait for the reluctant change of subject. What really irritated Jenny (when she thought about it) was that she was never quite sure what Aunt Jane had *done*. Aunt Caroline had explained to her once what Jane had *not* done, but she felt that there should have been more to it than that. After all, anybody might marry a French Count, and then find that he wasn't a Count, and that you hadn't married him, and that all that was left of him was that he was undoubtedly (oh, but *undoubtedly*) French. You wouldn't go on having bits in the paper about yourself, just because of a mistake like that. Would you, Aunt Caroline?

'My dear,' said Aunt Caroline, 'that was not all.'

'All what?'

'It is not a pleasant subject for a sister to discuss; it is not a pleasant subject for a girl of sixteen to discuss. My methods of bringing you up, Jenny, may be old-fashioned, but, to use an old-fashioned word, I want you to grow up a lady. We will now talk of something else.'

'Did Aunt Jane grow up a lady?'

'Aunt Jane', said Caroline proudly, 'would always be a lady whatever she did. She is a Windell.'

It occurred to Jenny that she also was a Windell and would therefore always be a lady whatever she did, even if she did all that Aunt Jane had done, whatever that was, so why—

'Touch the bell, please, and we will have tea. Is that a ladder coming in your stocking? Let me look. Yes. You had better go and change them now, and then you can mend them afterwards.'

So it was left to Jenny and her great friend Nancy to decide (over a box of chocolates) what Aunt Jane was doing. Jenny decided that she took Snow in Large and Increasing Quantities. Nancy decided that she played the harp with nothing on before All the Crowned Heads of Europe. Then they talked about something else.

And now, two years later, Aunt Jane was in the drawing-room of Auburn Lodge, and Jenny still didn't know what she was doing.

III

Jenny's first thought was 'How exciting!'—and then remorsefully 'Oh, but poor Aunt Jane!'—and then, being a sensible girl, she thought that, if it were really all true, all that was said, perhaps it was as well that Aunt Jane should be cut off before she could take still more snow, and play the harp before still more Crowned Heads, and perhaps even Presidents, with nothing on. And she thought that, since neither of these could be nice things to do, because anything up the nose was rather sickish, and the other would be very, very embarrassing, particularly if Presidents looked like their photographs in the papers, why, even Aunt

Jane must be glad that it was now all over. So, feeling a little excited again, she looked about the floor to see if there were any messages in cipher from the heads of any of the Greatest Criminal Organizations in Europe. Because, if so …

But there were none. Worse than that (or, as one would say, fortunately) there was no evidence of any sort of crime. Aunt Jane's high heels had slipped on the parquet floor, she had fallen to the ground, and her head had hit heavily against a valuable old brass door-stop. Nobody was to blame.

Jenny's next thought was to pick up the door-stop and restore it to its usual place upon the grand piano. The door-stop, which Aunt Caroline had previously picked up in Whitstable, was a representation of a slice of Conway Castle, and, though not actually beautiful, bore enough resemblance to a slice of Conway Castle to be ostensibly attractive rather than useful, and, as such, entitled to a place upon the piano, where it could be appreciated in comfort, rather than upon the floor, where it could only be appreciated when lying down. Jenny, then, picked this up; but noticing that it was a little stained, she did not immediately return it to its place between the General and Lord Roberts (under whom he had, at one time, served), but wiped it carefully first with her pocket-handkerchief. Then, since the handkerchief was also stained now, she made a little face at it and dropped it for the moment upon a chair, while she wondered what next she ought to do.

She had no time to wonder. There was a noise of a door opening below; there was a noise of voices on the stairs; and suddenly the awful realization swept over Jenny Windell, leaving her hot and cold, and red and white, sending her heart hotly up into her throat and then coldly down into her stomach, the awful realization that she had no business to be here at all—that six months ago she, too, had left Auburn Lodge for ever.

Chapter Two
Beginnings of Jenny

I

General Sir Oliver Windell, K.C.B., and so forth, was too good a Victorian to wish to survive his Queen. He had died, therefore, in March 1901; a little to the relief of the War Office (which had had him on its hands all through the Boer War) and greatly to the relief of his three children. Their attitude must have appealed strongly to the General, who had always deprecated damned sentimental nonsense.

The eldest child, and presumably the most relieved, was Caroline. She was twenty-seven, and for the last four years had been chatelaine of Auburn Lodge, thus enjoying not only the privileges of a daughter, but the daytime benefits of a wife. The second child was Young Oliver, who had had the advantage of attending a boarding-school during the greater part of those four years. He was now seventeen. The third child was Jane. She was seven, an age at which one can take refuge in the nursery and be damned by proxy.

This recurring interval of ten years between their births, which gave them the air of an Arithmetical Progression, and, as such, seemed to evidence some profound, but slightly unreasonable, military design on the part of the General, was in fact inevitable. When Caroline was one, she and her mother, in accordance with precedent, were returned to England. Here they settled down at Auburn Lodge, and waited anxiously for the General to join them on leave. Their anxiety was unnecessary. His unique capacity for provoking, and subsequently quelling, outbreaks of religious enthusiasm, kept him so occupied that it was not until eight years later that he could resume family life. Even now it was not safe for him to leave the country: Elaine was ordered to put Caroline out to school and join him at Chukrapoota. She obeyed; and within two years was able to escape again to England, this time with Young Oliver. Feeling more satisfied with her now, for the thought of some future India without a Windell was repugnant to him, the General returned to duty. Another eight years of religious enthusiasm followed, and Young Oliver was of age to be put out. But Fate intervened. The General was ordered home to receive the rewards due to him. He and her ladyship spent the winter together in the South of France; and when at last the uncanny quiet of India summoned him urgently back, it was obviously unwise for her ladyship to accompany him. She remained at Auburn Lodge; she died at Auburn Lodge four years later; and a General whose genius for provoking outbreaks had outlived his capacity for quelling them hastened home to protect his motherless children.

His first duty to them was to change the name of the house from Auburn Lodge to Simla. Caroline, lacking as yet the experience of the border tribes, dared to oppose him. She asked Why? The General replied shortly that one was a damned silly name and the other wasn't. Young Oliver, essaying his first schoolboy joke in the presence of the Indian Empire, murmured that anyhow the other sounded very Simla. When this had been explained to his father and Oliver had been sent to bed, the General announced that all this damned nonsense would now stop, and that Caroline would kindly oblige him by taking down a letter to the Postmaster-General; at that time a Mr. Hanbury.

Caroline obliged. The letter, a dignified compromise between the first and third persons, was dispatched; and in due course, and entirely in the third person, Mr. Hanbury regretted that it was impossible to adopt Sir Oliver's suggestion. The General, who was unaccustomed to having his commands mistaken for suggestions, then dictated a strong letter to *The Times*, but Mr. Hanbury was again too much for him. The letter was not delivered. Young Oliver, now up and back at school, did what he could for his father, without wasting a stamp, by writing every Sunday to:

Miss Windell
Simla
(née Auburn Lodge*)*
Brompton Road, S.W.—

but this was found not to be helpful. The General, in fact, was defeated.

Caroline was twenty-three, but not beautiful. The General looked over *The Times* at her across the breakfast-table, and felt uneasily that her face was familiar in some damned way; as indeed it was, for he had shaved something like it every morning for years. She was a Windell. Jane was not; but Jane was only three, and her future was not yet written on her face. Nurse said she would be a beauty when she grew up, but the General abandoned hope afresh with every inspection of Caroline over *The Times*. The Providence which had supervised so long and so wisely the suppression of religious enthusiasm on the Frontier had betrayed him now. Here he was, with that damned bloody feller in the Government, and the whole damned country all over the place, and in ten years' time he'd just be that poor old feller with the two damned ugly daughters.

Well, he supposed he must provide for them, for God knew no husband was likely to do it. Better leave 'em the house, and they could live in it together, two old maids with a tabby and a damned canary ...

He sent for Mr. Watterson, and issued his instructions. True to his tradition of never recognizing defeat, particularly when committing anything officially to paper, he bequeathed Simla to the absolute joint use and benefit of his two daughters, together with a sufficient sum for the proper upkeep of the same. Mr. Watterson was, not unnaturally, surprised at the munificence of the gift, and a little doubtful as to the validity of the title.

'Are you in fact,' he asked, 'I mean is it really—I had always understood that Simla—' and he tried to remember if anything in the lives of Warren Hastings and Clive formed a reliable precedent.

'This house', said the General coldly, 'is called Simla.'

Mr. Watterson, who had thought it was called all that messuage and hereditament known as Auburn Lodge, coughed and said: 'Quite, quite.'

'Then is that clear?' asked the General.

'Perfectly, my dear Sir Oliver,' said a greatly relieved Mr. Watterson.

So that was how Jenny's two aunts, Caroline and Jane, came to live together at Auburn Lodge. For the General's prophecy was correct; no husband ever did provide for them. But it is doubtful if, for that reason, Jane Latour could properly be regarded as an old maid.

II

Sir Oliver was not buried in the Abbey. He had expressed a wish to be put away without any of this damned flummery, and his wish was respected. All the obituary notices spoke highly of his services to the country, in some cases instancing what these were. High Commanding Officers had been under a cloud for the last eighteen months, and it was not difficult to feel enthusiasm for a General who had never been nearer to South Africa than the South of France, and now could never go. Indeed, one of the more patriotic organs said (and truthfully) that it was not generally known that Sir Oliver had been on the verge of taking up an important command in the Transvaal, and implied that any victories gained by the Boers in his now enforced absence were hardly to their credit.

Caroline was left in charge. Mr. Watterson had told her to be sure to call upon him, if in any difficulty she felt the need of a father. As she felt the need of nothing so little, she thanked him and said that she could manage quite well. She did. Oliver went to Sandhurst and then into the Hussars, where he looked extremely dashing in blue and yellow. Jane went to a succession of schools, and acquired a Catholic education; not so obviously in English History (for, as Chance would have it, each school was doing Henry VIII in the term that she was there) but in matters possibly as important. At eighteen she took her *bizarre* good looks, her cat-like indifference to others, and, of course, her knowledge of Henry VIII (which was by this time considerable) to a French finishing school. At twenty she was finished; and the Great War was beginning …

With the coming of the Great Peace, there were again three Windells at Auburn Lodge.

First, Caroline. She was now the forty-five which she had always looked to her father, and the old maid which he had always known she would be. She differed from others of her age and Parliamentary status in that she refused to take advantage of the new Cosmetic Era which had arisen. By looking the same in whatever light and (within the limits of a room) from whatever distance, she achieved a distinction which no Victorian could have foretold for her. There was only one Caroline Windell.

Then Jane. London was full of Jane Windells. She was now the twenty-five which she would have looked in any case. She had entertained the troops during the war; just how much, and in what direction, was not known. But her experiences with a Company of Players at Havre and Rouen had made it clear that the Stage gave her most scope for her natural abilities.

Lastly, the orphaned Jenny. She was five.

III

Since Edward had done so little for Jane, and George had not, in Caroline's view, been a conspicuous success with the modern girl, Jenny was brought up by Queen Victoria. She throve, under these auspices, in a world of her own.

She was the daughter of that dashing young Hussar whom she had never seen. She was glad and proud that he had been a Hussar. As she pointed out to God in one of her early prayers, he might have been in the Manchester Regiment.

Every night they talked together in bed.

'Well, Jenny, what shall we do to-night?'

Perhaps she had been reading *Robinson Crusoe*, by Mr. Daniel Defoe.

'Darling, I thought we might be wrecked together on a desert island.'

'Without the Aunts?'

'Just whatever you think, Hussar darling?'

'I don't like Aunt Jane,' said the Hussar dashingly.

Jenny called God's attention to the fact that it was the Hussar who was saying this.

'I do like Aunt Caroline, but I don't think she would be good on a desert island,' said the Hussar.

('We both like her,' explained Jenny, 'but we do *not* think she would be good on a desert island. You do see, don't you?')

'So it's just you and me, Jenny. Now the ship's breaking up, and I'm swimming to shore with you on my back. Go!'

When she was nine, she met Julian.

'Well, Jenny, what shall we do to-night?'

'Darling, I thought we might be the Dauntless Three, if you wouldn't mind very much. Do you mind very much, Hussar darling? You could be Horatius, and I could stand on your right hand.'

'But how about my left hand, Jenny?'

'I thought you might think of somebody, darling.'

'What about Julian?' said the Hussar, after racking his brain.

'Darling, what a *lovely* idea! You do think of lovely ideas.'

And then, a year later, Aunt Jane met the Comte de la Tour. At least, he said she did.

'Hussar darling?'

'Yes, Jenny?'

'Did you know about Aunt Jane running away with the French Count?'

'Yes, Jenny.'

'Why do you have to *run*?'

'He wants to get back to France quickly so as to say *"Vive la France!"* and it's a long way to go.'

'I thought that was it ... Hussar darling?'

'Yes, Jenny?'

'Why mustn't I talk about her any more?'

'Because they're carrying secret dispatches to the exiled King, and nobody must know.'

'I thought that was it. But I shan't tell Julian.'

'Oh, no, you mustn't.'

'Well, I don't tell him anything now. I think he's a silly little boy.'

'I think he is too,' said the extremely intelligent Hussar.

So Aunt Jane left Auburn Lodge ... and the Jane Latour who afterwards played the harp, and did other odd and exciting things, never saw Jenny again. But Jenny, as we know, saw Jane Latour.

IV

When Aunt Caroline died, Jenny was eighteen. The first thing that she did was to have her hair shingled. There was a great deal of it, parti-coloured like a straw-stack after rain, and as soon as it was safely off, she wondered if she had been unkind to her aunt's memory to proclaim her independence so quickly. Then she remembered that some tribes always shaved their heads as a sign of mourning, and if she had been one of those tribes she would have had to have had her hair shingled. This made her feel better. By the time she had called on Mr. Watterson (who was now nearly eighty) and Mr. Watterson had said nothing about her hair, because, being eighty, he hadn't noticed the difference, she felt quite comfortable again.

Mr. Watterson suggested that they should let Auburn Lodge (furnished) for a year, and that she should make her home with him and his dear wife for that time, while, as he put it, she looked round. Mr. Watterson lived in a house in St. John's Wood, with a garden, and, as he said this, he had a sudden thought of Jenny in the hammock between the two pear-trees, reading a magazine with a gay cover, while a thrush sang over her head, and beneath her on the grass lay a hat with cherry ribbons; which was how he remembered somebody in some other world; and two tears came into his two old eyes, and he knew that now nothing could ever happen, and in a little while he would be dead. Then he forgot all this just as suddenly, and remembered that there were six dozen of the port left and Victoria Falls Preferred were going up.

'You *are* kind,' said Jenny.

'You realize, my dear, that I am now your guardian?'

'Oh!' said Jenny, and thought: *'Another* guardian!' when all she really wanted was her dear Hussar.

She wondered what would be said about her hair, because Mrs. Watterson would be sure to notice it. Well, thank goodness, it couldn't go back.

'So I think that that's what we will do, my dear.'

Jenny agreed, as she always did when a guardian spoke to her.

So Auburn Lodge was let for a year (furnished) to Mr. and Mrs. George Parracot, who also wanted to look round. Mr. and Mrs. Parracot had lived for ten years at The Chestnuts, Chislehurst. They were great theatre-goers, and had missed the last five minutes of the Third Act of every play worth seeing since 1922. They had also missed in this way some five hundred renderings of the National Anthem. So when old Paul Parracot died suddenly (but not too suddenly, considering that they were only second cousins) they decided to take a house in London for a year, and see how they liked it. For whatever could be said about Chislehurst, it was not so central as the Brompton Road.

But Jane Latour knew nothing of all this. She did not even know that her sister Caroline was dead. Caroline was not News. No subeditor dropped a headline for her; in her name no vowels were wrung at Broadcasting House; and on that remote island in the South Seas at which the ex-President's yacht had just landed them, Jane Latour neither wept nor hung her harp upon the trees.

However, even ex-Presidents tire, and pleasure-cruises come to an end. Jane Latour was in London again, and, in the language of her profession, resting. She also, in a sense, was looking round. Taking stock.

In a year she would be forty—forty—forty. And now and at once and all the time she wanted money—money—money.

Forty ... money ...

Then, as she was lying one morning in the red-and-black bath in the red-and-black bathroom in the little red-and-black house in Stapleton Mews, comparing, as so often now, her overdraft, which was at the National Provincial Bank, with her assets, which, at the moment, were mostly under water, she remembered suddenly her sister Caroline. Caroline and she were joint-owners of Auburn Lodge; indeed, she still had the key to which joint-ownership entitled her. It was true that Caroline paid over to her yearly a half-share of the estimated rent, but why should not Caroline buy her out altogether? The house must be worth—what? Six—eight— ten thousand? Five thousand pounds for Jane Latour! She stretched out an arm and added another handful of bath-salts to the water. She could afford it.

So it was that Aunt Jane came again to Auburn Lodge. As she clicked up the little alley-way in her absurdly high heels, she fumbled in her bag for the latch-key, so long unused. To let herself into her own house was an assertion of her rights; it was to be a gesture, a reminder to Caroline that half of all this was hers; yes, even down to half of the silver photograph-frames on the grand piano. She would stand for no nonsense from Caroline.

She fidgeted the key into the lock, smiling a little scornfully as she thought of poor Caroline. And the child Jenny. Jenny must be nearly eighteen. What sort of a mid-Victorian miss had Caroline made of her?

But she did not smile scornfully as she thought of Jenny. Jenny was eighteen.

Chapter Three

Old Felsbridgian

I

There was a noise of a door opening below; there was a noise of footsteps on the stairs; and suddenly the awful realization swept over Jenny that she had no business to be here at all!

How could she have been so silly!

The answer was that to-day, for the first time since she had left Auburn Lodge, she had found herself in her dear Brompton Road. Old inhabitants of the North-West do their shopping in Oxford Street. Not exclusively in Oxford Street, for they may stop short at Wigmore Street, or venture as far south as Bond Street, Regent Street or Hanover Square; but they have a marked Oxford Street manner, which will never carry them across the Park. For six months Jenny had been striving to acquire this manner, and striving in vain. She had the stamp of Brompton Road upon her.

Brompton Road was particularly sweet to her, because it was the only London street in which she and her dear Hussar had been allowed to go about together. In Brompton Road, Aunt Caroline had felt, a young girl was Safe. However noisomely Danger might lurk in the side streets, waiting to pounce upon the divergent, along the straight way of Brompton Road walked only the Loyal and the Respectable. Jenny tripped up and down it untouched; but amid the perils of Beauchamp Place there marched by the side of Jenny her Aunt Caroline, or her Aunt Caroline's maid.

In St. John's Wood it was different. Mr. Watterson had the usual views about the modern young girl, but the fact that Abduction was Illegal made him indisposed to think that it could happen to a ward of Watterson, Watterson and Hinchoe's. There was no need for Jenny to have a latch-key, but (he assured Mrs. Watterson) she could safely run about London alone in the daytime. Indeed, in this way she could take some of the housekeeping off Mrs. Watterson's shoulders.

So at eighteen Jenny had been given the freedom of London. Moreover, unknown to Mr. Watterson, she had a latch-key in her bag. Admittedly it was not the latch-key to the house in Acacia Road, and therefore did not greatly enlarge her freedom; but a latch-key, brought casually to the surface when feeling for coppers in an omnibus, could only have one meaning, and her possession of it gave Jenny, if not the conductor, an authentic thrill. In fact, it was one of those in use at Auburn Lodge, which Jenny had been allowed to borrow on a certain notable occasion. She had gone to a dance without Aunt Caroline but not the less chaperoned, and the chaperones (there were several of them) had delivered her at the door of Auburn Lodge at an hour almost Edwardian. 'We'll just see you safely in,' had said the Colonel with a hearty laugh, and they had all gathered (a little humorously) round the front door, while Jenny felt proudly for her latch-key. The fact that it had slipped down behind the lining of her bag, and was not discovered until eight months later, had spoilt the joke at the time, but had left in Jenny's possession a key which should now have been with the Parracots.

She had this key, then, in her bag, and she had there ten pounds of her quarterly allowance, and it was a fine warm day in June, and all Brompton Road was calling to her as never before.

She went. She spent. She tripped backwards and forwards, and round and about—oh, the darling Brompton Road, how glad she was to get back to it again! Her dear Hussar was with her just as he used to be, and she was telling him all about Michael Alloway, the barrister by profession, who had found the body of a well-dressed woman in his drawing-room, and they were thinking how exciting this would be, and not really looking where they were going … and, before they knew where they were, they had come to the little alley-way together and, chattering as they had always done, turned up it. And there was the latch-key in her hand, and the key had fitted so easily, and now she was in the well-known house, and going dreamily up the stairs as she had gone a hundred, a thousand times before … 'Aunt Caroline! I'm back!'

II

The footsteps, the voices, were nearer. They were just outside the door. Only one thing to do. Hide!

In a flash Jenny was into the window-seat which went round the three sides of the big window over the lawn. She was curled up behind the curtains. As a child she had hidden here from Aunt Caroline or Aunt Jane and then popped her head out and said 'Boo!'—a joke in which, somehow, no grown-up had ever seemed able to join. But now it was not a joke; it was desperate. One simply couldn't let perfect strangers know how *idiotic* one had been.

'My God!' said Mr. George Parracot.

Jenny was neither surprised nor shocked. From a hundred detective stories, she knew that this was how men greeted the body of an unknown woman in the drawing-room.

'What is it?' called a voice from Aunt Caroline's bedroom.

'I say, quick!' shouted Mr. Parracot. And then commandingly: 'No—don't. Stay where you are!' Mr. Parracot had remembered that he was a Man and an Old Felsbridgian. One must keep The Women out of this sort of thing.

It was too late. Mrs. Parracot was in the doorway.

'George!' she cried.

There was just that something in her voice which made it clear that, from now onwards, whatever might happen, it was *his* body, not hers. Mr. Parracot, wearing the Club tie, recognized the note and accepted all responsibility.

'It's quite all right, old girl. You'd better go to your bedroom. Leave it all to me.'

'Is she—dead?'

'Yes.'

'Who is it?'

'Haven't the faintest. I say, old girl, you'd better—'

Mrs. Parracot came a little closer and said: 'Why, it's Jane Latour!' 'Good lord, not *the* Jane Latour?'

'Yes. I'm sure it is.' She looked up at him. 'George?'

It was not quite an accusation, not quite a question; and it said all about Jane Latour that was not going to be said in the obituary notices.

'I've never spoken to her in my life,' said George indignantly. 'I've never—Well, we've seen her act once or twice. But that's all. How on earth did she get *here?*'

'Poor thing,' said Laura Parracot, suddenly feeling an immense envy for one who had had such an exciting life, an immense pity for one who now would have it no more. 'Did she—kill herself?'

George looked about him in a puzzled way. 'Well, but—How?'

'Veronal or whatever—Oh!' She had come still closer.

'She couldn't have hit her head, because there's nothing—'

'George!'

'It's quite all right, old girl. You go to your bedroom, and I'll ring up the police.'

'But, George, don't you *understand*, she was *murdered*?'

'Yes, that's all right, old girl. *I'll* see to that.'

'But he may be in the house still!'

'Nonsense, old girl, he's far enough off by this time.'

'But he must have known the house was empty, or he wouldn't have been here with—her. And if we hadn't come in on our way to Mary's—Oh, I wish we'd gone straight through instead of—But I had to get some thinner things, and you wanted your Brilliantine, but don't you see he might be in the house *now,* looking for—for whatever it is they came here for.'

'Now now, old girl,' said Mr. Parracot quickly, 'this won't do.' He had an uneasy feeling that Laura was getting hysterical, and that the best way to stop it was to slap her face smartly with the open hand, an action so definitely un-Felsbridgian that he could not possibly bring himself to it. He fingered his tie anxiously, and said: 'If you go into your bedroom and lock the door, and if I'm here all the time, it *must* be all right, mustn't it, old girl?'

'All right, George,' said the old girl bravely.

She went out. Jenny was left alone with Mr. Parracot. For a little while there was silence. Then a voice began to speak.

'Hallo! I want the nearest police-station, please … Auburn Lodge. Brompton Road … Thank you … Oh, hallo! I'm speaking from Auburn Lodge, just off the Brompton Road. Er—there's a—there's a—a body here … A *body* … Yes … A well-dressed woman … I don't know … I don't know … George Parracot … Yes. But we've been away, and the house has been empty … Quite sure … Right … Right … Good-bye.'

Then there was silence again. Jenny looked round the corner of the curtain. Mr. Parracot was in an arm-chair, waiting. Jenny breathed a prayer to God or her Hussar, she wasn't sure which, to think of something. For if she were found now, not even the handsomest young detective could save her.

She had done *everything* wrong! Why, the first thing they told you was not to move anything until the police came, and she had moved the one thing which she ought to have left: the door-stop! Worse still, she had cleaned it with her handkerchief! Worst of all

('Oh, Hussar *darling,* isn't it *awful')* she had left her handkerchief in a chair for everyone to see! And it had 'Jenny' on it!

And then *hiding!*

Even that wasn't all. She was Aunt Jane's only relation, and so by law she would get all Aunt Jane's money, and the police would say that that was why she had done it!

JENNY WINDELL IN THE DOCK: DRAMATIC EVIDENCE

Jenny realized that there was only one thing to do. She must escape and fly the country. But how? And, more important, *when?*

When? Before the police came. There was just one moment when it could be done. There were no servants in the house, and Mrs. Parracot was safely locked up. So Mr. Parracot would have to go downstairs to let the police in. Then would be the moment.

How? That was easy. Through the window. The ground was higher at the back of the house than at the front, and there was a flower-bed not more than eight feet below her. Then out by the garden-door into the other little alley-way, and out through the far end into Merrion Place ...

Suppose Mrs. Parracot answered the door? *She* couldn't ...

Suppose the Police came in with a skeleton-key? *They wouldn't* ...

Suppose—

The front-door bell rang. There was a movement from the chair. Jenny, looking out, saw the disappearing back of Mr. Parracot, heard his 'All right, old girl, it's only the police'. She pushed open the casement window behind her, squeezed through, wriggled round and let herself down by her hands. There was only about eighteen inches to drop ... just enough to give Inspector Marigold, who had the case well in hand from the start, a couple of interesting footprints.

Chapter Four
Entry of Gloria Harris

I

In a tea-shop in Piccadilly, over a cup of coffee, half a toasted scone and two portions of honey, Jenny considered her position. It was half-past twelve. Twenty minutes ago she had escaped from Auburn Lodge, and for twenty minutes Inspector Marigold had been relentlessly finding clues. She wondered if he would stop for lunch, and hoped, if so, that he would have a nice long one.

She considered in her mind the Good and the Bad, as her old friend Robinson Crusoe would have done.

1.	*Bad.*	I've only got £2 5s. 9½*d*., and if I hadn't bought that hat, it would have been £6 9s. 9½*d*.
	Good.	But I might have bought the other one.
2.	*Bad.*	I've really got the wrong clothes for escaping.
	Good.	But I suppose I could buy some others.
	Bad.	But I've only got £2 5s. 9½*d*.
3.	*Bad.*	My handkerchief.

	Good.	But it's got 'Jenny' on it, and when the Inspector identifies Aunt Jane, he *might* think 'Jenny' is short for Jane.
	Bad.	Until somebody tells him it isn't.
4.	*Bad.*	Finger-prints. I must have left them all *over* the place.
	Good.	Still, that doesn't matter, if they don't know it's me.
5.	*Bad.*	I wish I could get some other clothes, and some more money and some cold cream and a toothbrush. I wonder if I *dare* go home for them.
	Good.	I think I might, because Mr. and Mrs. Watterson have gone down to Bath for a wedding.
	Bad.	All the same I daren't, because of the servants.
	Good.	I'm glad I said I would be out to lunch.
6.	*Good.*	It's lucky I never saw the Parracots when they were taking the house. They've simply never heard of me.
	Bad.	But the Inspector is sure to ask who lived there before the Parracots, and then he'll go to see Mr. Watterson.
	Good.	But Mr. Watterson is at Bath for the day.
7.	*Good.*	So I've probably got the whole of to-day to get away in, only I mustn't go home.
	Bad.	But I've only got £2 5s. 9½d.
8.	*Good.*	Still £2 5s. 9½d. is quite a lot *really,* if you sleep under haystacks.
	Bad.	But not nearly so much as £6 9s. 9½d. when you've got to buy all sorts of things.

And then, just as she was beginning her second portion of honey, Jenny had a most wonderful idea.

9. *Really* AWFULLY *Good.* Nancy Fairbrother! Of course!

This was that Nancy, who had supposed, mistakenly, that Aunt Jane played the harp with nothing on before all the Crowned Heads of Europe. She had been helpful and instructive in other ways, and in numerous imaginary adventures had been Jenny's sole female confederate. She had Jenny's romantic nature, very much Jenny's figure, and all of Jenny's passion for Crime. Probably she knew already what 'A K 17 L P K 29 Friday' meant.

Jenny paid for her lunch (leaving £2 5s. 1½d.) and walked to a telephone-box in the Piccadilly Tube station.

In her very deepest tones Jenny said: 'Hallo, is that Mr. Archibald Fenton's house?'

'Yes, Mr. Fenton's secretary speaking,' said a bright secretarial voice.

'Is that Miss Fairbrother?'

'Speaking.'

'Nancy,' said Jenny's voice urgently, 'this is Gloria Harris speaking. Do you remember? Say "Oh, yes, Miss Harris" if you do.'

'Oh, yes, Miss Harris,' said Miss Fairbrother primly.

'You sound as if you weren't alone, darling.'

'Quaite.'

'Is Mr. Fenton there?'

'Yes.'

'Listen, Nancy, it's terribly important. You mustn't see me, and you mustn't know that I've rung up, that's why I said Gloria Harris. But you *must* do something for me, if you'll be an angel. Will you be an angel, Nancy darling?'

'Of course, Miss Harris,' said Miss Fairbrother reassuringly.

'I want to go to your flat, and I want to change there, and I want to wear something of yours, something old and country-ish, and I'll leave you what I'm wearing instead. It's the green georgette. And nobody must know I've been. So if I call for your key now, will you leave it addressed to Miss Harris, but not so as people will guess it's a key, and I'll tie it on a piece of string and leave it hanging inside the letterbox. And you might say what you'd like me to wear of yours. Something you were going to sell, and you'll have my green georgette, so that *will* be all right, won't it?'

'That will be *quite* all right, Miss Harris. I'll do it at once.'

'You utter angel. You do understand, don't you?'

'Why, of course, Miss Harris. I assure you we're *quite* used to this sort of thing. *Good*-bye.'

'Good-bye, *darling!*'

Mr. Fenton looked up inquiringly.

'Autograph,' said Miss Fairbrother with a little shrug.

Until he had written *A Flock of Sheep* two years ago, Mr. Fenton had despised both those who asked for autographs and those who granted them. In those days he had been a reviewer and publisher's reader, a combination of professions not without its advantages, one of them being, in Mr. Fenton's case, immunity from the autograph-hunter. With the success of *A Flock of Sheep*, however, he had acquired a new set of values.

'Remind me,' said Archibald Fenton graciously.

'I wonder if you would mind just doing it now,' said Miss Fairbrother. 'She's calling for it directly. It came this morning.'

'Oh, very well.'

Nancy produced an autograph-book which had come that morning, and Mr. Fenton produced a gold fountain-pen with which he wrote 'Archibald Fenton, Kind regards' on a mauve page between 'Stanley Baldwin' and 'Kaye Don'. He always chose a mauve page, and preferred to be between

Rudyard Kipling and John Masefield, but this was not always possible.

'Would it be a bother', said Miss Fairbrother, 'if I just got this off, and then we shouldn't be interrupted again? I shall just have to write a letter; she wants a list of the titles of all your other books. She's ordered the new one, of course.'

'You've got some lists made out, haven't you?'

'I'm afraid I shall have to make it out again. We've run out of the last lot.'

Mr. Fenton looked at his watch.

'All right, we'll take five minutes off. I want to get this done before lunch. Who is she, by the way?'

'A Miss Gloria Harris,' said Nancy.

'Gloria? That wasn't the name in the book?'

Miss Fairbrother put a fresh sheet of paper into her typewriter, and said calmly: 'She's filling up the book for her little niece, as a surprise.'

'Oh, an Aunt,' said Mr. Fenton, losing interest, and went out of the room. It was time for a cocktail, anyhow.

At headlong speed Nancy typed the following list of titles for Miss Harris:

'Darling, I don't know what you've done, but it sounds as if you were leading a hue-and-cry. Take the beige stockinette about three from the left, and the brown beret, bottom drawer. Shoes? Stockings of course. How are you underneath, or doesn't that matter? You can have the beige knickers if you like, because unless you're going to wear two lots(!) I shall have yours. Shoes. There's a pound in the bead box in the dressing-table drawer, or you could have the old *crêpe* ones with a patch which leap to the eye, the only thing is, if you're going to be pursued for long, they mightn't go on fitting. So take the pound if you think you'll want it. *Disguise*. Most important. *Show your ears*, that will do it. Have you got time before you start, or must you wait till you're well away? There's a very good hairdresser in Tunbridge Wells, if you're making for the coast. Leave this stupid album in the flat, and I'll send it off to-night. All good luck, Jenny darling. You are a family, aren't you? My ridiculous Fenton will come back in a moment, and I must get this sealed up before he asks to read it. I wish I could have spoken to you properly just now, but perhaps it's as well, because now if the police come, I can say I don't know anything. Nancy.

'P.S. Burn this.'

Nancy took out her latch-key, tied a piece of string to it, wrapped the key and the string in this letter, put the letter in the middle of the album, put the album in a suitable envelope, addressed the envelope 'Miss Gloria Harris, *To be called for*' and hurried it down to the hall table. Then she went upstairs again, and almost immediately was joined by Mr. Archibald Fenton.

'Just let me make sure you've got that list right,' he said, holding out a hand.

'Oh, Mr. Fenton, I'm so sorry! I'm afraid it's sealed up now. I could open it if you like, but—'

'It doesn't matter. You didn't include *Lovely Lady*, of course,' said Mr. Fenton, referring to an earlier work of which he was now ashamed.

'No,' said Miss Fairbrother truthfully.

II

Jenny realized that the thing to avoid was taxis, because taxi-drivers always remembered when they had driven a fair girl in a biscuit-coloured hat and green georgette to Waterloo Station, and they nearly always heard her say to the porter: 'Bittlesham Regis, it's the three-ten, isn't it?' and then they always went to Scotland Yard and, after waiting a little while, were shown into the Inspector's room, and told him all about it. So she went to Bloomsbury by omnibus, and was very glad that omnibus drivers didn't remember so well, or want so much money.

It was wonderful of Nancy to have recognized Gloria Harris so quickly. *Gloria* (because it was the most glorious name Jenny could think of) *Harris* (as a slight tribute to Cook) and *Acetylene* (because it was a name Nancy had just heard about) *Pitt* (out of compliment to the Younger Pitt whom she was doing that term) had had their last adventure together six years ago, when they had served with Wellington in the Peninsular War, and, as far as was possible to two drummer boys, had rolled up the map of Europe at Waterloo. Now she was going to be Gloria Harris again, but not, thought Jenny, disguised as a boy. That always seemed to her so silly, because, however slim you were, you *were* different, and nobody could mistake that tight look that men's clothes gave you. Like that girl in Nancy's school in *The Young Cavalier*, all the wrong shapes and so silly. Why, the police would know at once she was escaping.

She came to Mr. Archibald Fenton's house and rang the bell. Nancy heard it, and longed to rush to the window and give one encouraging wave. But she could not. Mr. Fenton, who had been forced to the conclusion lately that success and artistic merit were not really incompatible, was dictating a kindly article on the novels of Mr. Galsworthy.

'It's Miss Harris,' said Jenny to the maid. 'I've called for a—a letter.'

'Oh yes, miss.' The envelope was shown to her. 'Would that be it?'

'That's it. Thank you very much,' said Jenny, a little surprised at the shape which Nancy's latch-key had taken. She hurried down the steps and across the square; and Mr. Fenton, carried on a slightly involved metaphor to the window, saw the back of her, and thought that, for an aunt, Miss Harris had kept her figure remarkably well.

Jenny sped round to the British Museum, and in a room where she was the youngest inhabitant by three thousand years she opened her precious envelope.

'Oh, Nancy darling,' she thought, 'Oh, Acetylene Pitt, you are wonderful!'

How marvellous it would have been if they could have escaped together! If Mr. Fenton had hurt himself badly on a dictionary or something, and Suspicion had rested upon his secretary! Perhaps Nancy could join her later, taking a ticket ostensibly to Earl's Court, but slipping out at Tottenham Court Road, and doubling back to St. Pancras.

She put the letter and the latch-key into her bag, and, with the autograph album under her arm, made her way back to omnibus country, and waited for something to take her to Victoria. But she was careful when paying for her ticket not to let the conductor see that she now had *two* latch-keys.

At Victoria she got into an omnibus for the King's Road, and all down the King's Road she was thinking to herself 'Hair'. Should she wait until she got to Tunbridge Wells, or should she get it done now? And if now, should she go into a hairdresser's and have a proper Eton crop, or should she try to cut it herself? She put two fingers at the back of her hat and snipped ... Yes, she could get the curls off easily—*and* the ones over her ears— but it would look rather funny, wouldn't it?

Bad.   It would look rather funny.
Good.   But I shall still have £2 4s. 5½d.
That settled it.

III

Gloria Harris came out of the little flat and looked cautiously round. The Inspector was obviously having his lunch. She walked into the King's Road and waited for an omnibus to take her back to Victoria.

Her plans were made. She would be a hiker. You couldn't very well start hiking in the King's Road, so she would take a train to Tunbridge Wells and start hiking from there. As far as she remembered, you either hiked in large companies or else in couples. She wouldn't be likely to find a large company, so she would have to do it by herself, but it would not really be by herself because she would always have her dear Hussar. So *that* was all right.

In the flat this letter was waiting for Miss Fairbrother:

'Darling Nancy,
    'You are an angel, darling, for understanding and everything. I have taken the stockinette, and two pairs of country stockings, and the beige knickers and chemise, but I *haven't* left you my green set because I *must* have two of everything, because I may have to wander about the country and I must have a change, and I haven't taken your pound, so I haven't very much money, so I can't afford to buy very much, and the shoes fit perfectly, darling. I am wearing the beige now, and shall dye the green later on if I can, because they might look rather funny getting over a stile, because the skirt is just the least bit short, but it doesn't matter because I shall be *hiking*, but a detective might notice and it's just the sort of *little* thing which makes them suspicious. Darling Nancy, do you mind, I've taken your pyjamas, I didn't know if you wore them, I never have, are they nice, there was only one pair, the blue,

which I've taken, because I suddenly remembered about that, and I must have something. I'm buying a knapsack to put them all in, and darling I've left you my watch, it's one Aunt Caroline gave me, but Mr. and Mrs. Watterson have never said anything, I mean they've never said 'What a pretty watch that is', so that means they've never really noticed it so as to describe it to the police, so I should think you could sell it quite easily, but not the bag, which I shan't want *hiking*, and people might remember it. So please do, Nancy, I mean the watch, because of the extra stockings and the knickers and the pyjamas and all the extra things I've taken, oh, and two handkerchiefs, and I hope you'll like the hat, it cost four guineas, so perhaps you could sell that too, I mean to a friend. Oh no, darling, I've just remembered, Mrs. Watterson *particularly* noticed the hat, so you'd better hide it altogether. Oh dear! and perhaps you oughtn't to wear the georgette either, oh *darling!* but you *will* sell the watch, won't you, and those are real little diamonds.

'I must fly, Nancy darling, because I daren't stay in London a moment longer, I've cut my hair myself, *quite* short, it looks awful, and I've found a lip-stick of yours, I didn't know you used them, I *never* have, are they nice, I've put a lot on for disguise, and I've taken it with me, so *mind you sell the watch*. And do just write to Miss Gloria Harris, Poste Restante, Tunbridge Wells, to say you don't mind what I've done. Your loving, grateful Jenny.

'P.S. Burn this.'

So, with a brown-paper parcel under her arm, and mixed emotions in her bosom, Miss Gloria Harris left London for Tunbridge Wells.

Chapter Five

Activity in London

I

Although Inspector James Marigold had had a long and varied career in the Police Force, he had never actually taken part in a Murder Case. It was almost the only thing in which he hadn't taken part. He had watched most of the Test Matches at Lord's from a sedentary position in front of the bowling screen, rousing himself in the intermissions to say 'Pass off the ground there, please' to those spectators who were delaying the resumption of play. He had joined hands with other members of the Force to keep back the crowd at fashionable weddings. In the Row on one occasion a horse which had suddenly caught sight of the Albert Memorial and was hurrying back to its stable was stopped by P.C. Marigold and returned to its lessee, and the fact that this gentleman was a Member of Parliament had brought the police officer a short but gratifying notice in the evening papers. On another occasion he had held the traffic up at Hyde Park Corner while a flock of sheep had transferred its grazing quarters to the Green Park; and though the photograph of him doing this (headed 'RURAL LONDON') had given the impression that it was the flock of sheep which was holding the traffic up while Sergeant Marigold went for a drink, it had all helped to fire his ambition, and to prepare him for what was to be his Greatest Case, the Auburn Lodge Mystery.

He had begun by arresting George Parracot. There were three reasons for arresting Mr. Parracot.

1. He had been the first to find the body.
2. He had called attention to Jenny's handkerchief in a Marked Manner.
3. He was obviously Concealing Something.

'There's this handkerchief, Inspector,' said Mr. Parracot almost as soon as they were in the room. 'I don't know if it has anything to do with it, but—'

'All in due course,' said the Inspector, holding up the hand which had stopped a thousand motor-omnibuses. 'We take things in order, Mr.—er ...'

'Parracot.'

'Mr. Parracot, and in that way we keep things orderly. Now then, over there, please, until I'm ready for you.'

The body was examined, photographed, removed. *Right* over there,' said the Inspector to Mr. Parracot, who had already got the legs of his trousers into two photographs. 'Sit right over there in that corner, and don't move until I tell you to come out.'

'About the handkerchief,' said George a little later on. 'I didn't want you to think—'

'When the moment comes to come to the handkerchief, Mr.— er ...'

'Parracot.'

'Parracot, we shall come to it.' He looked round the room. 'Now then, what were you saying about a handkerchief?'

'There's a handkerchief over there on that chair.'

'Well?'

'Well, you see, my wife—I mean it's got "Jenny" on it.'

'Well?'

'Well, I mean my wife's name is Laura.'

'We shall come to Mrs. Parracot later,' said the Inspector. 'Suppose we begin at the beginning, and try to get things into some sort of order.' He took out his notebook. 'Your name?'

'Parracot.'

'Just Parracot?'

'George Parracot.'

'Don't keep anything back. Now then, Mr. Parracot, if you would like to give some account of your movements this morning and to explain how you made this shocking discovery—'

'Well, it was like this,' said Mr. Parracot eagerly.

He gave an account. He explained. He made it perfectly clear that the responsibility was his and his alone; that though, as he maintained, he had not struck the actual blow, yet, if a Jury of his fellow-countrymen, some of them possibly Old Felsbridgians, held that the harbouring of a strange body in one's drawing-room was such bad form as to be practically indistinguishable from murder, then he was prepared to take what was coming to him, even if it meant the Supreme Penalty, so long as his dear wife, Laura—'

'Look here,' said Inspector Marigold, getting more and more suspicious, 'you say your wife's name is Laura?'

'Yes,' said George eagerly. 'Laura Mary Parracot.'

'And this,' said the Inspector, holding up the handkerchief, 'has "Jenny" on it?'

'Yes.'

'Then whose is it?'

Mr. Parracot was carried away on a wave of fine feeling. 'Mine,' he said simply, and fingered his tie.

'I thought you said your name was *George* Parracot,' said the Inspector, thumbing his way back to an earlier passage in his notebook.

Mr. Parracot returned to the surface. 'Er ... yes,' he said.

'And yet you have "Jenny" on your handkerchiefs?'

'Well, I don't exactly,' said George.

'How do you mean you don't exactly?'

'Well—' George wondered what he did mean.

'You mean somebody called Jenny gave you this handkerchief, and you always carry it about with you?'

'Good Heavens, no,' said Mr. Parracot hastily, realizing that he had gone much too far. 'No, no, of course not. As a matter of fact,' he said weakly, 'it isn't really mine at all.'

'Then why do you say it was?'

'Well—'

'Are you,' demanded Inspector Marigold sternly, 'endeavouring to Obstruct the Cause of Justice?'

'No, really,' said Mr. Parracot.

'Are you aware,' said Inspector Marigold severely, 'that Obstructing the Cause of Justice is an Extremely Serious Offence?'

'I—I misunderstood you. It isn't my handkerchief at all.'

'Then whose is it?'

'I don't— I mean I— Why, of course!' Mr. Parracot was suddenly inspired. 'Jane Latour! Jenny!'

'And who, might I ask, is Jane Latour?'

'Why, *she* was.' He jerked his head towards the door.

The Inspector moistened his thumb again and worked his way backwards.

'Five minutes ago you told me that you had never seen the dead woman before, and had no idea who she was.'

'Well, yes, in a way, but what I meant—'

'Mr. Parracot, in your own interests I advise you to be Very, Very Careful.'

'What I meant was my wife—' He pulled himself up. 'No, no, I mean *I*—I said to my wife, who—who just happened—as I say, I happened to call her in here, she was in her bedroom as a matter of fact, I should have said it anyhow, well really I just said it to myself, "It looks rather like Jane Latour," I said, and my wife said "Like *who*?" and I said "Nobody *you* know, old girl, it's just somebody I saw on the stage once," and photographs, you know, and—'

'I think', said Inspector Marigold, 'that I had better see Mrs. Parracot now.'

'Oh, I say,' cried George, 'must you?'

'Laura Parracot, didn't you say?' He got on to a clean page of his note-book.

'I say, you will spare her as much as possible? You know what I mean? She's only a woman, and—er—rather delicate and all that.'

Inspector Marigold's old school had no club tie, but he was a sportsman and a gentleman. His whole manner altered. For the first time he became friendly, human, understanding.

'That's all right, sir,' he said, with a look in his eye which was just not a wink. 'In a Delicate Condition, eh?'

'Er—yes,' said Mr. Parracot helplessly.

It was when he discovered that Mr. Parracot was lying for the third time that the Inspector arrested him.

II

If George Parracot had been taken in gyves to Merrion Place police station, then (a disturbing thought to many) this story might have been written differently. For the poster

FAMOUS ACTRESS
FOUND DEAD
WELL-KNOWN CLUBMAN
ARRESTED

would certainly have caught Nancy's eye in London, if not Jenny's in Tunbridge Wells, and Jenny, however absurd the arrest had seemed to her, since he was not a relation of Aunt Jane's, would have returned to save Mr. Parracot's life.

Fortunately Inspector Marigold had not as yet committed himself to publicity. Mr. Parracot, considering himself, as request-ed by the Inspector, under arrest, but as yet unmanacled, was waiting in the hall with Sergeant Bagshaw until investigations in the drawing-room were finished. Bagshaw, who always exerted himself socially on these occasions, was telling him about the last moments of the Edmonton murderer, but George could manage no more in reply than an occasional 'Fancy!' as horror succeeded horror. How, he wondered, was Laura getting on upstairs?

He need not have been anxious. Once the body was out of the way, Laura was her own woman again. Having removed the first misapprehension from the Inspector's mind, and excused him for a moment while he arrested George, she then put him right on one or two other points.

The dead woman was Jane Latour, the actress, as anybody with eyes in his head could have seen for himself …

Jane Latour was *not* called Jenny. Her intimate friends called her Toto, as anybody who could read would have known for himself …

They had taken the house through Harrods. The owner had died. No, not been murdered. Just died. Watterson, Watterson and Hinchcoe were the solicitors. Young Mr. Hinchcoe had met her at the house and gone into things with her …

Mr. Parracot had never met Miss Latour. He wouldn't. Not *that* sort of woman …

Now she remembered. She knew there was *something* about Jane Latour. Of course! Her real name was Jane Windell. She was the daughter of General Sir Oliver Windell …

It had *everything* to do with it. Auburn Lodge had belonged to a Miss Windell. The one who died …

She couldn't say everything at once. If the Inspector took that sort of tone, then she wouldn't say anything at all.

Inspector Marigold apologized humbly. Mrs. Parracot smiled at him sweetly. Inspector Marigold curled his moustache and smiled back; and metaphorically tied a knot in his handkerchief to remind him to release George, who was obviously not concerned in what, it was now plain, was a Family Job. Very handsome woman, Mrs. Parracot. Would have looked well at Lord's being passed gently off the ground after the luncheon interval.

'I'll tell you something else,' said Laura archly.

'Please do, madam.'

'I've only just noticed it, so don't ask me why I didn't say so before.' She said it so charmingly that the Inspector was not offended, but he did just wonder how personal a tone the conversation was going to take. Not, of course, a crumb on the moustache, but …

'The window,' said Laura.

'The window?' He turned in his chair.

Laura gave an apologetic little laugh.

'No, I'm being silly. Of course, *you* opened it.'

'No, madam, certainly not. Why?'

'Well, it wasn't open when we came in.'

'What!' The Inspector hoisted himself up and lumbered to the window.

'Of course, George might have done it, while he was waiting for you,' said Laura, trying to spoil it all.

She was too late. The Inspector was already at the window. He looked out. He saw the footprints. He beckoned mysteriously to Mrs. Parracot.

They looked out together.

'See that?'

'Footprints!' said Laura excitedly.

'The murderess,' said the Inspector solemnly.

'Jenny,' said Laura.

'Jenny it is.'

They drew their heads in and nodded to each other.

'And now,' said Inspector Marigold with grim determination, 'to find Jenny.'

He looked at his watch, and decided that he would find her after the luncheon interval.

III

Archibald Fenton had a wife and six children, and at first he had minded this a good deal. Not only were the seven of them expensive to maintain, but they formed, he could not help feeling, the wrong background for a critic of the Advanced School. The greeting which he was accustomed to receive from the less mathematical of his friends, 'Well, how's the family?' placed him definitely among the Victorians. So might Dickens have been addressed by Wilkie Collins; so, doubtless, he often was. But with the success of A Flock of Sheep, he realized that the family was just the background which he wanted. A man who had brought back 'heartiness', 'virility', 'the smell of hops', 'something of an Elizabethan tang' and 'a Rabelaisian robustness' to the English novel (to quote from different columns of the Observer review) was living well within himself in limiting his output of children to six; and though he did not go so far as to feel grateful to Fanny, he was now so far from blaming her that he insisted on accepting all the credit for himself. She was, so to say, merely her husband's publisher.

There was, he found, another advantage to him in the large family. As a young woman Fanny had been more admirable for her bank-balance than for her figure. It was natural that the needs of all these children should reduce considerably the one, and perhaps not surprising that the provision of them should have added considerably to the other, but certainly she was now much more noticeable for her figure than for her bank-balance.

In men Archibald had no objection to that heartiness of outline which could not—or, anyhow, should not—be called stoutness; indeed, he himself, to take a case, had an accommodating fullness of habit, a certain not unpleasing convexity of figure which sorted well with the robustness of his work. But Fanny was a woman; and Fanny, in any case, had gone too far altogether. It was as well, then, that the cares of the nursery should keep her so devotedly at home, at a time when her husband was, so conspicuously, going about. Even if Fanny had been slim and beautiful, yet in his new social system Archibald would have shone more brilliantly alone, the solitary focus of attention. Moreover, no real artist can preserve that mystery, that aloofness, which the laity demands from its artists, in the presence of one for whom he has lost all mystery ... and from whom he was never, strictly speaking, aloof.

This excursion into Mr. Archibald Fenton's family life is bringing us to no more than the fact that the house in Bloomsbury was full. Rightly Archibald had the largest room as his work-room, but it was a pity that there was no cupboard left over, however small, for his secretary.

At 9.30 Miss Fairbrother arrived, and looked through the letters which Mr. Fenton had left for her.

At 10.15 Mr. Fenton entered the work-room. Miss Fairbrother rose, and Mr. Fenton said something about the weather or his secretary's personal appearance.

From 10.15 to 1.10 Mr. Fenton dictated.

At 1.10 Mr. Fenton left for his club.

At 1.15 Miss Fairbrother joined the family for luncheon, thus enabling Mr. Fenton to pay her slightly less, and Miss Fairbrother to get an insight into the duties of a nursery governess, should she ever wish to be one.

At two o'clock Miss Fairbrother returned, alone, to the workroom, and typed all that she had taken down in shorthand in the morning.

At 4.30 Miss Fairbrother left, generally meeting Mr. Fenton on the doorstep; in which case he said to her 'Just off?' and she said 'Yes', these being the facts.

From 5–7 Mr. Fenton, alone in his workroom, prepared, either in his mind or in rough pencillings, the next morning's instalment.

At eight o'clock, complete from eye-glass to fob, Mr. Fenton went out to dinner.

At nine o'clock Mrs. Fenton put the last of the family (excepting, of course, Mr. Fenton) to bed.

At ten o'clock, when Mr. Fenton was just joining the ladies, she went to bed herself ...

At 4.30, then, on this day of late June, Nancy had begun her eager return to the Chelsea Flat. Jenny had been in her thoughts all through the long afternoon. The clack-clack of the typewriter went on; the rumble of Oxford Street, the gentler noises of the quiet square, drifted through the geranium-scented windows; but in her mind Nancy was at one moment in the heart of Kent, hiding among the hay-cocks while the pursuit went by, or fording a stream to give some blood-hound the slip ... and, at the next, back in London again, bidding a reluctant farewell to her beige knickers. If only she had been with Jenny (each, of course, wearing her own, and starting the thing properly) what fun they would have had! ...

Clack-clack-clack. Clack-clack. (*What* had *Jenny done?*) Clack-clack-clack. Clack.

She wondered how she would look in Jenny's green georgette. Not really her colour, of course. *Clack-clack-clack* ...

At last the afternoon was over, and she was free. Her mind still full of fancies, she hurried to her omnibus, and from the top of it began to get into touch with reality. A poster bore the words:

WELL KNOWN
ACTRESS
DEAD

Nancy wondered who it was, and hoped that it wouldn't be Gladys Cooper.

The next poster was more informative:

WEST END
ACTRESS
FOUND DEAD

Nancy was relieved, because now it was almost certainly *not* Gladys Cooper, who was much too West-end to be called a West-end actress. And 'Found dead' meant that nobody was there when you died, so you had probably done it yourself. Nancy wondered what it was like … doing it yourself. Anyhow Gladys Cooper wouldn't.

WEST END
MURDER MYSTERY
LATEST

That was that one at Notting Hill, wasn't it? The organ-grinder with the wooden leg.

ACTRESS DEAD
IN
WEST END
MANSION

That, thought Nancy, is the West-end actress. Gladys Cooper lived at Highgate. It would look funny if you had a poster 'ACTRESS ALIVE IN NORTH END MANSION'. What a lot of funny posters you could have if you tried.

FAMOUS
ACTRESS
MURDERED

I say! thought Nancy. So it isn't the organ-grinder! I *wonder* who it is! I expect her understudy did it! They always do. So as to play the part! I suppose the theatre will shut to-night. I wonder if—

And then, as she came into Sloane Square, two more posters told her all.

BROMPTON ROAD
MYSTERY
LATEST

said the one. And the other:

JANE
LATOUR
LATEST DEVELOPMENTS

'Jenny!' cried out Nancy's heart. 'Oh, Jenny darling!' And she rushed down the stairs of the omnibus, and out into the Square.

IV

Nancy drew the second sheet from the typewriter, placed it beneath the first sheet, and settled down to read. From time to time she nodded to herself approvingly. It was a good letter. She was prepared to bet that not even Archibald Fenton himself, with all his reputation, could have written a letter so good. It did everything which it had set out, six copies ago, to do.

It is possible that her early experiences in the Peninsular War had made Acetylene Pitt unduly cautious when communicating with a friend in the presence of the enemy; but certainly caution was necessary. For though the Englishman's home may still have the integrity, and to some extent (if desired) the exterior decoration, of a castle, his correspondence has long ceased to have any privacy at all. Once a letter gets into the hands of His Majesty's Postmaster-General, it is at the mercy of a Home Secretary looking for lottery tickets or a War Office searching for traitors. What more hopeful centre for their investigations, thought Nancy, than the Tunbridge Wells Post Office? Tunbridge Wells was notoriously the home of retired Admirals, Generals and Indian Civil Servants: admirable men, with a fixed but inadequate income, and an unconquerable belief in their ability to enlarge it. Who more likely than an Admiral to enter breezily for a sweepstake, or a General to sell to some treacherous foreign power his copy of *King's Regulations*, 1886? What more likely pseudonym for them to adopt than an innocent-seeming 'Gloria Harris'?

Nancy realized, then, that her letter to Jenny was a public rather than a private communication. Yet it had to answer Jenny's extremely private letter. It had to make the following points quite clear to Jenny without giving away anything to the police.

1. I know all about it, Jenny darling, and of course I'll help you.
2. It's perfectly all right about the clothes, and I don't mind a bit about the extra things.
3. I quite understand about not wearing the green georgette and hat.
4. I'll pawn the watch, and send you most of the money, because it's much too much just for the things you've taken.

So, with this in mind, Nancy sat down to her typewriter, and after six attempts, achieved the following:

'Darling Gloria,

'How nice to hear from you. I do hope you will enjoy your holiday. I haven't much news, except that two new exhibits joined the menagerie yesterday, but I haven't seen them yet. Sisters. Of course we are all very excited about the Jane Latour Murder, because one of the girls—Bertha Holloway — did you see her that time you came?—glasses and a protruding head like a tortoise—well, Bertha saw her in all those *Russian* plays, and had rather a crush on her, and of course we've all read all *sorts* of things about her, so it isn't really surprising, I mean being murdered, but Bertha says they aren't true. Apparently she wrote for her autograph once, but I don't see that that proves it. Bertha also says that the "Jenny" the police are looking for is *not* her illegitimate daughter, I mean Jane Latour's, as people are saying, but she doesn't know *who* she is—and neither does anybody else, not even the police, I mean, not *really*. But of course they're bound to find out soon, because of the handkerchief and the footprints, and then, I suppose, they'll begin to look for her properly.

'Well, that shows what London's like, with me listening to Miss Bertha Tortoise about a stupid murder, when I long to be out in the open sunshine, like you are, and listening to the birds. I got a new georgette—*blue*—and a ducky little hat at the sales, but I shan't be able to wear them yet, so I've put them away *very carefully*, and am sticking to the brown. (Well, really in this weather, *almost!*) And I've been selling one or two things, that stockinette, do you remember, and the undies that I always used to wear with it, but *quite* good still, and one or two other things, and have got a very good price for them, *quite* satisfactory in *every* way. I haven't actually got the money yet, but it's coming to-morrow, and what with one thing and another, spare-time work and Aunt Mary sending me a postal order on my birthday, I shall be able to pay you back *five pounds* of the money you lent me, darling, and *possibly more*. So this is very important, will you give me an address where I can send it, *and where you're sure to get it safely*, because I always say you can't have too much money on a holiday, particularly the sort of wandering-about holiday you're having now. So *don't forget.*

'Good-bye, Gloria darling, I *wish* I could be with you, but I expect I'm really better where I am, if you look at it all round. I mean just now.

'Your very loving A. P.

'P.S. Wasn't I right to insist on your taking pyjamas? I never wear them in London, but I think in the country, and *of course* if you sleep out, you simply *must* have them.'

The best of this letter, thought Nancy as she put it in its envelope, was that, not only was it an absolutely natural one to be waiting for anybody at the Tunbridge Wells Post Office, but that it gave Gloria Harris what Mr. Fenton would have called a Background. It would be safe for her, indeed it would be wise for her, to leave this letter lying about, so that whoever read it would know that Gloria Harris was a real person. With a Background.

Nancy had achieved the Background with her first six copies. What had made the seventh copy necessary was the problem of the address.

To put her real address at the head of the letter was to provide a clue. If the letter came into the Wrong Hands, then one of those hands could lay itself on Nancy's shoulder (if it should so desire) and lead her wherever it willed. But to put no address, as at first she had done, was to make Gloria Harris's background too indistinct altogether. A genuine letter would surely have *some* address. A false one then? Easy enough to invent, but also, in the wrong hands, easily proved false. Also, quite possibly, confusing to Jenny. And then, brilliant inspiration, she thought of 'The Menagerie'. It could refer to so many things. A boardinghouse, a Young Women's hostel, a shop, a secretarial college, a girls' school: from any one of these A. P. might be writing in very much the words of this letter. It needed a little alteration here and there; perhaps a slight reference to the Menagerie in the body of it; just enough to make a seventh copy advisable, but so little as to make it absolutely final—the Perfect Work of Art.

She stamped the letter and took it for a walk to South Kensington. South Kensington was so safe, and so full of menageries. As she walked, she wondered about A. P. Not Acetylene Pitt, which you couldn't really be called nowadays, but Alice Pitman. Thirty-five, she thought; good, earnest, slightly perspiring; half governess (without certificate) half matron at a large kindergarten with resident mistresses. The mistresses were young enough to think of themselves as 'the girls', and Bertha Holloway was the English mistress and taught the children to act plays, and Alice Pitman (secretary, of course, to the Head, as well as the other things, because of using a typewriter) was really called Miss Pitman, but she liked to think that they called her Alice and thought of her as one of the girls too; and Gloria Harris ...

But how would Miss Pitman have a friend like Gloria Harris? Oh, well, that was easy. An old pupil ...

It was really quite a story ...

Might write a story one day, thought Nancy. I know most of the tricks ...

Why not dye the green georgette? Why ever not?

Why not? ...

She would ...

The letter went into the box, but, before it came to Gloria Harris, Jenny had got a new background altogether.

Chapter Six

Jenny at Tunbridge Wells

I

With two brown-paper parcels under her arm and mixed emotions in her bosom, Miss Gloria Harris left Tunbridge Wells by omnibus.

It was five o'clock in the afternoon, such a mellow, gracious June afternoon as Jenny had never known. In one of her parcels were a green set of underclothes, a pair of blue pyjamas, a pair of beige stockings, two handkerchiefs and a lipstick. In the other were a knapsack, a small towel, a cake of soap, a comb, a pair of scissors, a toothbrush, a small sponge, a tube of toothpaste, a pair of pink garters, some cold cream, a large slab of chocolate, a box of dates, and Watson's Wonderful Combination Watchdog-and-Water-pistol. The first parcel contained all that she had taken away from Nancy's flat; the second contained all that little Mr. Sandroyd, of Sandroyd's Stores and General Depository, had sold her as soon as he heard the magic word 'knapsack'.

'A knapsack? Certainly, madam,' said Mr. Sandroyd, brushing up the cascade of his moustache with the back of his hand, as if to make himself more audible. 'Going hiking, if I may be permitted the phrase?'

'Yes,' said Jenny.

'Ah!' He beamed at her through his glasses. 'Then perhaps you will allow me to bring to your notice this list which I have compiled for the convenience of our customers.' He handed her a gaudily printed bill headed: 'HIKERS. BEWARE!'

'Beware of what?' said Jenny a little nervously.

'A little ruse of mine, madam,' said Mr. Sandroyd reassuringly, 'for calling the attention of ladies and gentlemen to the articles which they so often forget to take with them. You will notice'—he leant over the counter and jabbed at the list with a stubby and reflexed thumb—'that I have ventured to divide the articles into two columns headed *Optional* and *Obligatory*. Far be it from me', said Mr. Sandroyd kindly, 'to dictate to ladies and gentlemen what they should take and what they should not. My only purpose—if you will allow me one moment'—he swooped down on the list, made a mark with a finger-nail against one item, and leant back complacently—'there! Soap!' He twinkled at her. 'I am not going too far in suggesting that *soap* is an article for a young lady's toilet ...? Even in the give-and-take of camp life ...? Well, one wouldn't *quite* say "*optional*", would one?' He put his head on one side and looked at her comically over his glasses.

Jenny nodded confidingly at him.

'I do want some,' she said.

'A dainty cake of freshly scented soap,' he agreed. 'Verbena, lemon, rose, sandal-wood—a matter of personal choice for the customer, but we have them all—'

'Verbena,' nodded Jenny.

'Dainty and distinguished,' said Mr. Sandroyd approvingly. 'Now suppose we decide upon the knapsack first, and then place each article as bought into its proper receptacle. I have here —excuse me one moment'—he disappeared behind the counter and came back almost at once —'I have here', said Mr. Sandroyd, holding it up and turning it this way and that, 'a superb specimen of the knapsacker's art.'

Jenny gasped.

'Oh, I'm *sure*,' she began, 'I mean— You see, I haven't really very much money.'

'Ah!'

He put the knapsack down, and looked at her commiseratingly, holding his elbow with one hand, and scratching his ear with the other. 'Well now, let me think.' He nodded to himself. 'Yes. How would this be? We buy the soap and other articles first, and then we know how much money we have over? We can then suit the knapsack to our means. How would that be?'

Jenny agreed that that would be a very good idea, and said that she *did* want a tube of Kolynos, and in fact—er—well, perhaps a—

Mr. Sandroyd held up a kindly hand. He understood perfectly. Having the—how should he put it?—the publicity of camp life in their minds, many young ladies took this opportunity of renewing certain of their toilet accessories. A sponge, for instance, after quite a short use which had in no way impaired its properties, frequently proved to have lost its air of freshness when brought, as it were, into competition with a more newly purchased article ... Quite a small sponge? Certainly ... And the next?

Jenny told him ...

'And that really *is* all,' she said at last.

Mr. Sandroyd held up a finger, and shook his head. 'Food, madam. What in the Army we used to call the emergency rations. My own recommendation to my clients is a packet of chocolate and a box of dates. Dates,' said Mr. Sandroyd, lovingly stroking a box, 'from Tunis. A most sustaining food, as many travellers can attest who have crossed the desert on no more than a handful of dates.'

'Oh, thank you, yes,' said Jenny. 'I did want something. And that really *is* all, thank you. How much does all that come to?'

Mr. Sandroyd pushed his spectacles on to his forehead, and involved himself in the necessary addition. He emerged, after a short struggle, with a total of 18s. 4½d.

'I see,' said Jenny, but without much hope.

'Now what would that leave us for the knapsack?'

'What is the very cheapest you have?' asked Jenny anxiously.

'I shouldn't care to let you have one for less than five and sixpence.'

Jenny tried not to show her relief, and, having asked to see a five-and-sixpenny one, said that that would do beautifully. 'That's one pound three and tenpence halfpenny, isn't it, so if I give you one pound four—' She took out her purse.

'Excuse me a moment, miss.' Mr. Sandroyd disappeared into the western recesses of his counter, and came back a little mysteriously, one hand hidden. 'Now, madam,' he went on solemnly, 'I feel bound to ask you and I trust you will forgive the liberty, are you making this pleasure-jaunt in a large company of both sexes, or, as I might say, more intimately?'

'I—I'm meeting somebody,' stammered Jenny. 'I—I mean I shall be *with* somebody,' and told herself that she would always be with her dear Hussar whatever happened.

'Far be it from me to intrude,' said Mr. Sandroyd, holding up his free hand. 'All I wish to bring home to you, madam, is that there will be times, there must be times, when you will be separated from your companion. He—or she— *or* she,' he said again, to show how little he wished to intrude, 'will have gone to a neighbouring farm for eggs, while you remain in camp and boil the kettle. Or you yourself will have gone down to the stream to fill the kettle, while she— or, as it might be, he—remains in camp. However it is, you will be separated. You will be alone. Am I not right?' He waited anxiously.

Jenny agreed that there would be times when she would be alone.

'Ah!' He gave a sigh of relief. 'Then in that case I must insist on selling you a Watson's Wonderful Combination Watch-dog-and-Water-pistol.' With which words, he whipped it out from behind his back and presented it at an imaginary enemy in the doorway.

Jenny screamed, thinking that a gang was breaking in, thinking that he was going to fire. Mr. Sandroyd, taking the scream as a tribute to the alarming appearance of Watson's Wonderful Combination Watch-dog-and-Water-pistol, turned to her with a happy smile. 'Only five and six,' he said, 'the same price as the knapsack,' as if, in some way, this made it more of a bargain.

'Oh, but I daren't,' said Jenny. 'I should be afraid—why, I might—' She remembered that she was already being held responsible for one body, and she couldn't, she simply couldn't, take the risk of having to explain another.

'It is not a real pistol, madam,' he said delightedly.

'Oh, I thought it was.'

'Precisely! Now allow me to explain.' Without waiting for permission he brushed up his moustache, took a deep breath and launched himself on his favourite recitation.

'The watch-dog. Now what is the function of the watch-dog? He has, we may say, two functions. To alarm the intruder by his bark, and to arouse the household. Watson's Wonderful Combination Watch-dog-and-Water-pistol performs these two functions. It alarms the intruder, the marauding tramp, by the volume of its explosion, an explosion of similar volume to that of an ordinary pistol, and at the same time it summons help from the passer-by. But it does more. Let us suppose that some prowling ruffian has demanded a lady's purse, or—' Mr. Sandroyd modestly closed his eyes— 'something even dearer to her. She produces her Watson, and says "Leave me or I fire!" He laughs brutally; he realizes that she will never have the courage. She fires! And now comes in the real beauty of the invention, amply meriting in my opinion the word Wonderful. She pulls the trigger again, and a thin stream of water is discharged. Now consider, as Watson has considered it, the psychology of the marauder. He sees the pistol; he hears the explosion; instinctively he closes his eyes; then suddenly he feels something streaming down his brow. *Blood!* He has been hit! He will be hit again if he stays! He flies! Watson's Wonderful Combination Watch-dog-and-Water-pistol. Invented,' added Mr. Sandroyd kindly, the recitation over, 'by a man called Watson. A Benefactor. With six cartridges and full instructions, five and sixpence.'

'Oh,' said Jenny. 'I see.'

'No daughter of mine', said Mr. Sandroyd sternly, 'should go hiking without it.'

'I hadn't thought of—of tramps and things.'

Mr. Sandroyd hesitated for a moment, and then risked all his profit from five and sixpence in one large reassuring smile. She was so young and, in spite of her painted lips, so simple.

'And ten to one you won't need to, miss,' he said comfortingly. 'But just in case?' he pleaded. And, indeed, he was going to sleep happier tonight, if he could think of her under Watson's protection.

'But where would I carry it? I mean if you had it on your back in your knapsack—'

'In the pocket, madam? As you see, it is very small and handy. Or some ladies carry it in the garter, in the Spanish fashion, strapped, as it were, to the leg.'

'Oh, but I'm wearing suspenders!' said Jenny.

'Allow me, madam.' He went away and came back with a pair of cheap pink garters.

'Oh, but—' began Jenny.

'If you will allow me,' said Mr. Sandroyd with a fatherly beam, 'we will say nothing about —let me see, it was one pound three shillings and tenpence halfpenny, and five and sixpence for the pistol. That makes one pound nine shillings and fourpence ha'penny altogether. Are we putting the knapsack on now, or shall I wrap them all up?'

'Oh, wrapped up, please. Oh, but I—oh, but are you really? Oh, but it *is* good of you. Thank you so much… Thank you … Good afternoon and—and *thank* you.'

Mr. Sandroyd accompanied her to the door. At the door he ventured to pat her shoulder gently—two little pats so gentle that they hardly reached her.

'Take care of yourself, my dear young lady,' he said solemnly. 'In every way.'

'Oh, I *will*,' said Jenny earnestly. 'I *promise* I will.'

II

Jenny's one idea now was to escape from Tunbridge Wells. In Tunbridge Wells there were policemen; she had just seen one. In the fields there were none. Was there anything else she wanted before she made for the fields? There was. A shop across the road was calling out CREAM ICES, and this was always a trumpet-call for Jenny. She crossed the road and went into the Olde Kent Kreamery (F. Searle, Proprietor) for what would probably be the last cream ice she would ever eat.

It was the magic hour of tea, and the Olde Kent Kreamery was full of women who could have refreshed themselves more comfortably, but less noticeably, at home. Jenny shared a table with two friends, May and Nina. May lived in Tunbridge Wells with Aunt Jane— obviously another one; Nina had come in for the day, and was coming in again next week, and would be sure to let May know, so that they could have the whole day together this time. 'I did ask you how Mrs. Anderson was?' said May, and Nina said Yes, she had … and Mrs. Anderson was left there, so that Jenny never really knew how she was. May said that there was no doubt the busses were *awfully* convenient, whatever people said about spoiling the country, and Nina said that now that Daddy had had to give up the car, if it wasn't for the busses—but of course they did spoil the country rather, at least, when you weren't riding in one yourself. They both laughed at this, and May went into a reverie, her teaspoon idly chasing a stranger round her cup. As soon as her ideas were solidified, she said: 'Don't you think Life *is* rather like that? I mean things seem different according to how you look at them? I mean it's like looking at two sides of a wall.' Nina wrinkled her forehead, and said that she saw what May meant, and she supposed it *was* rather. Like two sides of a penny. 'Y-yes,' said May, a little doubtfully, feeling, perhaps, that Nina had not advanced the idea as much as she might have done; and then shook a dozen bangles off her wrist, and looked at her watch, and said: 'Good gracious, oh but there's plenty of time. I'll come down to the bus with you. We needn't go for five minutes yet.' Nina, looking at her watch, agreed, and asked for the bills, adding 'Separately, please,' just as May was beginning to say: 'Oh no, dear, you really mustn't.'

'Of course there's something about the country,' said May quickly, to hide her embarrassment, 'I mean the real country, that does make it different, I mean from a place like Tunbridge Wells, I mean *right* in the country, I mean like you are.'

'Well, of course,' said Nina, 'I do think you want to be one or the other. I mean—'

It was at this moment that Jenny came to a decision. Even at the cost of a pain in the forehead, she must finish her ice in four minutes so as to follow Nina into the real country, where it was different from a place like Tunbridge Wells …

The three bills were paid. May gathered herself and her bangles together and came out of her seat. There was a good deal to come, and Jenny, following her to the door, thought: 'Of course a lot of it's bone, but I believe if she *did* something, but I suppose it's too late now. Anyhow I shan't lose sight of her, which is lucky.' She lingered at the next shop window, so that she should not seem to follow, and then hurried up the hill, a little anxiously at first, but, reassured by unmistakable glimpses of May from the south, soon more leisurely, until she found herself again within earshot of the bangles and the voices, and knew that she was safe. They came to an omnibus.

'Well, we're in time all right,' said May, looking at her watch, and Nina, looking at the omnibus, agreed. Nina said: 'Don't bother to wait,' and May said that perhaps she *had* better get back, as Aunt Jane generally liked to be read to about that time. Nina asked her if she had read *A Flock of Sheep*, and May said wasn't it funny she was just going to ask Nina if *she* had. Apparently they had both read it, and thought it was lovely. May said that some friends of theirs, the Graysons, knew a great friend of Archibald Fenton's, and that he was just like that himself, and that all the Circus part was drawn from his own experiences, when he had run away from school. Nina said: 'Oh, I thought he was at Eton,' and May said she didn't *think* so, but she might be wrong. They both seemed to feel that nobody would want to run away from Eton.

Meanwhile Jenny was walking round the omnibus, to see if it would tell her where it went to. Not that she minded, so long as it went away from Tunbridge Wells; but she felt that a girl with two large parcels under her arm would not just be taking the parcels for a drive into the country, but would have some definite destination for them in her mind. She might sit next to Nina, but on the far side of the conductor, and say whatever Nina said. But then that would fix her in Nina's mind, and she didn't want to be fixed in anybody's mind. Besides, Nina might have a return ticket, if they had return tickets on country omnibuses. They didn't have them on London ones, of course.

The omnibus said that it was going to Maidstone. One of the less useful things which Jenny had learnt with her second governess was that Maidstone was the capital of Kent, and what was now proving to be one of the more useful things which she had learnt with her third governess was that the capital town of a county was where the county gaol was. So she decided not to go to Maidstone. In fact she had almost decided not to use the omnibus at all, owing to its unfortunate connexions, when a little woman in black came up to the driver and said 'Do you go through Endover?' and the driver said 'Near as may be, mother,' and she said 'Thank you' and went inside. There and then Jenny made up her mind to sit as far away from the little woman as she could, and whisper Endover to the conductor as quietly as possible, and get out at the next stopping-place after the little woman had got out, *and* (most important) pay for her ticket with half a crown to be on the safe side. Because anybody going to Endover with two parcels obviously lived at Endover, and ought to know how much the fare was.

Nina was getting in. May was saying 'Tell Mrs. Anderson I asked after her,' and Nina said 'Yes I will,' this further glimpse of Mrs. Anderson leaving Jenny much where she was. The omnibus started. May and Nina waved to each other, May with the more abandon, as befitted one in the more spacious surroundings. Then May went slowly up the hill to her Aunt Jane, jingling as she went, and telling herself that Nina wasn't exactly stuck-up, but wasn't nearly as nice as she used to be; and Nina sat in the omnibus, looking as if she had never waved at anybody, and telling herself that May wasn't a bad sort, but a little —*you* know, and perhaps it was as well that they needn't meet again ... And the omnibus went on; and by and by the little woman got out, and went off down a side-lane, and a quarter of a mile farther on they came to a village. This, then, thought Jenny, must be Endover. So she got out with her parcels, looking as if she had known the village all her life, and the omnibus growled its way out of sight ... and Jenny Windell stood there, watching it go, and telling herself that so far everything had worked out beautifully.

She was just preparing to take to the fields, when the dashing Hussar had one of his most dashing ideas. He whispered to Jenny, who was standing outside the village stores, and pointed to something in the window. Gurgling to herself she went in and bought it. She also bought two oranges.

Chapter Seven

Hussar's Daughter

I

Jenny sat down, not unwillingly, by the side of the little river, and unpacked her parcels. Not until everything was safely in the knapsack could she consider herself a real hiker. But with the contents of the parcels on the ground beside her, she asked herself 'What would a real Hussar do first?' and knew by instinct that the answer was: 'He would load and place in position Watson's Wonderful Combination Watch-dog-and-Water-pistol. '

She took it from its box. She followed the instructions with a solicitude which would have charmed the author of them; doubtless Watson himself. No pistol was ever more tenderly loaded. But all the instructions of the armament ring would not solve the problem which now faced her. *Which leg?* Hero and villain alike, as she well knew, drew from the hip. Hips, however, were not in the picture. If Jenny drew, it would be from the calf, or no, not the calf, since Nancy's skirt was a little short for the fashion, but from a point six inches above the knee. Which knee? The fact, impressed upon her by her second governess, that Madrid was the capital of Spain, gave her no clue to the romantic Spanish mode, but she knew (who better?) where English Hussars carried so dashingly their swords. Over the left hip. Bother! Hips again. Well, then, romance must make way for the practical. A simple trial urged the claims of the knee which came nearest. The right ... So the pistol was fixed there, and for the first time in the history of the elastic trade a pair of garters found themselves, to their surprise, upon the same leg.

It was a practical Jenny also who packed the knapsack. Change of clothes at the bottom; then the pyjamas; then the articles of toilet; then the towel; then the food. There! The knapsack was strapped up; the brown paper and string pushed down a rabbit-hole—('It's all right,' Jenny told herself, 'because they do have another way, because of ferrets'); the knapsack hoisted on to her shoulders; and there was Gloria Harris, complete from head to foot, from shoulder to knee, the bachelor girl on holiday.

Now to walk and walk and walk. She walked round a bend of the river, no farther, and stopped dead. A little cry escaped from her. His boots by his side, his back against a tree, the most unattractive man she had ever seen was taking his siesta.

At the noise of Jenny's cry, he opened his eyes.

'Gor',' said this unattractive man slowly, 'two ruddy females.'

Jenny stood there. Her heart was beating ridiculously, right up in her throat. It was silly, because she was the daughter of a soldier; not just a soldier in the Manchester Regiment, but a real Hussar. 'Courage, Jenny,' he was saying. Or was this Gloria Harris, to be so frightened?

She greeted him bravely.

'Good afternoon,' she said with a gulp.

'*One* ruddy female,' said the Tramp, correcting himself.

'Good afternoon,' said Jenny, but with the intonation now of one who was leaving. She took a step forward.

'What's the hurry?' said the Tramp.

Jenny knew, but thought it bad manners to explain. She smiled apologetically, and stopped.

'Fellowship ruddy road,' said the Tramp, and as a development of the theme, added 'Ships parss night.' He was silent for a little, and then explained 'Ruddy night,' in case Jenny hadn't understood.

She had seen him somewhere before: on the stage or in the pages of *Punch*. His nose and eyes were inflamed; he had a month's beard all over him; his hands were horrid, his feet showed through his socks ... and yet ... and yet ... somehow through the mat of hair which hid him there gleamed— something. Something, as it were, alive, human, companionable; or something of this that would be there when he was sober.

'*Siddown*!' commanded the Tramp with sudden violence.

Jenny sat down shrinkingly.

'Stannup!'

Jenny stood up.

'Do what you ruddy well like,' said the Tramp, exhausted by so much authority. He closed his eyes.

Jenny sat down. It was now or never, she felt. If she were frightened now, then she might as well go back to London. But it was idiotic to be frightened. She and Hussar and Watson— three to one! She sat down and took off her hat ...

'Wojjer think I've eat to-day?' asked the Tramp with his eyes closed. And he answered: 'Two ruddy chesnuts.'

'Is that all?' asked Jenny.

'Two ruddy 'orse-chesnuts.'

Jenny said that she had always thought that horse-chestnuts weren't ripe until September.

'*Ripe?*' said the Tramp scornfully. 'Two ruddy unripe ruddy 'orse—' he paused for a moment as if not quite sure about this, and then added 'ruddy chesnuts.'

'Would you like some chocolate?'

'No,' said the Tramp with absolute conviction.

There was another silence. It was very peaceful by the little river, and Jenny decided that she was not afraid of anybody now.

'Two ruddy 'orse-chesnuts off of a nolly-tree,' he mumbled, 'and I ses to 'er "Is this the way to Paradise?" and she ses—' He opened his eyes suddenly and shouted 'Stannup!'

'Why?' asked Jenny bravely, not moving.

"Cos you're sitting on a ruddy wopses nest.'

Jenny jumped to her feet with a scream.

'*Siddown*,' said the Tramp, "cos it's a false alarm.' He chuckled to himself 'Ruddy female,' and closed his eyes.

'I've a good mind to go altogether,' said Jenny severely, 'if you can't behave properly.'

She sat down again, a little farther away, having made quite sure that there were no nests of any kind underneath her.

'I've got a wife and six starving children,' said the Tramp with his eyes shut. 'Don't be 'ard on me.' He wagged a hand at her by way of withdrawal. 'Seven,' he amended. 'I was forgetting ruddy 'Orace.'

'What are the names of the others?' asked Jenny.

'Wot others?'

'The other six.'

'Six wot?'

'Six children.'

"Oose children?'

'Oh, never mind,' said Jenny.

'I don't,' said the Tramp. 'Not one ruddy barnacle.' He roused himself and came to business. "Ow much money 'ave you got?'

'I—I haven't counted,' said Jenny. She put a hand under her skirt—ready.

'Got the price of a pint?'

'A pint of what?'

'Gor'! These ruddy females. Better 'and it all over, and I'll give you back what I don't want.'

'No,' said Jenny.

'Owjer mean No?'

'I mean, Don't be silly.'

'Look 'ere,' said the Tramp reasonably, 'jer *wornt* to be strangled?'

'No.'

'Or 'it over the 'ead with a banana-skin?'

'No.'

'Jer *wornt* to wait until I've got me boots on, so's I can jump on yer defenceless stomach?'

'No.' *(Suppose it didn't work, didn't fire properly!)*

'Then 'and over.'

'Not like that,' said Jenny bravely.

'Like wot?'

'If you ask nicely, and say "Please," I might give you sixpence. That's a penny for each of your family.'

'Wot family?'

'Oh, never mind.'

'Wot about ruddy 'Orace?'

Jenny realized that the conversation was getting them nowhere. She slipped the pistol out of her garters, and held it behind her back. Then she stood up, her hat in her left hand.

'Good-bye,' she said. 'I'm going now.'

'Well 'and over first.'

'*Please* don't be silly.'

The Tramp hoisted himself with care and dignity to his feet.

'Boots or no boots,' he said, 'I've got to strangle one ruddy female.' He spat on his hands, and shuffled towards her.

With a prayer in her heart to Hussar, to Watson, to Mr. Sandroyd, to God—'oh, *please* let it be all right'—she pointed the pistol. 'Go away,' she said, 'or I shall fire.'

('He laughs brutally. He realizes that she will never have the courage' … *Jenny waited for the brutal laugh. It didn't come.*)

'Gor',' said the Tramp, surprised, 'she's got a ruddy gun.' He took a quick step back, trod firmly on a thistle, yelled, jumped high to avoid another one, and sat down heavily. 'Now then, now then,' he said, 'none o' that.'

'I've a good mind to shoot you,' said Jenny severely.

'You can't,' said the Tramp, feeling his foot tenderly.

'Why not?'

''Cos I've trod on a thistle and 'urt the ball of me toe.'

'That's no reason.'

'Wot isn't?' He was peering at his foot.

'Lots of people get shot when they've hurt their toes.'

'Trod on a thistle and 'urt the balls of their toes?' said the Tramp surprised.

'Yes,' said Jenny.

'Their ruddy big toes?'

Jenny nodded.

'I suppose', said the Tramp, leaving it there for the moment, 'you 'aven't got a tweezies in that bag o' yours.'

'I'm afraid not.'

'Not got a tweezies?'

'No.'

'Then *'ow*,' said the Tramp, returning to his foot, *'ow'* does a ruddy superfellus female remove 'er ruddy superfellus 'air, if she don't twitch it out with a tweezies?'

Jenny decided not to go into this.

'I must be going now,' she said firmly.

'Bye-bye,' said the Tramp.

'Good-bye,' said Jenny.

She walked off. At the next bend of the river she looked round. The Tramp was still deep in the mysteries of his foot. Jenny turned the corner, her heart, her whole body, singing with happiness ...

II

Jenny came to a haystack at about 9.30 that evening, and decided to sleep there. Almost immediately she made her second discovery of the day. The first had been that Tramps were Harmless—and this of course depends on whether or not you have Watson's Wonderful Combination Watch-dog-and-Water-pistol strapped to your leg. The second discovery was unconditionally true: being the notorious fact that it is always the other side of a haystack which affords invisibility.

As soon as Jenny saw the haystack, she decided to undress behind it. She went behind it ... and found that she was visible to the whole of Kent. Realizing that, by a silly mistake, she had got, not behind, but in front of the haystack, she went round to the back, and again found herself in front of it. The remaining two sides, promising as they seemed, proved to be no more trustworthy. She realized that you cannot undress behind a haystack.

She now began to wonder what people meant when they talked about 'sleeping under a haystack'. Not only had a haystack no behind, but it had no underneath; it seemed to be strangely ill-equipped. Did they mean sleeping on the top of a haystack? She walked round it again ... and there was a ladder! She sat down, caring nothing for visibility, and thought it out.

The hayfield ran down to the river, and by its banks there were still a few haycocks uncarried. The unfinished haystack meant not only that a farm was near, but that early in the morning men would be coming back to the field. It also meant, thought Jenny, that the farmer was not afraid of rain, and farmers always knew about the weather. Moreover, and this was important, they always got up very, very early. So what it came to was: she could sleep without fear of rain at the top of the haystack, but she would have to wake up very early, so as to get away before the farmer came.

Right. The Hussar's daughter began to make her plans.

1. She would get ready for bed by the side of the river. With a haycock behind her, and the stream, sheltered on the other side by trees, in front of her, she would be perfectly safe.

2. She would wash in the stream.
3. Teeth! (*She thought for a little.*) Yes. She would eat an orange for supper, and cut it with her nail-scissors, so that she had two orange-peel cups, and clean her teeth out of one of them.
4. She must be ready to start *at once* in the morning, with the knapsack already packed, so that if she suddenly saw the men coming, she could fly.
5. So she would have to sleep in her clothes. But wouldn't that be rather horrid next morning?
6. Sleep in her clothes and change into the green set as soon as she was up and away? But she didn't want to wear the green until they were dyed, because of getting over stiles.
7. Lovely idea! Sleep in the pyjamas with the stockinette over. Pack everything else in the knapsack, and have it ready by her side. As soon as she woke up, roll the pyjamas above her knees and slip on knapsack and shoes; then it would just look like the stockinette and bare legs, which anybody might wear.
8. Dress properly a little farther on after washing in the stream.

Jenny supped. The orange was good, the chocolate was good; but the dates, at close quarters, were disappointing. It seemed impossible that anybody should cross, or want to cross, the desert on a handful of dates; Mr. Sandroyd must have been misinformed about that. Jenny, licking her fingers after handling only two of them, turned with relief to her orange, and thought with pleasure of the wash which was to come. The orange cups made, she picked up her knapsack and went down to the river …

It was the hour between sunset and the dark. The flush had faded out of an innocent sky; pinks and blues were merged into a dappled grey; the world had lost its colour suddenly, its song, its laughter. Under the alders the river met the night, and began to send out tentacles of darkness towards the ghostly Jenny who leaned over it. Quickly she slipped on her clothes and hurried back to the haystack. Quickly, before the blackness was upon her, she prepared everything for the morning. Then Night came down and greeted her ... enfolded her while still she knelt, a child on her castle, saying her prayers to God and her Hussar.

WEDNESDAY

Chapter Eight

Further activity in London

I

It was a pity that, from the nature of them, Aunt Jane would never read the best notices of her career. Everything, of course, was in her favour. To begin with, she was an actress; and in acting, alone among the arts, a certain standard of ability is assumed, so that the artist has to be found out, rather than discovered. Partly because (for this or that reason) she had accepted few engagements, partly because most of these engagements were limited to single performances on Sunday nights, Jane Latour had never been found out. On the contrary, this obvious reluctance of hers to commercialize her art seemed a sufficient guarantee of its purity; and, taken in conjunction with her surprising death (and the fact that most of her authors had been elaborating a new technique, which would really account for anything), it more than justified the enthusiasm of the obituary notices.

In dealing with the other side of Jane Latour's life, criticism was naturally more restrained. If she did take snow in large and increasing quantities, certainly nothing more was said of it than that 'she was a well-known social figure, particularly among the younger set', and her ability as a harpist can only have been implied in the statement that 'she was always ready to offer her services on behalf of any charity'. As for her matrimonial adventure with the Count, it lost itself so easily in a summary of her distinguished father's services for the Empire that a careless reader would have supposed that she had married a Colonial Bishop.

So much for Jane Latour among the obituary notices. Jane Latour murdered had the front page to herself.

There was never any doubt that it was Murder. In inviting the co-operation of the Press and the Public, Inspector Marigold had not only been photographed in four different positions, but had put our readers in full possession of all the facts. Dr. Willoughby Hatch (the well-known expert) had yet to conduct his *post mortem*, or, at least, to communicate his findings through the Coroner to the nation. Opinion, therefore, to some extent was to be reserved. But the absence of a weapon and the presence of strange footprints and a strange handkerchief made the nature of the crime obvious.

Who was the mysterious Jenny? Was she indeed the murderess; or was she (a theory held in many well-informed quarters) another victim? Suppose (said Our Special Investigator beneath a photograph of Chukrapoota, where the dead woman's father had resided at one period), suppose Jenny had been lured by somebody engaged in the White Slave Traffic to what he had thought to be a deserted house. Suppose that the dead woman, who, as Jane Windell, had herself resided there at one time, had interrupted them. Suppose—and nobody who knew Miss Jane Latour would be surprised at this—that she had bravely intervened to save the intended victim. What happens? Callously the ruffian strikes her down. Then hastily rendering Jenny unconscious with a whiff of chloroform, he lets her out of the window, jumps after her, and half-drags, half-carries her to where his car is waiting. But he has made two little slips, just those little slips which have brought so many murderers to the gallows. Unknown to him, she has dropped the handkerchief with which she was endeavouring to stanch the injuries of the dead woman. Unknown to him, she has left her footprints in the bed. [*'Flower-bed,' corrected the Night Editor, feeling that the sex-interest was getting too strong*] ... This theory, held as it was in many well-informed quarters, might or might not be the correct one; but obviously, correct or not, the first thing to do was to identify the mysterious Jenny. *Who was Jenny?*

Miss Nancy Fairbrother knew the answer to that. Reading a paper on her way to Bloomsbury this morning, she saw that it would not be long before the police knew. The afternoon papers would give a full description of Miss Jenny Windell in the clothes which she was wearing on that fatal morning; the clothes which were now hidden away in Nancy's flat. Everybody would be looking for a fair girl of medium height, grey eyes, attractive appearance, in green georgette with a biscuit-coloured picture-hat. Well, that wasn't going to help anybody. And even if they caught her, she could still persuade certain well-informed quarters that she was victim, not villain.

But could she? Not Jenny Windell. Jenny was too simple, too straightforward for that. If only it had been Nancy Fairbrother!

For nobody could pretend so well as Nancy. She combined the imagination of the novelist with the technique of the old-fashioned actress, transmuting herself into everything which went through her mind. She thought, as it were, in inverted commas. If, in her imagination, she met the Prince of Wales, and they talked together, then she was the Prince of Wales, talking like a Prince (of Wales) who had just met the secretary of an author, and she was Miss Nancy Fairbrother, talking like a girl who was secretary to an author, who had just met the Prince of Wales ... which was all very different from the Prince of Wales just meeting Miss Nancy Fairbrother. So, had she been in Jenny's position, it would have been easy for her to have told Inspector Marigold the whole story of that terrible scene in Auburn Lodge; but she would have found it difficult, if asked for Miss Latour's actual words to the leader of the White Slave Gang, not to have given a much too brilliant impression of Miss Latour actually saying them.

Well, she was not Jenny. But she was Jenny's right hand; the girl who was to save Jenny. Also she was Mr. Archibald Fenton's private secretary, and somehow she had to pawn Jenny's watch to-day. Walking from the omnibus to Mr. Fenton's house she became a girl with a watch to pawn; a watch that had once belonged to her little sister Joyce.

II

Mr. Fenton was feeling pretty pleased with himself this morning. There were several reasons for this. First of all, it was his day for weighing himself, and owing to some mechanical defect in the bathroom weighing-machine, he had gone down to thirteen stone seven. Secondly, Ursula had now definitely got measles, so that her three little sisters would have to be taken by their mother to Bognor Regis to keep out of danger. Thirdly, Stephen's half-term report had just arrived, and he was top in Divinity. To one who had to leave all that sort of thing to his wife and children, this was extremely gratifying. Fourthly, the photographs in the Bookman had come out well, particularly the one of himself and Lady Claudia and Fanny at Brocken, in which Fanny, being partially obscured by the fountain round which they were grouped, looked younger than she had been for many years. Lastly, and most importantly, he began to see his way through the new book. It was going to be All Right.

'Good morning, Miss Secretary,' he said cheerily to Nancy, as he came into the work-room.

'Good morning, Mr. Fenton,' said Joyce's sister bravely.

'Hallo!'

'Yes, Mr. Fenton?'

'What's the matter with our Miss Fairbrother this bright and breezy morning?'

'Matter, Mr. Fenton?'

'Come on, let's hear all about it.'

'Really, Mr. Fenton, if you think I'm going to interrupt your morning with my own silly troubles—'

'You'll interrupt it much more, if you sit there looking like St. Agnes or St. Agatha or somebody, just before the lion came in.'

'A lion *has* just come in,' said Nancy, with a flutter of her eyes.

'That's better. Now then, what is it?'

Nancy swallowed and said: 'It's my little sister, Joyce.'

'I say, not dead? I'm terribly sorry. I wouldn't have said that, if I'd known—'

'Oh no, no!' said Nancy. She thought of saying 'Worse than death', in a sad sepulchral voice, but stopped herself just in time. If once she began like that, there was no knowing where she (and her little sister Joyce) would get to. 'But she's in trouble.'

'Ah!' said Mr. Fenton sympathetically, quite understanding. A pleasing picture of Nancy also 'in trouble', and himself the cause of it, flashed through his mind.

'Not that sort of trouble,' said Nancy primly.

'Oh!' said Mr. Fenton, disappointed. 'Well, what?'

'Money.'

'Ah!' said Mr. Fenton coldly. He might have known.

'She's sent me her watch to pawn, and I—I don't know how to do it, and—'

A revived Mr. Fenton held out his hand.

'Let's have a look at it.'

As he examined it, and noted the little 'J' in diamonds (for 'Joyce'), Nancy went on hurriedly: 'You see, she's in an office in a cathedral town, and I don't know if they do have pawnbrokers there, but Joyce daren't go to one, because she might be seen,

79

and if once it got about, I mean her employer is so very *strict*, and besides it looks bad, doesn't it, I mean it shows that you're spending more money than you ought to, and—'

'Real diamonds?' said Mr. Fenton.

'"m.' Nancy gave another gulp. 'Uncle George gave it to her on her birthday. She was his favourite. He's dead now, so— I mean he wouldn't mind, but I've never been to a pawnbroker, and—'

'D'you know how much he paid for it?'

'I *think* twenty pounds,' Joyce said 'Aunt Emily told her, because she was rather annoyed about it, I mean Aunt Emily, but I don't *know*. It looks very good, doesn't it, and if only she could get ten pounds, because you generally get half, don't you, and—'

'When you say "pawn", do you mean you want to redeem it later, or do you just want to sell it?'

'Sell it to a pawnbroker, I thought,' said Nancy.

Mr. Archibald Fenton was thinking. Until two years ago he had been a Realist, thus sharing with most critics and Court Painters the conviction that photography is the highest form of art. To describe with such accuracy that even the village idiot, looking over the artist's shoulder, would say 'Danged if it tident Farmer Bassett's old sow': surely authorship could go no higher than this. He discovered that it could. It could bring back a Rabelaisian robustness to the English novel; even if in so doing (as the man who looked after them in Langley's circus wrote to tell Mr. Fenton) it made three distinct errors in the toilet of a female elephant. Mr. Archibald Fenton ceased to be a realist ... but at times he had misgivings. What it came to, he decided at last, was this. Elephants didn't matter because very few people knew about elephants, but with horses you would have to be careful.

Would you have to be careful with pawnbrokers? Hardly ... except, of course, for the cheap editions ... And serial rights ... Serial rights: that settled it.

'How would it be', said Mr. Fenton, 'if I took it to a pawnbroker for you?'

'Oh, Mr. Fenton!' said Joyce's big sister.

'That's all right,' said Mr. Fenton airily. 'I'll do it this afternoon.'

'It *is* good of you. Joyce—' she gulped. 'I hardly know how to thank you.' She just touched her eyes with her handkerchief. Pretty little thing she was.

'That's all right.' He patted her shoulder encouragingly. 'Well, let's get on with Chapter Five.'

It is, of course, at the end of Chapter Five (as Nancy well knew) that Eustace Frere pawns his cuff-links.

III

Mr. Watterson's authority for what was happening in the great world had always been *The Times*. Mrs. Watterson's authority for what the Radicals were up to had always been Mr. Watterson. At Bath Station, on the morning after the wedding of his grandson, Mr. Watterson proposed to buy a copy of *The Times* and take it and Mrs. Watterson into a first-class carriage with him.

'What do you want *The Times* for, dear?' said Mrs. Watterson.

'To read,' said Mr. Watterson, in the voice of one who thought the question unnecessary.

'But it's waiting for you at home, dear. It seems a pity to have two copies.'

Mr. Watterson had been married for fifty years, and knew that the urgency for his need for *The Times* was one of those things which his wife would never understand.

'My dear, I can afford the extra twopence,' he said mildly.

'It seems such a waste. Why not get one of the other papers, dear?'

'There *are* no other papers,' said Mr. Watterson, believing it.

'Nonsense. There are plenty. Look, there's the *Morning Post*.'

From time to time Mr. Watterson had read the *Morning Post* at his club, and from time to time Mr. Watterson and the Editor of the *Morning Post* had agreed upon this or that, but not until the Editor of *The Times* and Mr. Watterson had agreed upon it first.

'Very well,' he said, 'I won't get a paper.'

'Oh, but you *must* have a *paper,* dear. Only it seems so silly to—'

'I *don't* want a paper, I don't *want* a paper, *I* don't want a paper,' said Mr. Watterson fretfully.

'Oh well, dear, you know best. Will you get me the *Illustrated London News?*'

The wedding champagne still disagreeing with him, Mr. Watterson bought two copies of the *Illustrated London News*, one for each of them. Mrs. Watterson sighed and said nothing. She had been married for fifty years, and knew that men would always go on being children. This accounted for War and Politics and Sport, and so many things.

They reached home a little after midday, and as soon as Mr. Watterson had opened the door, Cook and Hilda and Alice were in the hall. There had been an argument about this at breakfast.

Cook said that it was *her* place to break any domestic news, good or bad, to the Mistress.

Hilda said: 'When I broke that what d'you call it varse, *you* didn't break it, catch *you.*'

'Well, *you broke* it,' said Cook unanswerably.

Alice said: 'It's me the Police will want to know about what she's wearing what I put out for her being her maid as you might say.'

Cook said: 'All in good time, Alice. I'm not talking about when the Police comes, but when the Mistress comes.'

Hilda said: 'Well, I've got to be in the 'all to get the luggage in and all, 'aven't I?'

Cook said: 'I'm not saying for that.'

Alice said, sniffing slightly: 'I'm the only one as reely cares about poor Miss Jenny, being her maid, as you might say.'

Cook said: 'Alice! How *can* you sit there and say things like that, knowing what we all think about Miss Jenny, and never was a sweeter, more innocent young lady, and Dear knows what—'

Hilda said: 'Well, I've got to be in the 'all, 'aven't I, to get the luggage in and all,' just as Alice was saying: 'Well, I was the one as wanted to ring up the police, only you wouldn't let me, being her own maid, well almost.' So naturally Cook said: 'Well, if we all speak at once like that, nobody will know *'oo's* missing. That's all I'm thinking of.'

'Well, I've got to be in the 'all,' said Hilda, 'that's all there is to it, and you two can do what you like.'

This was what they did; and so, as soon as the door opened, Cook and Hilda and Alice were in the hall crying: 'It's Miss Jenny, ma'am!'

'Miss Jenny?' said Mrs. Watterson. 'What?'

'She never came home, ma'am.'

'Never came home?' said Mr. Watterson, edging towards *The Times*. He picked it up, as if accidentally, and opened it, but still with the air of one listening to something else, in the middle, at the leading articles.

Cook and Hilda and Alice were explaining vociferously. They had nothing to explain, save the fact that Miss Jenny had said she would be out to lunch, and had never come back again. For, like Mr. Watterson, they had read no papers.

'Hubert,' said Mrs. Watterson, 'are you listening? Jenny went out yesterday morning and hasn't come back.'

Mr. Watterson was not listening. The name Auburn Lodge had called to him from the page opposite the leading articles, and he was reading about the death of Jane Latour ...

'Hubert!'

'Yes, dear, I know.' He went to his study.

'What are you going to do?'

'Ring up the police.'

He shut the door behind him. Alice's triumphant eye caught Cook's reluctant one. 'What,' said Alice's eye, 'did I tell you?'

IV

Mr. Archibald Fenton lunched, as usual, at his club. After luncheon he found himself involved in one of those unending literary discussions, whose like he had set rolling so often and so happily in the past. Now he found them embarrassing. A man with a Fentonian reputation, particularly if he be still an occasional critic, has to be careful. As a novelist he could have afforded, and would have preferred, to be generous; to leave behind him those who would say to each other: 'What I like about Fenton is that he's always so enthusiastic about other novelists.' As an occasional critic in the monthlies his one care was not to commit himself in private to anything which might be said more cleverly in public. For instance, Blair Sturge's name was mentioned. Awkward. Sturge's book was coming out next month, and Fenton had not yet decided what he was going to say about it. It depended upon certain unknown quantities, one of them being, of course, the actual quality of the book. He might use that phrase, which had come into his mind the other day, about 'the pen of a highly certificated governess who had just learnt the facts of sex'— supposing, of course, that the new book was sufficiently like the previous one to justify it. On the other hand, Sturge and Ramsbotham were bosom friends—which made it all very difficult ...

He temporized. He temporized so successfully that it was teatime before the discussion died out. The others thereupon ordered tea. Fenton felt that it was up to him, as one who had brought the smell of hops back to the English novel, to do something hearty with a tankard of beer. Never having liked beer very much, he felt depressed afterwards. London was a beastly place. Where was he dining to-night? He looked at his engagement book, and found that he wasn't. Hell!

He turned over a page or two, and saw that he had a blank week in front of him, except for next Tuesday when he was dining with the Moberleys. Oh God, he had forgotten all about that!

It was at a cocktail-party. Well, what did people do at cocktail-parties? How many hundred books had he read— well, reviewed—about cocktail-parties, in which people— And Good Heavens, it was only a kiss at most, and where else could you put your hand? Really, for a modern young girl and an art-student at that … And she had been absolutely all over him until that moment.

Damn Cynthia Moberley!

He tried to think of one or two good things for a short, stout man to say to a girl who had slapped his face the last time they'd met … There weren't any.

He tried to think of one or two good things for a man to say, who was reviewing a novel in which a young girl slapped a man's face just because he had kissed her … He thought of several. Delightfully contemptuous, ironical things …

It looked as if life were too many-sided to be pinned down to any however realistic novel. Face-slapping in the nineteen-thirties! Who would have guessed it?

No, he couldn't dine with the Moberleys. That was certain.

He had a renewed internal awareness of what had once been a tankard of beer, and decided again that London was beastly. Why not leave it, and go down to the cottage? And really get on with the book? Authors were allowed these sudden decisions, and they always made a good paragraph for one's publishers. He would write to Mrs. Moberley. He would get away from London this evening ...

It was then that Mr. Archibald Fenton remembered about the watch. Oh well, that was all right. He would pawn it now on the way home, and send the money on to Miss Fairbrother, and tell her to take a fortnight's holiday. He took out his pocket-book. Luckily, for the bank would be shut by now, he had enough. Two five-pound notes, and three ten in addition. And of course, if he sent Nancy a cheque, he would have the watch money.

He went off to find a pawnbroker, well pleased with himself as a man of sudden moods; a man also, when necessary, of decision. He returned to the house in Bloomsbury, rang up his housekeeper at the cottage, and wrote three letters.

To Fanny at Bognor Regis he wrote:

'Dear Fanny, Hope you all arrived safely. Chapter Five is sticking rather, and I'm just off to the cottage for a fortnight to get it cleared up.
Archie.'

He read the letter through and added: *Love to you all.*

Fanny read the letter and said to herself: 'I wonder what *that* means.' And then aloud: 'No, darling, not marmalade *and* jam.'

To Mrs. Andrew Moberley in Seymour Street he wrote:

'Dear Mrs. Moberley, Will you ever forgive me? Well, yes, I am encouraged to think that you might, because you too have the artistic temperament, and know what slaves it makes of us. I have got to get down to the country, away from everybody, and wrestle with the new book in solitude. It is now or never. You know how that can be, as few women would know. Am I wrong in putting my work first, even above courtesy to one who has shown so much kindness to me? Somehow I feel that I am not; and that you will understand why, very regretfully, I ask you to excuse me from your so charmingly hospitable table on Tuesday.

'Yours most sincerely,
'Archibald Fenton.'

He read the letter through, and regretted the unfortunate assonance of 'hospitable table'. But he was damned if he would write the thing out again.

Mrs. Moberley read the letter and passed it to her daughter. Cynthia read it and said: 'Oh well, as long as he doesn't wrestle with *me* in solitude, I don't mind.'

Mr. Fenton began his third letter. To Miss Nancy Fairbrother in Elm Park Mansions he wrote:

'Dear Miss Fairbrother, I must get away into the country and work on that chapter by myself. It is really the crucial chapter of the book. I enclose a cheque for £15 10s.—i.e. £12 10s. for your sister's watch, plus a week's salary. I suggest that you take a fortnight's holiday, on half-salary (as you have had no time to arrange anything) and perhaps in these circumstances you wouldn't mind attending to my letters, which I shall send on to you, say twice a week, with instructions. I had a job to get the £12 10s. and I doubt if anybody else would have got more than a tenner, so I hope Joyce will be properly grateful to you. You can tell her from me to be more careful in the future! Look after Miss Nancy Fairbrother while I am away, and don't let her get into mischief!

'Yours, A. F.'

He read the letter through and added: 'P.S. I sold the watch outright, as you said you wanted this.'

Nancy read the letter, and said: 'Thank the Lord *he's* out of the way. Now I can really *do* something.'

Chapter Nine
Arrival of Naomi Fenton

I

Jenny had never slept out before, but she knew all about it. Lady Barbara, escaping in the guise of a boy from an unwelcome marriage, had spent many a night in a hay-stack; so had Ned Tregellis, escaping from an unwelcome prison in the guise of a girl. Both of them had spoken enthusiastically of the experience. 'By'r lady,' had said young Tregellis, 'but it shall go ill with me if ever again I spend the night within the confines of four walls'; and (on other occasion) Lady Barbara had declared: 'An I cannot pass the night beneath God's canopy, I vow I will not bed me at all.' It would have been convenient, this being so, if they had married each other, but unfortunately they were in different books. Jenny, who had been kept awake by a night-jar who went to bed at two, and, when at last she fell asleep, woken up by a blue-bottle who started the day at four, was not so enthusiastic. Long before the farmer thought of getting up, she was down from her haystack, feeling uncomfortable and unrefreshed, and telling herself that she supposed one got used to it.

Still she had done it. She had slept out—alone. How many girls could say that? And here she was, by the side of her river again, a new day beginning. However tickly and wriggly she felt, she had this confidence in herself to sustain her. She was doing a very exciting thing.

Dare she bathe? She would never feel comfortable again unless she did. Here was a little bay in the stream where the banks went steeply down to a gravelled floor. Nobody would be up so early, nobody was about. Should she? She looked all round her. She was alone. She scrambled down the bank and took off her knapsack, shoes and dress; put the towel ready. Now she was in her pyjamas, and people often went about in pyjamas. She washed. Now for it. She hurried up the bank and took a last look round. All safe. Down again. One, two, three—go! ... She was down on her back in the water, the water was playing round her and over her, the sun was coming through the alders at her, birds were singing above her—By'r lady, but it shall go ill with me, an ever I lave myself again within the confines of a porcelain bath.

She lay there, exulting in the fact that it was she, the authentic Jenny, who had so escaped from Miss Windell and the world. But it was cold. She let the water go right over her head, and sat up with a gasp, and came out. In a little while she was dried and dressed. She sat on the bank in the sun, munching chocolate happily. Now she was comfortable, inside and out, and ready for anything. Oh, Hussar, *isn't* it fun? Aren't I different? Soon she was walking on again and wondering about breakfast.

It must still have been an hour before her usual breakfast-time when she met the Painter.

'Oh!' said Jenny to herself, 'somebody sketching.'

She would have passed behind him with perhaps a 'Good-morning', but he spoke to her, and his voice was nicer than the Tramp's.

He said, without looking up: 'Are you an artist's model, by any chance?'

'I'm afraid not,' said Jenny, and stopped for a moment.

'Dear, dear, how very unlucky one is.'

'Did you want an artist's model?' said Jenny, an idea suddenly coming to her.

'Well, I did rather.'

'What for? I mean what as?' She would have to earn money somehow, soon.

'A nymph or water-sprite. I suppose you wouldn't care to be a nymph or water-sprite? In other words a naiad?'

'What do they wear?'

'Nothing,' said the Painter.

'Oh, then I'm afraid I couldn't,' said Jenny reluctantly.

'I thought you probably couldn't.'

'Would an artist's model?'

'I think so. If I asked her nicely.'

'It seems funny,' mused Jenny. And then in explanation: 'I suppose you get used to it.'

'That's it. We both get used to it.'

'How funny.'

'Well, looking at it in another way, clothes are funny.'

'Well, it depends how you look at it.'

'That', said the Painter, 'is really what I mean.'

Jenny was silent for a little, and then said: 'I couldn't possibly, could I?'

'No,' said the Painter, 'not possibly.'

'All the same, it seems different in the open air somehow. I mean it's like saying "Will you marry me?" and you say "Oh, I don't think I could," and it's quite all right asking, and it's quite all right saying "No," only it just happens you can't.'

'Exactly.'

'I'm so sorry. Do you mind if I sit down and watch you?'

'Not a bit. Do you know anything about painting?'

'Nothing, I'm afraid.'

'That's good.'

He went on painting, and Jenny went on watching him.

'What a lot of things one doesn't know anything about,' she said.

'Practically everything.'

'Do you live near here?'

He dabbed with his brush over a shoulder.

'I'm at the farm there. A mile or two back.'

'Oh! How funny!'

'Why?'

'I slept on their haystack last night. Do you think they'd mind?'

'I am sure they would have been delighted, if they had known about it.'

'I thought perhaps they wouldn't mind.'

The Painter, looking in a depressed sort of way from his canvas to the river, and back again, said: 'Is that how you live?'

'How do you mean?'

'On haystacks.'

'Oh, no! I'm hiking,' said Jenny proudly.

'Just how does one do that? I've often wondered.'

'Well, you walk about with a knapsack—'

'What we used to call walking?'

'Well, yes. And you sleep in haystacks and things—'

'What we used to call sleeping out?'

'Yes. Well—well, that's about all, I suppose.'

'I see … I'm glad I know at last. And you're doing all this entirely by yourself?'

'Yes,' said Jenny. 'It's rather fun.'

'It must be. What do you call yourself when you talk to yourself?'

'Do you mean, what is my name?'

'Well, it comes to that, I suppose.'

Jenny stopped herself from saying 'Jenny Windell' just in time.

'Gloria Harris,' she said.

'You can't seriously want to be called Miss Harris,' said the Painter, after considering this for a little.

'Oh no!' agreed Jenny eagerly.

'I thought not. If it comes to that, I'm not so set on Gloria as some.'

'Isn't it funny,' said Jenny, 'I used to think it was a lovely name, and now it seems rather silly.'

'What did they call you at school?'

'I never went to school.'

'A pity. That might have given us a wider choice.'

Suddenly Jenny remembered that she had two handkerchiefs with 'N' on them. Supposing she dropped one!

'Gloria Harris isn't the whole name,' she said.

'I thought it couldn't be.'

'It's Gloria Naomi Harris. I'm really Naomi. I mean to special friends.'

'That's much better. And now,' said the Painter, 'although you have expressed no interest in the subject whatever, I shall tell you *my* name.'

'Oh, I *do* want to know. Really I do,' said Jenny earnestly. 'What is it, please?'

'Derek Fenton.'

'Oh!' said Jenny.

'Quite so.'

'Are you related to Archibald Fenton?'

'No. He's related to *me*.'

'I mean—'

'It so happens that we are brothers. I', explained the Painter, 'am the nice one.'

'How funny.'

'Not if you've seen Archibald,' said the Painter.

'I mean it's funny because—' Jenny stopped. She couldn't be sure whether Gloria Naomi Harris knew Nancy Fairbrother or not. Perhaps safer not. 'I mean, well, everybody knows Archibald Fenton. I mean *A Flock of Sheep,* and everything.'

'Have you read *A Flock of Sheep?*' asked Derek.

'Oh, yes!'

'You must tell me about it.'

'You mean you haven't *read* it?' said Jenny, in astonishment.

'No.'

'Oh, but *oughtn't* you to have?'

'Well, *he* hasn't seen this picture,' Derek pointed out.

'It's funny,' said Jenny. 'Two of the people in the bus were talking about it only yesterday.'

'About this picture?' asked Derek, surprised.

'Oh, no, I mean about the book.'

'This picture', said Derek impressively, 'will be talked about in taxi-cabs.'

It was funny, thought Jenny, that they hadn't really seen each other yet. She had been going to pass behind him; she had sat down behind him; and never once had he turned round to her. She was looking now at the back of his sunburnt neck; he was looking from the picture to the river, from the river to the picture, to the palette, to the picture, to the river again; throwing remarks to her, as it were, over his shoulder. Occasionally she saw the line of his jaw, brown and hard. His hair was very short at the back—not at all what you expect of a painter, but perhaps he wasn't a very good painter—and it went to a point in what was really rather a fascinating way. It was funny to have lived all these years—eighteen—and never to have seen the way a man's hair went at the back before.

'You're much younger than your brother, aren't you?'

'Yes.'

'Don't you ever read his books?'

'No.'

'Why not?'

'In case I might like them.'

'But—but—that's a reason *for* reading them, isn't it?'

'Well, you see, I don't like Archibald.'

'Oh!' She thought this over for a little, and then said 'Why?' It seemed so funny not to like your brother.

'Well, there are a lot of people in the world, and you can't like them all. So *I* ... don't like Archibald.'

Jenny tried to think of any other brothers she had known who hadn't liked each other. She could only think of Jacob and Esau.

'Did he rob you of your inheritance?' she asked.

'Well, I suppose he did in a way.'

'How? Or don't you like talking about it?'

'I love talking about it.'

'Then how?'

'Well, you see, I inherited the name of Fenton, and he's gone and spoilt it.'

'Spoilt it?' said Jenny indignantly. 'He's made it famous.'

'That's what I mean. He's spoilt it for *me*. As soon as I mention my name, people say— well, what Gloria Naomi Harris said.'

'What did I say?' wondered Jenny, wrinkling her forehead. 'Oh, yes, I remember. Well, but you ought to be *proud*.'

'I am. Too proud to bask in the back-wash of Archibald's fame, if you follow my metaphor. I look forward', he went on in a dreamy voice, 'to the day when a complacent and hopeful Archibald is shown by a butler with a bell-like voice into a crowded ducal drawing-room, and, as soon as they hear his name, all the guests rush up to him and say: "Oh *do* tell me, *are* you any relation to *Derek* Fenton?" That', said Mr. Derek Fenton, indicating his canvas with a circling gesture of the brush, 'is why I am doing this. In private life I am in the wine-trade.'

II

At first it was a little disappointing to Jenny to find that he was in the wine-trade. A young girl whose alcoholic experience has been limited to one cocktail has not that sensitiveness which enables her to appreciate the gulf fixed between the selling of Burgundy and the selling of oatmeal biscuits. But a renewed study of the back of his neck convinced her that he couldn't be the man who actually sold the bottles, but was more probably the owner of the château in France where the grapes were grown—a sort of gentleman-fruit-farmer, which was rather an exciting thing to be. But she decided not to discuss the wine-trade with him, in case he wasn't.

'You won't mind my asking,' said the Fruit-farmer suddenly, after an anxious five minutes with Art, 'but in the intervals of being—or rather,' he added hastily, '*not* being a water-nymph, you live somewhere?'

'St. John's Wood,' said Jenny, without thinking.

'Oh, I see, a wood-nymph. Well, what I wanted to say was, do dryads in St. John's Wood have an occasional breakfast from time to time?'

'Well, of course,' smiled Jenny.

'Tell me', said Derek, 'all about it.'

'Do you mean what do I eat for breakfast?'

'And drink, and contemplate, and reject, and turn up the nose at, and have two helps of.'

'Well, it depends. I generally have grapefruit and toast and a scrambled egg and marmalade and an apple. *And* coffee, of course.'

'This is not my lucky day,' said Derek. 'I was hoping that you would say an orange and scones and a hard-boiled egg and butter and a banana. *And* milk, of course.'

'Oh?' said Jenny, puzzled.

'If you *had* said that, we would have opened that string-bag over there, and seen what somebody's sent us.'

'Oh!' said Jenny ecstatically. 'Are you inviting me to breakfast?'

'I certainly am, as we say in America.'

'Oh, have you been to America?'

'Yes and No,' said Derek.

'But either you've been or you haven't,' laughed Jenny. 'I mean, mustn't you?'

'No and Yes, if you follow me.'

'I don't quite, I'm afraid.'

'I started in the direction of America once, but there were sixty Americans on board who talked to me so much and so loudly about Archibald that I saw that it was hopeless to try and settle down with a hundred and fifty million of them.'

'What did you do?'

'Came back again.'

'Do you mean at once?'

'As soon as they could turn the boat round.'

'Then you never saw America at all?'

'I saw New York from the river. New York from the river,' said Mr. Derek Fenton enthusiastically, 'at a moment when the sun has just set, and no one is asking you what Archibald looked like as a child, is enough for anybody. Tell me, are you accepting my invitation?'

'To breakfast? Please!'

'Good.'

He stood up. Now they were facing each other. She tried to tell herself what he looked like; to remember what he looked like, feature by feature, so that when she went on, and saw him never again, she could think about him sometimes. Was he good-looking or ugly, tall or short? She hardly knew. All she knew was that she liked him, that you couldn't help liking him; that, if you told him about Hussar, it would be all right, that even if you told him about Aunt Jane, it would be all right. Her thoughts went back to the Tramp, and she thought that *he* was nice too, I mean *really*, if you got to know him. Derek Fenton made everybody seem nice ... And then suddenly she felt herself going hot all over, and she turned away quickly to hide her face; because suddenly she remembered that they had been talking about water-nymphs, and that just for one funny moment in that early morning sunshine, when the world was so remote from all that she had ever been taught, she had felt that being a water-nymph for him to paint would not have been such a terrible thing to do, but simple and natural and beautiful. Now, suddenly, she knew that he was the one man in the world for whom she could never, never do it.

III

'This', said Derek, cracking an egg on his shoe, 'is a breakfast, not a Passport office. If I ask you anything which is inconvenient, just pass me the butter in a casual way, and I shall know that I am on slippery ground. Is that all right?'

'Yes,' said Jenny. 'Thank you.'

'Then, roughly and in a general way, where do we go from here?'

'Do you mean, where am *I* going?'

'On whose haystack are you resting to-night?'

'Well,' said Jenny guardedly, 'I'm sort of making for the coast.'

'As you were heading when we met, you would have struck it at about Northumberland. You aren't going on to Norway by any chance?'

'No. I don't think so.'

'Keep the butter handy for this one. Are you running away from anybody or anything? ... Thanks. *And* the salt, if you wouldn't mind.' He buttered a scone, dipped his egg in the salt and munched.

'I'm sorry,' said Jenny, looking at him with pleading eyes.

'Perfectly all right. Now just one more question, and we can get on to the orange. How old are you, Naomi?'

'Eighteen.'

'You're sure you're not six?'

'Eighteen, *really*.'

'Or six hundred?'

'Well, eighteen and a half, actually.'

'Then who cares? Have an orange?'

'Thank you.'

'If one can't do what one likes at eighteen, when can one? The answer is, Never.'

'Can't one at thirty?'

'*I'm* thirty, and *I* can't do what I like.'

'Can't you really?' asked Jenny in surprise.

'No. I should like to paint sunlight on water, and I can't. I should like to murder Archibald, and I mustn't. I should like—' he gave her a quick glance and ended, 'oh, lots of things. Well now, listen, Dryad.'

'Yes?'

'Are you listening?'

'Yes.'

'Well now, here we are. You're going to wander from haystack to haystack, and very nice too. I'm staying at Bassetts, and very nice too. You are thinking of Mrs. Bassett entirely as a scone-baker, and you are saying to yourself that a woman who bakes scones like Mrs. Bassett has no room for any of the other virtues. You are wrong. She has all the virtues. She is a mother to those who want mothers, and an aunt to anybody who likes aunts. My portrait of her,' said Mr. Fenton, becoming enthusiastic, 'which now hangs in her parlour, depicts all these qualities. Even the scone *motif* runs through it in what I can only call—and so far only I *have* called it—a masterly way.'

'I *wish* I could see it,' said Jenny, quite carried away by this.

'Well, that's what we're working up to. In order to do this properly we must now go back to haystacks. Hay undoubtedly makes an excellent bed. The Americans, as I discovered in the course of my travels to and from that astonishing country, have an expression "to hit the hay".'

'How funny! What does it mean?'

'It means to go to bed. You, on your way to Northumberland, will hit the hay at this or that point for the next month or so. If this Northumbrian pilgrimage is merely an excuse for hay-hitting, it can be done equally well in the neighbourhood of Bassetts, as you discovered last night. We will tell Farmer Bassett not to thatch his haystack until Miss Harris has finished with it. But if one's object were simply to be out of London, or,' said Mr. Fenton carefully, 'as it might be incognito and unobserved, to fade into the landscape as the pursuit goes by, well then, again I ask you, what more eligible site than Bassetts?'

'Do you mean,' said Jenny eagerly, 'that I could stay there?'

'Why not? But I suggest, in the romantic and subterfugitive way which befits a Dryad, Naiad and—and assuming you to have ascended Constitution Hill—Oread. Now listen: How would you like to take a false name?'

Miss Harris blushed.

'Rightly you are shocked,' said Derek, 'but sometimes it's rather fun.'

'Oh, it is!' said Miss Harris.

'Good. Then how would you like to be my sister?'

'Your sister?'

'I know what you are thinking. You are saying to yourself "Good Heavens, then Archibald will be *my* brother too," and you quail at the idea.'

'Oh no!' said Jenny eagerly. 'I think it's a lovely idea.'

'One of the bravest girls I ever met. But there are limits to what one can ask. You shall be my half-sister, and Archibald your half-brother only. Have you finished your breakfast?'

'Yes, thank you.'

'Do you smoke? Obviously not, if you're a Dryad?'

'No, thank you.'

'Then now I'm going to think for two minutes.'

By the time his pipe was alight, he was ready.

'You are Miss Naomi Fenton. You were going on a walking-tour with a friend. Name of friend?'

Nancy Fairbrother? No, he might recognize her as his brother's secretary. Acetylene Pitt? Nobody would believe it.

'Nancy Pitt,' said Jenny.

'Good. You and Miss Pitt have walked to—where shall we say?—'

'Endover?'

Derek looked across at her quickly.

'Do you know Endover?'

'I came through it yesterday. Why?'

'I see. Could you find your way back to it?'

'Oh, I think so.' She began to think. 'Oh, I'm sure I could.'

'Splendid. Then at Endover—'

'But why did you look at me like that?'

'Did I?'

'As if you didn't like it very much.'

'You're very clever.'

Jenny's second governess, who had taught her the capitals of Europe, had said that she was industrious and full of promise, and her third, who had gone on from these to the Life of the Bee, had said that she was easily interested and that her conduct was extremely satisfactory; but nobody had called her very clever before. She glowed.

Derek explained. 'A man whom I dislike intensely has a cottage at Endover. Fortunately he isn't there now.'

'Your brother?' said Jenny cleverly.

'A relation by marriage,' said Derek guardedly, 'of the name of Archibald. To continue: at Endover your tour is interrupted. Does Miss Pitt sprain her ankle—or is she summoned to the sick bed of her Uncle Thomas?'

'Ankle. Because how would her Uncle Thomas know she was at Endover?'

'You think of everything.' (Jenny glowed again.) 'She sprains her ankle, and returns by omnibus to Tunbridge Wells, and thence to town. She refuses to spoil your holiday, too, and insists that you shall not see her home. But you can hardly continue your walking-tour alone—'

'Why not?' interrupted Jenny.

'Why not? Because', said Mr. Fenton after deep thought, 'you had promised your half-brother Derek that you wouldn't.'

'Oh, I see.'

'Very well then. Bassetts, you will be surprised to hear, is on the telephone, but not, for which God be thanked, on the wireless. At Endover you remember that half-brother Derek is staying at Bassetts. Having seen Miss Pitt into her omnibus, you go into the post office and ring up Bassetts. Derek is out, so you speak to Mrs. Bassett. There is a lot of Bassett in all this, but no matter. You ask Mrs.

B. to tell your brother that you are coming to tea, and you wonder if by any chance she has a spare bedroom, as you have been on a walking-tour with a friend who has sprained—but we needn't go through all that again. Are you keeping up with me?'

'It's easy,' said Jenny. *'Has* she got a spare room?'

'She has. Now then. We have got to get you, in a surreptitious sort of way, back to Endover. How did you come yesterday?'

'By the river after about the first mile, except when I had to leave it to go through gates and things.'

'Meet anybody?'

'Only one.'

'Man or woman?'

'Man.'

'Speak to him?'

'Yes. We—we talked a little,' said Jenny hurriedly.

'What like?'

'Rather a nice middle-aged, elderly sort of man,' said Jenny.

'Like to go back that way, or would you rather go round by the road?'

'I think I'd rather go by the road,' said Jenny. She felt in some extraordinary way that her Hussar had left her, and that she could not brave again the dangers through which, yesterday, she and he had come. Somehow she knew that, from now on, she would have to depend on the physical presence of this other man, who had taken Hussar's place. Without him there were terrifying places in the world—by the banks of streams and on haystacks.

'Safer,' nodded Derek. 'It wouldn't do if you met old Bassett down by your haystack, when you're supposed to be Tonbridge way with Miss Pitt. All right then, I'll tell you in a moment how to go. But don't hurry. You want to ring up from Endover about half-past twelve. Tell Mrs. Bassett that you are coming through the fields by the river, and will I meet you as you don't quite know the way. I'll walk along after lunch and bring you back. Meanwhile you have lunch yourself, and come the way you came yesterday. How?'

'Lovely,' said Jenny, nodding eagerly.

IV

Miss Naomi Fenton picked up the receiver.

'Is that Bassetts Farm?' she asked.

'Yes, Mrs. Bassett speaking,' said a comfortable, motherly, scone-baking voice.

'This is Miss Naomi Fenton. Could I speak to my brother, please?'

'Mr. Fenton's out at the moment, miss. Could I give him a message?'

'Oh! I'm speaking from Endover. I was wondering if I could come along this afternoon and have tea with him?'

'I'm sure he would be delighted, miss. About what time shall I tell him to expect you?'

'Well— Is that Mrs. Bassett speaking?'

'Yes, miss.'

'Well— You see, I've been on a walking-tour with a friend, and she's had to go back suddenly, and I was sort of wondering if I could stay with my brother for a few days, because I'm all alone, and I wondered if—but I suppose you haven't got a spare room—'

'That I have, miss, if it's only just the bedroom you're wanting.'

'Oh, yes, just the bedroom.'

'Mr. Fenton has the sitting-room, you see, so you could have your meals there together, and sit of an evening, and if it's just the bedroom, I've got a nice room I could get ready—'

'That would be lovely.'

'Very well, miss, then I'll tell him to expect you, and we shall look for you about teatime.'

'Oh thank you. Oh, and Mrs. Bassett?'

'Yes, miss.'

'I've been asking the way here, and they tell me if I get down to the river by the mill, and then walk along it, I can get quite close to you—'

'That's right, miss. If you follow the river, it's about six miles, but—'

'Well, will you tell Mr. Fenton I'm coming that way and ask him to meet me, and tell him I'll start from the mill about half-past one, and—'

'Yes, miss, then you'll be sure of meeting, and he can bring you back with him. It's very pretty down by the river.'

'Yes, isn't it? I mean we came along that way this morning, and then my friend sprained her ankle—"

'Oh *dear*, miss, I *am* sorry to hear that.'

'Well, sort of ricked it, so she thought she ought to go back, and then her uncle hadn't been very well, and she thought she oughtn't to be away from him any longer, and then—'

'Yes, miss. Well, I'll tell Mr. Fenton, and I'm sure we shall do our best to make you comfortable.'

'Thank you so much. Good-bye, Mrs. Bassett.'

'Good-bye, Miss Fenton. And I'll see that your room is all ready for you.'

'Thank you so much. Good-bye.'

'Good-bye, miss.'

Mrs. Bassett went back to her cooking.

Chapter Ten

Entry of a Short, Stout Gentleman

I

By three o'clock that afternoon Jenny Windell, had she but known it, was cleared of the major suspicion. It was always obvious that Jane Latour had been murdered, but as the result of Dr. Willoughby Hatch's masterly post-mortem examination of the deceased, it was now certain that no woman had struck the fatal blow. On the contrary, it had been delivered from behind by a short, and probably stout, left-handed man, and there were certain subcutaneous indications that the murderer, though possessed of considerable strength, was not in the best of training. The absence of certain other indications made it quite clear that the deceased was on friendly terms with her assailant.

'Here, wait a bit,' said the Inspector. 'How d'you get that?'

'There was no sign of any struggle,' said Dr. Hatch patiently. 'On the contrary—'

'Well, but if the Shah of Persia was to walk into this room now, and I was to catch him suddenly on the head with an inkstand, that wouldn't hardly prove I was on friendly terms with him, would it? I'm not, anyway,' he added, so as to have it quite clear.

Dr. Willoughby Hatch put up an eye-glass and surveyed the Inspector dispassionately. He nodded to himself, as if he had expected to see something like that, but had thought it his duty to make sure. He stood up.

'Is there anything more you want to know?'

'Here, wait a bit, Doctor. I'm not disputing anything you say'—a faint smile curved the Doctor's lips—'but I've got to look at it all round.' He began to write. 'Short, stout man, left-handed—sedentary occupation?—' He looked up with a question in his eyes.

'That's in your department,' said the Expert, sitting down again. 'I merely state that he was stout and not in good condition. Make any deduction from the facts that you feel are justified.'

'"Sedentary occupation",' wrote the Inspector, feeling that it was justified. '"*And* known to the deceased." Now can you give us anything about the girl?'

'I understood you to tell me that you knew all about her.'

'I know who she is, if that's what you mean, but that doesn't say I know what she did.'

'Ah! Well, Miss Latour and Miss Windell were engaged in conversation when the murder took place. As Miss Latour was struck she fell against the girl's shoulder, and from there to the floor.'

'Certain?'

Dr. Hatch began to feel for his eye-glass again, and the Inspector hurriedly held up a large, preventive hand.

'All right, all right,' he said. 'I just wondered how you knew, that's all.'

'There was a minute bruise on the right wall of the chest made at the moment of death. As there was nothing against which she could have fallen—'

'The floor,' said the Inspector, but not really hopefully.

'In that case the area of the bruising would have been more extensive. Moreover, the absence of any marked contusion on the knees—'

'All right, all right,' said the Inspector. 'Well, but this looks as if she might have been an accomplice, eh? Held the dead woman in talk, while the murderer—'

Dr. Willoughby Hatch shrugged. Facts, not deductions, were all that concerned him.

'Or, of course, *not* an accomplice,' said the Inspector, wishing to do himself complete justice. 'As you say, we've got to look at it all round.'

The Doctor, who had said nothing of the sort, stood up.

'Inquest to-morrow,' said the Inspector. He looked at his notes. 'Well, we're getting on.'

They were indeed getting on. A complete description of Miss Jenny Windell in walking costume and picture hat was in all the evening papers. This description, in order to leave nothing to chance, was supplemented by yet another photograph of Inspector Marigold, and by a camera-study of Miss Windell, in evening costume and without a hat, showing how delightfully the curls clustered round her head and over her ears. By some sort of gentleman's agreement among the editors, however, the name 'Windell' was discarded thereafter as unhelpful, and the public was asked to look out for 'Jenny', and if it saw 'Jenny' to communicate immediately with Scotland Yard or the nearest police-station.

WHERE IS JENNY?

asked one poster, and another announced:

JENNY IDENTIFIED: WHERE IS SHE?

A more direct appeal was made by a third, which put it squarely to the passer-by:

HAVE YOU SEEN JENNY?

There was now no sort of suggestion that Jenny was an accessory to the murder. The Law being what it was, no gentleman would hint such a thing against a ward of Watterson, Watterson and Hinchcoe's. Jenny, it was assumed, was a fellow-victim, now probably on her way to the Argentine. A well-known Harley Street physician discussed the possibility of drugging (and removing to the Argentine) a girl of Jenny's build, and seemed to think that, unless she had been deceived into thinking that someone dear to her had been suddenly taken ill in the Argentine, and was calling for her, it was impossible that the trans-shipment could be effected safely, a certain amount of cooperation on Jenny's part being almost essential. On the other hand, a lady novelist of repute, in an article entitled 'Are Our Girls Safe?', gave one or two remarkable instances of what had nearly happened to the daughters of friends of hers when walking up Regent Street and passing a hospital nurse. It was obvious that, if the murderer had been disguised as a hospital nurse, almost anything might have happened.

In these circumstances it was a comfort to know that the ports were being watched …

Nancy read all this in a tea-shop in Bloomsbury. She had stayed at her work a little later than usual, so as to be sure of not missing Mr. Fenton; for Mr. Archibald Fenton was not merely returning from his club this afternoon, but from the pawnbroker's, with money in his pocket for Joyce's big sister. At five o'clock, she decided that she could wait no longer. In any case, she told herself, the money could not be sent to Tunbridge Wells, until she had heard from Jenny. She went out, bought all the papers, and settled down to them over a pot of tea and a Bath bun.

She tried to imagine herself searching for the Jenny of the description and the photograph. Hopeless, with no more knowledge of her than this, to identify the real Jenny. The photographer had caught Miss Windell in one of those unfortunate moments when one is wearing evening-dress in the afternoon, and looking at a very ugly little man in a large bow-tie, and Nancy felt that too many girls had been surprised in just this position for any one of them to excite attention. And then, reading of all the horrible things which hadn't happened to Jenny, another thought came to her. Wouldn't Mr. and Mrs. Watterson be feeling rather *anxious*?

Mr. Watterson, of course, was a Guardian and a Solicitor, thus belonging to the two classes which were most notoriously unanxious when a ward, whose money they were handling, disappeared. Moreover, he was eighty, and at nineteen Nancy felt that the only things an old gentleman of eighty would be anxious about were the conditions and prospects in the next world. Still, even so, and even though he and Mrs. Watterson were no sort of relation to Jenny, they *might* be worrying about her. Oughtn't she to relieve that anxiety?

But how? An anonymous letter in a disguised handwriting? Safer than typing, because detectives always recognized the faulty '*e*' in a typewriter, and then searched London until they found it. She wouldn't post it in Chelsea, but would buy a letter-card in the nearest post office, and send it off now.

In capital letters, written with the left hand, the message said:

'YR NEICE SAFE AND ZOUND CANOT SAY MORE NO FAKE RENTON FRERS IN SHOSE A FREIND'

Once more Nancy felt rather pleased with herself as a writer of letters. First the 'neice'. Nobody, by reading the papers, would suppose that Jenny was Mr. Watterson's niece, but anybody meeting Jenny, and hearing her talk of 'Uncle Hubert', might make just that mistake. Then the shoes. Jenny's shoes, bought from Renton Frères, were now in Nancy's flat. Without some sort of identification the letter might be dismissed by Mr. Watterson as the work of any half-witted humorist; with its reference to the shoes, which one of the servants could confirm, added to the mistake about the niece, it became convincingly genuine. She dropped the letter-card into the box, and made her way home. On her omnibus she wondered about A FREIND, and decided that he was the captain of a sailing-barge now making its slow way to Newcastle.

II

Alice said, 'Well! If I didn't go and forget 'er watch.'

Cook was telling them about a friend of hers called Alfred Truby, whose thumb had been taken right off by a circular saw.

'What did it look like, Mrs. Price?' asked Hilda. 'Hot, this tea is,' she added, pouring it into her saucer, and blowing on it.

'Not nice,' said Cook, shaking her head. 'Unnatural, as you might say. Well, I'm just telling you. You never know *what* may happen. Five minutes before the hour, there he was, and the last thing he was thinking of was losing his thumb—five minutes after, and there's his thumb gone, and not all the finest surgeons in the country can put it back for him.'

'Wouldn't take ten minutes for a saw to get it off, would it?' said Hilda, who had now discovered a most attractive way of blowing ripples. 'Be like in a flash. Look, Alice, see that?' She blew again. 'Like sort of little waves.'

Alice said: 'Well, fancy *me* going and forgetting 'er watch. 'Tisn't like *me*.'

'Watch?' said Cook, ready for a change of subject.

'Your telling us about that saw suddenly put it into me 'ead. Miss Jenny's watch.'

'Look, Alice, see that?' said Hilda.

'D'you mean her watch that she wears?'

'That's it. Covered with diamonds and all. And I never told that Mr. Marigold nothing about it.'

'*Now* look, Alice! I got it lovely.'

'Never mind that, Hilda,' said Cook sharply. 'This is something we've got to think about. Her watch, Alice? Well, how *could* you have been so silly?'

'It just didn't come into me 'ead.'

'What does the silly old watch matter?' said Hilda, annoyed, as any artist would be, at interruption just when perfection was reached.

'Why of course it matters.'

'Well, if you ask *me*, I should say if you can't reckernize a person by 'er hat and dress, you aren't going to do it by asking 'er the time and then taking a snoop at 'er watch.'

'It isn't that, Hilda,' explained Alice. 'It's just that if anything—if poor Miss Jenny—if she *is*—' She gulped, and had to leave it to Cook.

'First thing they'd do', said Cook impressively to Hilda, 'would be to sell that watch. He'd get a good price for a watch like that. Reel diamonds, wasn't it, Alice?'

Alice nodded.

'That's right. And what the Police would do is to send round to all the—'

'Fences,' said Alice, knowing about it from Jenny's books.

'To all the pawnbrokers, to say "'As anybody been trying to sell the aforesaid watch?" and then they get a description of him, and that's a clue, d'you see?'

'Oh, all right!' said Hilda, and drank up her tea.

So when Mr. Watterson came back from the office at six o'clock, Alice went up and told him what she had forgotten. Mr. Watterson rang up the Inspector; and then Alice told the Inspector exactly what Jenny's watch was like; and then Inspector Marigold did just what Cook had said he would do. And at about ten o'clock Mr. Watterson rang up Inspector

Marigold again, and again the Inspector went round to Acacia Road. Once more Alice went into the study, but this time only to be asked a question about Miss Jenny's shoes. When she had answered it, the Inspector and Mr. Watterson nodded solemnly at each other, and a little later Inspector Marigold left; and at eleven o'clock, under the impression that he had now cleared the ground as thoroughly as he had ever cleared it in the old days at Lord's, he went early to bed, in readiness for a full day's play to-morrow.

III

At twenty minutes to seven Mr. Archibald Fenton crossed Chelsea Bridge in his Sandeman Six on his way to Endover. As a critic had said, the success of *A Flock of Sheep* had raised many problems—one of them being whether one should have a chauffeur or drive the car oneself. Mr. Fenton decided against a chauffeur, on the very reasonable grounds that if one drove the car oneself, one always had it, whereas if a chauffeur drove it, one's wife might want it at some inconvenient moment; and he felt that a wife could not go on admiring a husband, if he were continually explaining to her how necessary it was for his art that he should have the car this afternoon. Of course he did not say all this to Fanny. He explained quite simply that it was necessary for his art that they should live well within their means, and that, however inconvenient to both of them, he thought that they should try to do without a chauffeur. Fanny then, rather foolishly, offered to learn to drive a car too, but her husband said that he knew it was absurd of him, but he would feel horribly nervous to think of Fanny driving about alone, particularly in London.

Mr. Fenton drove well. It was his one physical attainment, unless pure stoutness is to be reckoned as such; for, though in these last two years he had become an enthusiastic cricketer, he excelled as a bad player rather than as a good one, doing so with the air of one who preferred it this way, as being more in the literary tradition. As he drove, he thought with the pleased satisfaction which occasionally eluded him, of his negotiations with the pawnbrokers. He had been, he thought, completely in the character, even to the detail of removing his tie, but secretly, before going in, and turning up the coat of his collar. His poverty being thus apparent, he had told the story of a sick wife, Jessie, to whom he had given the watch as a wedding present, and the urgent necessity of taking her into the country for a fortnight. His name was William Makepeace Thackeray—*and,* thought Mr. Fenton, a very good name, too. The pawnbroker, who didn't seem to mind how many sick wives Mr. Thackeray had, reluctantly doled out twelve pounds ten. Mr. W. M. Thackeray left the shop, the pawn-ticket in his waistcoat pocket. He found his car. He put on his tie again and turned down his collar. And it was not until then that he remembered Julia, and the urgent necessity of taking *her* into the country for a fortnight.

Julia Treherne was an extremely beautiful and intelligent actress, who had been wedded to her Art and Mr. Allison for ten years, and had no intention of being unfaithful to either. In fact, she loved them both devotedly. But Mr. Allison and she equally recognized that an actress is not as other women, and that, within certain specified limits, it was necessary for her to be all things to all men, particularly if they were, or might be, connected with the theatre. Julia kept exactly within the limits, enjoyed herself considerably, and saw as much of her husband as was possible without being ostentatious. Mr. Archibald Fenton (who did not, however, quite know the rules) was her latest conquest, and he had just remembered that it was her birthday on Friday.

Friday. To-day was Wednesday. Easy to get her a present now before he left London, but too late to make it the personal gift which, if he had remembered earlier, he would have chosen with such loving care. And now here it was waiting for him: the watch with 'J' in diamonds for Julia!

He went back to the shop. With the excuse of a suddenly remembered Uncle Makepeace from whom he had not yet borrowed, he redeemed the watch. He realized that, if he had thought of all this before, he could have bought it direct from Nancy at less expense, but he was oddly scrupulous about money matters, and was not sorry that the cheque which he was sending her had, as it were, the countersign of authority. He took the watch home with him. It was in his pocket now as he climbed up to the Crystal Palace. To-morrow he would send it to Julia with a letter ... such a letter ... and then!— who knew? Even next Sunday perhaps ...

As he came down River Hill he stopped thinking of this, and began to compose the letter. At Tonbridge it was almost a poem ...

THURSDAY

Chapter Eleven

Use for the Fourth Governess

I

Jenny, half-waking, half-sleeping, turned restlessly on to her back, and saw above her head the dim skeleton of some enormous animal.

She had seen it before somewhere ... in that Natural History Museum to which she had been taken so often by her third governess. It was a mega-something. Not a megaphone, that was the other thing. 'Now this, Jenny, is one of those animals I was telling you about who lived long, long before there were any little girls in the world. They are called prehistoric animals, because they lived before history books were written. You see, history books couldn't be written because there weren't any men or women to write them!' 'Not Adam and Eve?' had asked Jenny, and the third governess, not being quite sure what to do about that, because it was all very difficult if you weren't to destroy a child's innocent faith, decided that it was now time to go home. But, before they left, they spent a few minutes with a case of humming-birds, because humming-birds were perfectly safe, and wouldn't put ideas into anybody's head ...

To Jenny one skeleton more or less in the ridiculous confusion of her brain did not matter. She turned over to her left side, snuggled herself down and let herself back into her dream. In a moment she was asleep again. But not for long. The sun climbed slowly above the trees at the bottom of the meadow, and seeped through the curtains; outside the open windows starlings imitated themselves and other birds untiringly; kitchen stoves were being raked out below; animals were shifting slowly at the sound of men's voices, and a hoof would hit suddenly and restlessly upon stone. Against the new insistent day Jenny's sleep could not prevail. She woke ... and wondered where she was.

Even in the daylight the centre beam and crossbeams of the ceiling looked like the backbone of a giant sole. This had been in her dreams, and adventures with tramps who were policemen, and going about in the more public places with nothing on. Now she began to remember things more sharply. Derek Fenton ... Bassetts ... and what was her name? Naomi Fenton. She was in a bedroom at Bassetts. It was still almost like a dream.

There was a knock at her door, and an 'Are you awake, Miss Fenton?' 'Come in,' called Jenny, and Mrs. Bassett came in.

'I've brought you a cup of tea, miss. It's a lovely morning. Shall I pull your curtains?'

'Oh, thank you. Oh yes, please. What a *lovely* day.'

'Looks like it's going to be hot. Now what would you like to do, miss? Your brother always has a bathe in the river. He's just back from his, and he said I was to say if you'd like one too, he'd show you the best place.'

'Oh!' said Jenny. 'I—I haven't got a bathing-dress.'

'Bless you, miss, that doesn't matter, there'll be nobody there to see, not at this time. I'll have some hot water ready for you by the time you get back.'

'Oh, thank you.'

'Then I'll tell Mr. Fenton you'll be ready as soon as you've drank your tea.'

'Oh, thank you.'

Mrs. Bassett bustled out.

Jenny had so many things to think about that a new problem was almost welcome, since it distracted her mind from the old ones. How did one get to the river if one hadn't a dressing-gown or anything? And how did one come back? And would Mr. Fenton— Derek—of course he wouldn't really—but would he—

There was a whistle from beneath her window —definitely not a starling—and then a call 'Na-o-mi!' She got out of bed, took her tea to the window-sill, and looked out.

'Hallo! Good-morning, sister,' said Derek.

'Good-morning.'

'Have you slept well?'

'Very, thank you.'

'And did you do it in a nightdress or pyjamas?'

'Do you mean what have I got on now?'

'That's what I'm leading up to.'

'Pyjamas.'

'Good. I was wondering how to get you down to the river. I've got Mrs. Bassett's second-best gum-boots for you, and there's no disguising the fact that they *don't* go with a night-dress. You're only going to meet two cows and a rabbit, but one must consider everybody. Are you more or less ready?'

'Just on,' said Jenny, and sipped her tea.

'Right. Then I'll show you the place, point out the ants' nest, and leave you to it. Here, wait a bit, I'll throw up the boots. Got anything breakable just under the window?'

'No.'

'Then withdraw yourself and cup of tea, and watch.'

Thump! … Thump!

'Well done!' cried Jenny, returning to the window.

'Tuck your trousers into those and you'll look like a musical comedy producer's idea of a midshipman. Have you got two towels?'

'One,' said Jenny, looking at the towel-horse.

'I'll have another ready for you. I've told Mrs. Bassett over and over again that the secret of a contented life is two towels. Don't be long.'

He went into the house, and Jenny finished her tea. This had suddenly become fun. She put on the boots and looked at herself. She had never seen Nancy's pyjamas in daylight. They looked rather nice. She didn't at all mind Derek or anybody seeing her like this.

She took the towel, and went downstairs.

'As I thought,' said Derek. 'Midshipman in charge of swabbing party. Here you are.' He gave her the other towel.

As they walked through the fields, Jenny said: 'I think I know the place.'

'Sure?'

'I think I passed it yesterday.'

'You must have done that, but you certainly didn't bathe there.'

'How do you know?' asked Jenny, and had the sudden thought that perhaps he had seen her yesterday. It was funny; now she felt quite different to him again; now she didn't mind if he *had* seen her. It was funny that his first question to her yesterday had been 'Are you an artist's model by any chance?' Almost as if he had seen her, and thought her beautiful. 'How do you know?' she asked again.

'Intuitive deduction. I depend upon it a good deal, particularly in the wine-trade. As soon as I sip a glass of Burgundy, no matter what the vintage may be, I take one look at the bottle and say to myself "Burgundy". Sometimes it's claret, but the principle is the same.'

They came nearer the river, and Jenny pointed and said 'Is that it?'

'That is it. Here, then, I leave you, Miss Fenton. A parting word, and I am gone. Can you swim?'

'Yes,' said Jenny, for her fourth governess had insisted on this.

'It takes a good three strokes to get across the pool, *and,*' added Derek, 'a good three strokes to get back again. So husband your strength. Good-bye. We shall meet at breakfast.' ...

Ten minutes later, with a towel round her waist and another over her shoulders, Jenny sat drying in the sun. If only she could let herself be quite, quite happy, how happy she would be! 'True happiness', one of her governesses had said, quoting possibly from some other thinker, 'lies only in memory or anticipation.' In Jenny's case it was memory and anticipation which were troubling her present happiness.

Memory: Mr. Watterson.

Anticipation: Mrs. Bassett.

Present Happiness: Derek.

Mr. Watterson was eighty, but even at eighty you could be anxious. Besides, he was her Guardian by Law, so he was responsible for her, and would get into trouble if he lost her. She *must* let him know that she was safe ...

Mrs. Bassett was—fifty? But even at fifty you wanted money for rooms. Jenny had nine-and-threepence left. Next Wednesday Mrs. Bassett would want—how much? Well, more than nine-andthreepence ...

Derek was thirty. And she was safe with him, and he understood things ...

It was so lovely here. If only it could go on for ever ...

He couldn't let her go now, could he? Not even if she told him everything?

She dropped the towel from her shoulders and stood up. He couldn't let her go now? ...

It was a happy midshipman who came across the fields to the house, singing a little French nursery-song.

Frère Jacques, frère Jacques,
Dormez-vous, dormez-vous?
Sonnez la patine,
Sonnez la patine,
Bim, bom, boom!

After breakfast Derek said: 'In half an hour I am going to fish.'

'Oh, are there fish in the river?' said Jenny.

'That is what I am trying to find out.'

'What do you fish for? I mean what sort of fish?'

'There again we are in the dark. It might be mermaids and it might be eels. But I like sitting on the bank and watching nothing happen, and if you like it too, we should be certain of not missing anything.'

Jenny liked it too. She lay on the bank and watched the gay little float twisting in the eddies, and told herself that as soon as it was quite still, she would say 'Derek' ... But it wasn't *quite* still ... Not yet ... nor yet ... nor—

'Derek.'

'Naomi.'

She had called him Derek. The worst was over. She gulped down her nervousness, and said: 'Would you mind very much if you got mixed up in something?'

He understood that this was the end of the day's fishing.

'Do you mean something like marmalade?' he asked. 'Or more like a wasp's nest?'

'Murder,' said Jenny bravely.

'You mean you want me to murder somebody?' said Derek. 'I suppose', he went on wistfully, 'it couldn't be Archibald?'

Jenny shook her head.

'You see,' she said simply, 'I'm Jenny Windell.'

'*Not* Gloria Naomi Harris?'

'No.'

Derek nodded.

'I felt certain that there was some mistake. I know all the Harrises—there are only seventeen thousand of them left now—and you aren't in the least like any of them.'

'You see, it was my handkerchief.'

Derek frowned.

'Your handkerchief,' he said.

'Jenny,' she explained.

'Jenny.'

'Because of Conway Castle.'

'Conway Castle,' nodded Derek. 'Leave nothing out, however unimportant it seems. Once I have all the facts, then I can fit them together.'

'Well, of course I oughtn't to have been there at all. That's why I hid, you see.'

'That's why you hid. I must now interrupt, in order to narrate a sad story about a relation by marriage. Many years ago, before he became famous, Archibald wrote a long blank-verse poem. Or anyhow a long poem. Or anyhow,' said Derek, 'it was long. He forgot, however, to number the pages, and it so happened that they were dropped two or three times before they got to the printer. The printer then dropped them again, and the printer's boy, who was given the job of searching for, and collecting them, abstracted a page here and there so that he might make paper darts. The residue was published under the title *Ariadne in Stoke Newington*, and, I am bound to say, received high praise from Archibald's fellow-critics. *But*,' said Derek emphatically, 'and this is the point, *Archibald's poem was not what it was*. So now, Jenny Windell, *could* you get the pages of your murder story in the right order, and begin, unoriginal as it may seem, at the very beginning?'

'But haven't you read the papers?' cried Jenny.

'Not one. We get nothing but the Sunday papers. So begin by telling me who Jenny Windell is.'

Jenny told him …

When she had finished, Derek said 'Gosh!'

Jenny said: 'It is rather awful, isn't it?'

'Awful? Not a bit. It's terrific.'

'Do you mind?' asked Jenny timidly.

'Mind? O Robert Louis Stevenson, O Arthur Conan Doyle, O Freeman Hardy and Willis, I mean Freeman Wills Croft, I thank thee. I mean ye.'

'Have I been *terribly* silly?'

'You have been enchantingly wise. If there is one thing which stands out more than another in this world—and of course,' said Derek, 'one thing always *does* stand out more than another—it is that there are some things which you cannot explain to a policeman. To make it clear to a policeman, an inspector, a coroner, a solicitor, a barrister *and* a judge, one after the other, that you and Hussar were so wrapped up in each other's conversation that you went into the wrong house without looking, would take about nineteen years, and then leave you just where you were at the start. Far, far better a life of exile.'

'Yes, *I* thought it would be difficult.'

'Impossible. Another anecdote of the Fenton family occurs to me. When I was a small boy I had an Aberdeen terrier. One day I lost it, and my father asked the local policeman to let him know if anybody found it. Next day the policeman came up to the house, saluted and said: "Sir, I have to report that the animal in question was last observed proceeding in the direction of Chorlton-cum-Hardy." If you can imagine to yourself the back-view of an Aberdeen terrier doing this, you will realize how very matter-of-fact we are in the police force.'

But it was not at an Aberdeen terrier proceeding in the direction of Chorlton-cum-Hardy that Jenny was looking; she was trying to see Derek as a small boy, unhappy because he had lost his friend …

'And now', said Derek, 'to business.'

'Business?' said Jenny, waking up with a start.

'Yes. What are we going to do?'

'I don't know. I thought perhaps *you'd* know.'

'Then let me think.'

Jenny let him think. She wanted to think, too. Just of how lovely it was to let somebody else think for you like this …

'Obviously the first thing', said Derek, 'is to find out what's happening in London. This afternoon, therefore, I shall be observed proceeding in the direction of Maidstone, where I shall get all the morning papers.'

'Oh!' said Jenny suddenly.

'Why "Oh!"?'

'I've just remembered! I asked Nancy to write to me at the Tunbridge Wells post office.'

'Oh! Very well then, I shall proceed in the direction of Tunbridge Wells, and get all the morning papers.'

'And my letter?'

'And your letter.'

'Will they give it to you?'

'I hope so.'

'Couldn't I come with you?'

'Safer not. Sleuths may have tracked you to Tunbridge Wells.'

'I do look different. Really. I mean my hair—it makes a tremendous difference.'

Derek looked at her.

'I should know you anywhere, Jenny Windell, Gloria Harris, Naomi Fenton, Dryad, Naiad and Oread. No matter what you did to your hair.'

'Oh, *you,*' said Jenny, as if that were natural.

'Yes, me. Or, as Archibald would say, I. No, what you shall do is to give me a note saying that your brother Wilbraham Harris, of Wilbraham Harris Ltd., preserved fruit importers, is calling for a letter for you. I will bring the letter and the papers back here, and we will spend a long evening with them. That all right?'

'Yes,' said Jenny.

'Good. Now then, what about the Wattersons?'

'Oh, *please*!'

'However old they are, they must have noticed that you have left St. John's Wood.'

'Oh, I know. They must be anxious.'

'Well, they ought to be told that you're safe. Shall I ring Mr. Watterson up? Anonymously?'

'But then, wouldn't he go to the police? He's a solicitor, you know. He'd find out where the call came from—they always do—'

'Yes.' Derek thought this over. 'A telegram would be safer.'

'Oh, but they trace telegrams! Always! They get an authorization from the Postmaster-General—'

'What a lot you know, Naomi. All right, then, let's think of something else.'

He thought. Jenny frowned. Between them they were baffling the police...

'Where is Mr. Watterson now?' asked Derek. 'Office or Home?' 'He goes to the office every morning.'

'And gets home?'

'One o'clock. Regularly.'

'Sure?'

'Oh, but it used to be a joke how regular he was.'

'Then if I rang up the house now, who would answer it?'

'The cook. Mrs. Price.'

'Is she quick? Intelligent?'

'Not very,' smiled Jenny. 'Of course it might be Hilda, the house-parlourmaid.'

'You're sure it wouldn't be Mrs. Watterson?'

'It goes to the kitchen first, and then upstairs. Besides, she generally goes out for a drive at eleven.'

'Good.' He looked at his watch. 'Half-past ten. Mr. Watterson gone?'

'Oh, yes. He's at the office by ten.'

'Then I think that's fairly safe. Now listen. We go back to the house in a quarter of an hour, and at five minutes past eleven, you ring up.'

'Me?'

'You. Cook answers—or Hilda. Do you know their voices on the telephone?'

'Oh, yes, easily.'

'What do you call Mr. Watterson?'

'Uncle Hubert.'

'Right. Then you say, "Hallo, is that Mrs. Price?"—or Hilda, or whoever it is. Don't say who you are, but let her recognize *your* voice, and if she says: "Well I never, is that Miss Jenny?" you can say "Yes". But all you've really got to say is, "Will you tell Uncle Hubert when he comes back that I'm quite, quite safe?" And then you ring off quickly. And when Uncle Hubert gets the message two hours later, not all the Postmaster-Generals in the world are going to find out where the call came from. At least, not nearer than Tunbridge Wells. How's that?'

'Perfect,' said Jenny admiringly. And though Derek didn't think that it was perfect, he thought it was the best they could do, and not too bad at that.

II

Up till now the one love of Jenny's life had been Hussar. But just as many grown-up people prefer to concentrate their religious emotion on some material representation of their God, so the child Jenny had found that her passion for Hussar could most easily be worked off on the current governess. The expression of this passion took many strange forms, one of them being an earnest imitation of the handwriting of the loved one. It was with the pen of her fourth governess that she wrote a letter of authorization to the Tunbridge Wells post office.

> *'Please give the bearer any letters addressed to Miss Gloria Harris, Poste Restante, Tunbridge Wells. Gloria N. Harris.'*

The fourth governess had been the most uncertificated of them all. She didn't really know anything. Not for her the Greek 'e', the modern script, the clerkly, undistinguished style. She wrote home to the vicarage in a round, rolling hand, full of Victorianly feminine curves and flounces, saying that she had a bedroom on the top floor, which looked quite homey now that all the photographs were up, and Jenny was a funny little thing, but sweetly pretty, and they were going to be great friends. Jenny had loved her dearly; and, while waiting for the day when she would save her darling Miss Withers from being run over, and be taken to St. George's Hospital and have her life despaired of, and be slowly nursed back to health by a more than ever devoted Miss Withers, who would now let Jenny call her Grace, she had occupied herself in adapting to her own needs all of Grace Withers that was accessible: her movements, her speech, her handwriting.

'Do you always write like this?' asked Derek.

'No,' said Jenny; 'look.' She wrote the message out again, this time in her own hand. Derek compared the two.

'There's nothing you can't do. It's marvellous. We really *ought* to murder Archibald between us. Think it over. We'd get away with it easily.'

Derek drove to Tunbridge Wells in his two-seater *coupé,* and parked his car opposite the Wesleyan Methodist Church. An earnest-faced, spectacled young woman was at the entrance to the post office as he went in. They got in each other's way, apologized, smiled at each other. For a moment he thought that he recognized her, but perhaps it was only because she seemed for a moment to recognize him. Then she moved away, and he went inside. The combination of Gloria Harris and Grace Withers brought complete conviction to the clerk, and the letter was given to him. As he turned to leave he seemed to feel, rather than to see, that the young woman was now inside the post office, writing at the telegraph-desk. He went out, and walked to the station for the papers.

A poster outside the bookstall said:

WHERE IS
JENNY?
STARTLING DEVELOPMENTS

'So it's like that,' said Derek to himself. 'What fun we're going to have.'

Chapter Twelve

Miss Pitman at the Wells

I

In Lovely Lady, the novel of which he was ashamed, Mr. Archibald Fenton describes his heroine, Barbara Wilmot, in what he thought at the time were a few well-chosen words. She was at the threshold of life, standing with reluctant feet, as Mr. Fenton pointed out, where the brook and river meet, and already the slender lines of her figure indicated the gentle promise of womanhood. One could hardly put it more delicately. She had a vivacious, mobile face which lit up when she talked, and on one occasion, but fortunately only in the first rough copy, it went so far as to make a delicious little moue at Leslie Brand, the hero. This face was framed in a mass of unruly hair, stray tendrils of which escaped from time to time, and had to be pushed back beneath the hat where customarily they nestled. Whenever Leslie Brand let fall an epigram, and he seemed unable to let fall anything else, she either trilled or else bubbled with happy laughter. Altogether she seemed to be a delightful creature, and Archibald's engagement to Fanny a few days after publication came as a surprise to his friends.

It may have been because she reminded him of Barbara Wilmot that Mr. Fenton chose Miss Fairbrother, rather than one of the stouter and less mobile applicants, as his private secretary.

Nancy hoped that this was so, because, in order to obtain the post, she had, in fact, modelled herself on Miss Wilmot. In the game which she played with life, it was almost a necessity for her to model herself on somebody; so that, hearing of Mr. Fenton's need, it was natural for her first to wonder what sort of applicant would most appeal to him. Obviously one who had read all his books. She read them, and, as she read, looked out for further clues. The heroine of *A Flock of Sheep* was fair, and, in a nice sort of way, generously proportioned, but this was outside Nancy's range. The heroines of the two intermediate books (omitting, of course, the essays and the critical studies) were, in her opinion, much better left there. One of them had a pimple on her chin, which Mr. Fenton had described so lovingly and so often that he would certainly miss it; the other had a horselike face, which had so stamped itself on the man's mind, that nothing short of a horse (or, rather, a mare) could expect to awaken the necessary tender memories. Nancy made her personal application, therefore, as Barbara Wilmot, hoping that the sight of his first love would strike a chord in the Great Man's heart. Apparently it struck it, for she was engaged at once.

The post obtained, she dropped Barbara Wilmot, and became the Complete Private Secretary. This was a disappointment to Mr. Archibald Fenton. Gone were the trills, the bubbles of happy laughter when he let fall an epigram; Miss Fairbrother had nothing for him now but a prim 'Yes, Mr. Fenton'. If *moues* were still made, they were made behind his back, and, in any case, were no longer delicious. But the tendrils still escaped, the hair still was unruly. The face remained mobile, though its vivacity seemed to be gone. It may be that there is no vivacious way of taking down shorthand or clacking on a typewriter; it may have been that the poor girl had troubles at home which she hid from him. In any case no possible fault could be found with her work—nor with the slender lines of her figure. These, as Mr. Fenton noted from time to time, indicated the gentle promise of womanhood ...

On this Thursday morning Mr. Fenton (thank the Lord) was out of the way, and Nancy was going to 'do something'. What it was she would do was not yet certain, but she had decided that it was Alice Pitman who would do it. Miss Pitman, it may be remembered, was good, earnest and slightly perspiring; half governess, half matron at a large kindergarten in South Kensington. What else? A little fuller in the figure than Nancy, which would mean padding of some sort. That would be uncomfortably hot in this sort of weather, but then Miss Pitman was always uncomfortably hot in this sort of weather, which would make it just right. Glasses? Glasses undoubtedly. And probably a white, full, silk petticoat, which showed a little …

At ten o'clock Miss Nancy Fairbrother entered Mr. Fenton's Bank, and cashed her cheque.

At 11.15 Miss Fairbrother returned to her flat with several brown-paper parcels.

At 12 Miss Alice Pitman looked at herself in Nancy's glass with a satisfaction which the real Miss Pitman could never have felt.

At 12.30 Miss Pitman left London for Tunbridge Wells. She was going to find Jenny.

'Now,' said Nancy to herself in the corner of a third-class carriage, 'let's think it out.'

Whatever Jenny was doing, she couldn't go on doing it without money. If she had had Nancy's letter, she would have written to give an address to which the money could be sent. Therefore, up to yesterday evening she had not had Nancy's letter. But she might have got it this morning. Obviously the first thing to do was to find out about this. If Miss Gloria Harris's letter was still waiting for her in the Tunbridge Wells post office, and if she did not come for it to-day, then Jenny was not in the Tunbridge Wells district, and would have to be tracked.

How?

As far as her studies had gone, Nancy had learnt of only three ways of tracking. The first way was by following the spoor of the wanted person; which could really only be done over snow or sands, or (if one was an Indian) through trackless forests. Tunbridge Wells was obviously unfavourable ground for this. The second way was by showing a bloodhound some garment belonging to the fugitive; but even if she had had the garment with her, and could have bought a bloodhound in Tunbridge Wells, Nancy felt that this method was too public for her purposes. It did happen sometimes that, owing to the fact that the fugitive had accidentally stepped into some aniseed before starting out, the pursuit could be made with a less noticeable dog, but Nancy felt that it was unlikely that Jenny had done this. The third method was by asking questions in a round-about way in the bars of public-houses. This method was clearly unsuited to Miss Pitman.

What was left?

'Well,' said Nancy to herself, 'let's see when we get there.'

'Care to look at the paper, miss?' said the young man opposite, seeing that she was now disengaged.

'Oh, *thank* you,' said Miss Pitman, instinctively gushing a little. 'That *is* kind of you. I quite forgot to *look* at it this morning.'

'Queer business this Auburn Lodge murder.'

'Yes, *isn't* it queer?'

'There.' He folded back the paper and handed it to her. 'See that? That's funny, isn't it?'

Nancy took the paper eagerly. Her heart beat a little more quickly under its padding. She was looking at a reproduction of her letter-card, and feeling as so many authors have felt when they first saw their own work in the press.

'What does it mean?' she asked. 'Renton Frers?'

'It tells you down below. Name of a boot-shop. French, you know, for Renton Brothers. It tells you there.'

'Oh, I see. Frères.'

'That's right. Brothers. Tell you what *I* think?'

'Oh yes, *do,* please.'

'I'll tell you. All this about White Slave Traffic—if you don't mind my mentioning it to a lady—'

'That's *quite* all right,' said Miss Pitman earnestly. 'I've just come back from Geneva as secretary to a gentleman—'

'That so? Well, you can take it from me that most of the talk you hear is just bunk. Bunk,' said the young man, making a discarding movement with his two hands. 'Nothing in it. D'you know the first thing I say, when I read about a murder?'

'No.'

'I say, who's *this* going to do a bit of good to? See what I mean?'

'You mean who's going to profit by it?'

'That's right. And the answer's plain. Jenny.' 'Oh, do you *think* so?'

'Well, she's Jane Latour's niece, isn't she?'

'Yes, but—'

'*And* only relation?'

'Yes, but—'

'Well, it really isn't quite fair of me talking like this, because I happen to be a bit in the know. But you can take it from me—' 'Oh, are you a detective? How *exciting!*'

'Well, yes and no. More in an amateur way, if you see what I mean. I've studied this sort of thing a lot. But it just happens that a friend of mine happens to be in with the Scotland Yard people, and he told me for a fact that they *know* in Scotland Yard that it was the niece who did it. That doesn't mean that they can prove it, mind you. But they know.'

'Oh, but how awful to think of a young girl like that being a murderess! I still can't quite believe it.'

'Fact, I assure you.'

'Then does that mean she wrote this letter-card herself?'

'That's right. Put 'em off the scent.'

'Yes, but wouldn't it have been better if she hadn't said anything at all, and then everybody would have thought she was dead?'

'Well,' said the young man, after thinking this over, and finding that it was too much for him, 'you've got to look at it all round. See what I mean? I'm only telling you what they say at the Yard. Well, I get out here. Sevenoaks. Good-morning, miss. No, that's all right, thanks, I've finished with it.'

Left alone, Nancy went back to the paper. She read her own contribution again, and then passed on to the inferior work of other contributors. Well, no; not so inferior. Suddenly the paper dropped out of her fingers, and she gave a whistle of dismayed astonishment, quite outside Miss Pitman's range. 'Lordy!' cried Miss Fairbrother. 'What do you know about that?' She had just discovered that they were looking for Jenny's watch ...

What would happen? They would find the pawnbroker. The pawnbroker would reveal Mr. Fenton. Well, no need for that. Fenton would read the papers and recognize for himself that 'J' in diamonds. He would go to the police. The police would go to Elm Park Mansions ... and in twenty-four hours the papers would be saying 'Where is Nancy?'

'Well, after all,' said Miss Pitman complacently, 'where is she?'

II

At Tunbridge Wells Nancy got out of the train, and put her bag in the cloak-room. Then she walked down to the post office.

So that was the post office.

It was half-past one. Should she go in and ask about Gloria Harris?

Yes ...

No ...

Obviously no. If Jenny had not called for her letter, then there was just the one chance of finding her. Hang about the post office until Jenny came. Sooner or later she was bound to come. But if Nancy asked about the letter now, and went away and had lunch, and came back again, then all through the afternoon while she was waiting, she would have the uneasy feeling that perhaps Jenny had come and gone in that luncheon interval, and that now she was waiting for nothing. For it would be quite impossible to make a second innocent inquiry about the letter.

She walked up to the High Street and lunched. She came back to the post office and went in.

'Good-afternoon,' said Miss Pitman, with a nervous but friendly smile. 'Is there a letter for me? Pitman. Miss Alice Pitman. You see, I'm camping, and I didn't quite—oh, thank you *so* much.'

The clerk had gone away to look. He came back to say that he was sorry, there was no letter for Miss Pitman. Miss Pitman looked disappointed.

'Oh!' she said. 'Oh, thank you.' She hesitated; and then, taking courage, gave the clerk another nervous smile, and said: 'I'm *so* sorry to trouble you, but I *wonder* if you would mind telling me if there are any letters for my friend Miss *Harris*? We're camping together, you see, and she—'

'Have you an authority from Miss Harris to—'

'Oh, no, no, no,' interrupted Miss Pitman quickly. 'I didn't mean *that*! How silly of me! No, all I meant was, she's coming into the Wells to *tea*, but it's right the other side of the *town*, you see, and I *know* she talked of seeing if there were any letters for her, and I thought if I could tell her there weren't any, then it would save her all that walk, you see, and if there *were* any, then of course she would come for them herself. I knew I couldn't take them without an authority, of course, but I thought if I could just tell her, you see—oh, thank you *so* much.'

The clerk had gone away to look. With his back to her, he said: 'Any name or initials?'

'Gloria,' said Miss Pitman eagerly. 'Miss *Gloria* Harris. It *is* kind of you. It will save her all that *long* walk, and—'

'Miss Gloria Harris,' read out the clerk. 'Yes. There is.'

'Oh, thank you *so* much, then he *has* written. I'll tell her. Unless of course she may have started to walk in *earlier* than she said, but then I expect she'd come anyhow, but of course she *may* have changed her mind and not be coming in this afternoon at *all*, but it is nice to *know*, isn't it? Thank you *so* much, good-afternoon.'

So far, thought Nancy, so good. Now all she had to do was to hang about the post office until Jenny came.

All! It was enough. Up to now the adventure had been exciting, but there was nothing exciting in walking up and down outside a post office, lingering a moment here and a moment there, pretending to look in at this shop-window and at that. In books the hero always engaged a room opposite the house he was watching, and so gave himself a chance of sitting down, but in real life there was no reason why the owner of any house opposite any house which anybody happened to suspect should want to take in lodgers of a suspicious nature. It might be worth trying, of course; she would have to sleep somewhere; but she dare not begin to make inquiries until her vigil for the day was over. Three o'clock. She must not leave before six at the earliest. Six would be fairly safe. She continued to walk up and down ...

With the idea of increasing the amenities of an attractive town the authorities have had the vision to place a demobilized Tank just outside the post office, where it serves equally as an inspiration to the young, a tender memory to the middle-aged, and a token of their faith to the elderly. After nearly an hour in its company, Nancy, a little capriciously, began to feel that Tunbridge Wells was practically all Tank (all of it, that is, which was not post office) and she wished that Jenny had chosen some other town to escape to, one, for instance, which had been content to decorate itself with an odd howitzer here and there, or a handful of bombs. Then she felt ashamed of herself for thinking this, because, of course, a Tank was really a very beautiful thing, and it wasn't meant to be next to the post office at all, it only just happened to be there because they wanted to have it opposite the Wesleyan Methodist Church ...

Next to the church were two hotels. At six o'clock, she would get her bag from the station, and take a bedroom in one of the hotels, and then to-morrow she would be able to sit down ...

The bother was that she was now cut off from London. She had meant to send her address to Mrs. Featherstone, who 'came in' every morning, so that if Jenny wrote from some other town, the letter could be forwarded; but now it was impossible. WHERE IS NANCY? Definitely not giving the police an address at Tunbridge Wells. Let them find her there if they could.

She came to the post office again, looked idly in through the swing doors, and came out.

Bump!

'Oh, I'm *so* sorry,' said Miss Pitman, confused and earnest.

'I *beg* your pardon,' smiled the young man, taking off his hat.

For a moment they looked at each other, and with a sudden pleasurable shock Nancy recognized him.

His face was not very familiar, but to one who, hour after hour, as it seemed, had been eagerly looking out for a friend, and had seen nothing more responsive than a Tank, even the sight of a recognizable stranger was in some way reassuring. She had seen him in Bloomsbury once—twice, wasn't it?—he had called for Mr. Fenton and they had gone out to lunch together. She wasn't introduced. Secretaries weren't. He had just walked in, so she didn't hear his name. Archibald had been rather annoyed about it, and the other man had said, 'My dear Hippo, I assure you—', and had been hurried out, leaving Nancy to wonder whether Hippo was short for Hippolytus or Hippopotamus. Either way Archibald hadn't liked it. The other time was in the hall, as she was going out, and he had smiled and said 'Good-afternoon'.

There was no reason why he should have anything to do with Jenny, but on an impulse she followed him into the post office ...

Nothing like being impulsive.

She heard him say: 'Have you any letters for Miss Gloria Harris?' She saw him hand over a piece of paper to the clerk ... She followed him out.

He walked to the station. He looked at the posters outside the bookstall. He bought all the papers. He put five under his arm and stood reading the sixth. He went back to the car-park below the Tank, still reading. He dropped the papers into a blue *coupé*, and walked up to the High Street ...

What did it mean?

The simple explanation (always the best, said the books) was that Jenny had settled down somewhere as Gloria Harris, and being unable, or afraid, to come into Tunbridge Wells herself, had asked some newly met acquaintance to call for her letter. By one of those odd coincidences he happened already to be an acquaintance of Nancy's. That was all.

Should she wait until he came back and then say 'I think we *have* met—' But they hadn't. She was Alice Pitman. Bother! Yet somehow she *must* get a message to Jenny. How?

In the days when Gloria Harris and Acetylene Pitt had been drummer-boys together in Wellington's army, it had been necessary for them to communicate with each other (or with Wellington) in code, in case, as Nancy pointed out to Jenny, their communications fell into the enemy's hands and gave away the position of the British forces. The code had been invented by Nancy, and would certainly have baffled Napoleon. Indeed, for a moment it had seemed as if it would baffle Jenny.

You wrote your message out thus:

'AM AT CASTLE HOTEL WITH MONEY FOR YOU
ALICE PITMAN.'

Then you wrote down the number of letters in each word.
Thus:

2265453356

Then you took away the first letter of each word and put down
the result thus:

MTASTLEOTELITHONEYOROULICEITMAN

You divided this up, however you liked. For instance:

MTAS TLEOT ELITHON EYORO ULIC EITM AN

You put in the figures in ones or twos between the groups, and
on each side of the figures you put any letters you liked. Then,
at the end, you added all the first letters. Thus:

MTASK22RTLEOTF6EELITHONS5BEYOROO
45EULICD33LEITM05QANW6EAACHWMFYAP

When Jenny first saw this, or something like it, at the age of
eleven, she said 'Oh!' Nancy explained to her that it was very
easy to uncipher, and that her uncle Mr. Pitt, the Prime Minister,
thought it was clever.

'How do you *begin?*' said Jenny, frowning at it.

'I'll show you,' said Nancy. 'First you count how many
figures there are, and there are ten of them, so you take away
the last ten letters, but don't lose them because you'll want

them directly. Then you make a circle round the figures and the letter on each side of the figures, and you don't bother about the circles any more, except for looking at the figures, and the first figure is 2, so the first word has two letters, and the first letter is the first of the ten you took away, so that's A, and the first word is AM, do you see, Jenny darling? And the next is AT. And the third has six letters, and it begins with C, so you take the next five, leaving out the circle, which is ASTLE, so it's CASTLE, d'you see, darling? It's easy, isn't it, and my uncle said Napoleon would never guess even if he knew English *perfectly*, so now we needn't *eat* messages any more, even when we get surrounded.'

'Oh, *I* see,' said Jenny suddenly. 'Where's a pencil, quick! I'm going to write *you* one.'

Now sometimes it was necessary that a message should be hidden in a secret place, and if you knew it was there you went and looked, and if you didn't, then you might miss it. To guard against this Nancy arranged that each of them should have a special sign, which meant: 'Look out for something from me,' and it had to be something which you could leave about, and other people wouldn't notice. They wondered about this for a long time, and Jenny thought their initials ought to come into it somehow, like monograms. And then Nancy said *I* know! I'll have "Cap" because it ends in A.P., and you have "Bough" because it ends in G.H.' Jenny said: 'Do you mean leaving your tammy about, because you're always doing that?' and Nancy said: 'Well, I never will again, except when it's a Sign, and every one will say: "How tidy the dear child is getting" and that will be a great joke between us, because I shan't be really.' Jenny said: 'Well, they won't think *I'm* getting tidy if I have to leave *boughs* about everywhere,' but Nancy explained that it need only be a *twig*. One day A.P. had been escaping from the licentious soldiery with the help of a pistol which really fired,

144

and she had to hide a message for G.H. in the secret place, so she dropped one of the caps which they used for the pistol, and Jenny saw it and guessed at once, and found the message. So, after that, they both knew that, whatever happened, they would always be all right.

Would Jenny remember all this? Of course!

Nancy hurried to the station and bought a *Daily Mail*. This was the paper which the man had been reading: the paper, therefore, which he would be most ready to lend Jenny. Jenny, of course, would want to read everything she could about herself, and would almost certainly try to borrow all the papers, but, even so, it would be better if the secret message were in the paper which the man had already read, so that he would not be likely to see it. On the outside of the *Daily Mail*, then, she drew a cap, and in the margin of the page which said WHERE IS JENNY she drew another. Then, hidden away in the most uninteresting part of the paper, she wrote her cipher message MTASK22R ... It took her a little time to get this done, and she ran from the station waiting-room and down the street in panic lest the car should have gone, but it was still there, and she slowed down and looked about her, wondering just how to do what she had to do. Should she go boldly up to the car from the roadside, or secretly from the common?

As always, Nancy was for boldness. Be natural, she told herself, and, whatever odd thing you are doing, nobody will suspect you. Be unnatural, and the most innocent action looks suspicious. Nancy walked along the cars swinging her paper; stopped at the *coupé;* put her head and shoulders in at the window; dropped her *Daily Mail* on to the seat, and took away the one that was there; smiled, nodded and walked away, still swinging her paper, still smiling. She had recognized a friend in the car and had stopped to shake hands. That was all. Absurdly simple.

She went back to the station for her bag. At the Castle Hotel she engaged a room, tidied Miss Pitman up, and went off to the Pantiles for tea. Only one thing prevented her from being completely happy. From her bedroom window she could see that dreadful Tank.

Chapter Thirteen

Feverish Activity in London

I

'ALL right, all right,' said Cook damply from the scullery.

The telephone-bell went on ringing.

'*All* right, I'm coming,' Cook reassured it.

'Telephone, Mrs. Price,' said Alice helpfully from the kitchen.

'Well, I'm not deaf,' said Cook, coming out of the scullery still drying her hands. 'Shut the window, there's a good girl, there's so much noise blowing in—Hallo! ... Yes ... *Window*, Alice! ... Yes?'

'Is that Mr. Watterson's house?' said a distant voice.

'Yes, madam.'

'Oh—is that Mrs. Price speaking?'

'Yes, who is it, please?'

There was a note in Cook's voice which made Alice come away from the window, and say—

'*H'sh!*' said Cook, waving her back before she could say it. 'Yes, madam, who is it, please?'

'Oh, Mrs. Price, will you tell Uncle Hubert, please, when he comes in, that I'm *quite, quite* safe.'

'*Miss Jenny!*' shrieked Cook.

'Miss Jenny?' cried Alice.

'Here, what's the matter?' said Hilda, poking her head in from the hall. 'I say, Alice. I *wish* you wouldn't leave all your—'

'S'sh!' said Cook imperiously. 'Hallo ... Hallo! ... Hallo! ... Miss Jenny! ... *Hallo!*'

'What's it all about?' said Hilda. 'That Marigold again?'

'Miss Jenny on the telephone,' said Alice eagerly. 'What did she say, Mrs. Price?'

'Hallo!' said Cook, refusing to give in. 'Hallo!'

'Here, let *me,*' said Hilda, taking the telephone from Cook. 'Hallo!'

Mrs. Price sank into a chair.

'Well, I never,' she panted.

'Cut off,' said Hilda, putting back the receiver. 'P'raps she'll ring again. Sure it was her?'

Cook told them.

Alice nodded eagerly, understanding it all so well.

'And at that moment', said Alice, carrying the story on, 'the Leader of the Gang came in surreptitiously, and put *one* hand over her mouth, and the *other*—'

'Queer,' said Hilda thoughtfully. 'Sounded like as if she was quite all right?'

'Well, I'm telling you. Those were 'er very words. "Tell Uncle Hubert when 'e comes in that I'm quite, quite safe."'

'And then, before she could say more, the Leader of the Gang—'

'Oh, *shut* up, Alice!'

'Now, now, Hilda,' said Cook, 'you don't want to take Alice up like that.'

'Well, what's she want to be so silly for with 'er silly gangs?'

'*You* wouldn't mind', said Alice, ''ow many gangs carried 'er off.' She sniffed, and went on, 'I'm the only one as reely—'

'Now, Alice, we don't want to go into all that again. Those were her words, and if you ask *me*, she's quite safe, but doesn't want anybody to know where she is.'

'That's about it,' said Hilda. 'Gone off with somebody.'

'That I *won't* have said,' declared Cook firmly. 'Not in my kitchen. Miss Jenny's *not* the sort, as you know well—'

'Oh, isn't she? Well, look at 'er aunt!'

'What aunt?'

'Well, Jane Latour's 'er aunt, isn't she? 'Er reel aunt by blood. So it's in the blood, y'see, and what's born in the blood, as they say—'

'I s'pose voices 'aven't never been imitated before,' said Alice sarcastically to nobody.

'That won't do, Hilda. You might as well say that because your Aunt Lucy had the dropsy—'

'Never mind my Aunt Lucy,' said Hilda, a little shrill suddenly. 'If you think it's manners to bring up my Aunt Lucy, which I only told you about, talking in secret confidence about aunts—'

'I s'pose voices 'aven't never been imitated before,' said Alice on a slightly higher note.

'I'm not one to break a confidence, Hilda, as you know well. And if you overheard anything, Alice, about Hilda's Aunt Lucy having the dropsy, then you'll remember, please, it's a sealed book between us three. All I'm saying—'

'Then say it to yourself,' cried Hilda, and slammed the door on them.

Cook's lower lip was trembling, but she got possession of it again and said kindly to Alice:

'What was that you were saying, Alice, about voices?'

'Nothing,' said Alice, 'only I s'pose voices can be imitated, can't they?'

'This wasn't. It was Miss Jenny 'er very own self. I'll swear to that. 'Er own voice.'

'Well, hadn't you better ring up Mr. Marigold? He said to ring up if we heard anything.'

'Miss Jenny didn't say anything about any Mr. Marigold. She said "Tell Uncle Hubert", and if that's what she said, it isn't my place to tell anybody else. First thing he comes back I go out and tell him.'

But she didn't. At a quarter to one Mrs. Watterson came back, bringing her husband with her. Hilda was waiting for her, and hurried into the hall.

'Oh, madam,' she cried, 'oh, sir! Miss Jenny's rung up, and says she's quite, quite safe!'

'What's that?' said Mr. Watterson.

Hilda gave him the story at full length. It wasn't really her story, of course, but cooks who drag in people's Aunt Lucy's dropsies have got to be taught their place.

II

Mr. Bernard Morris, his story ended, twiddled his hat. Inspector Marigold continued to write. Sergeant Bagshaw continued to watch him writing. Mr. Morris looked at Inspector Marigold and at Sergeant Bagshaw, and decided that he didn't like either of them. There was something about policemen's faces that made an honest man sick.

'H'm,' said Inspector Marigold. 'And you think it was the actual watch?'

'Well, I'm telling you, aren't I? Holy Snakes and Ladders,' said Mr. Morris to the ceiling, 'what d'you think I came here for? Company?'

'I don't want comments, Morris. Just answer the questions. It had "J" on it in diamonds?'

'That's what I said. That's all I do say. I don't know who's milky watch it was, and I don't care. It had a "J" on it in diamonds. Standing for Julius Caesar, I dare say.'

'Now then, Morris,' put in Sergeant Bagshaw dutifully.

'And you say he pledged it with you, and then half an hour later redeemed it? Now I wonder why he did that?'

'Wanted to know the time per'aps,' suggested Mr. Morris unhelpfully.

'Cold feet,' said Sergeant Bagshaw, nodding at the Inspector.

'That's about it,' agreed Marigold. 'You took his name, of course?'

'I did. What d'you think?'

'Well, come on, let's have it.'

Mr. Morris searched for, and found, a dirty piece of paper in his waistcoat pocket.

'William Makespeak Thackeray,' he read.

'Ah! Think it was his real name?'

'Suffering Chorus-girls!' said Mr. Morris to Heaven. 'D'you think I looked at his passport, or asked to see the monogram tattooed on his chest?'

'Don't be a fool, Morris. You know well enough by now when a man's giving his real name or not.'

'Sweet Potatoes,' said Mr. Morris, *'how* many—'

Sergeant Bagshaw cleared his throat and looked self-conscious.

'After you,' said Mr. Morris courteously.

'It wasn't,' announced Sergeant Bagshaw.

'Wasn't what?' asked the Inspector.

'Wasn't his real name.'

'How do you know?'

'Because he's a northor.'

'Who is?'

'What he was saying. William Makepeace Thackeray.'

'Well, why shouldn't he be? Think a northor can't commit a murder as well as anybody else?'

'I mean he's a classic.'

'Who is?'

'William Makepeace Thackeray.'

'How d'you mean a classic?'

'Like Shakespeare.'

'That's right,' said Mr. Morris, thinking it was time he joined in again. 'Like Shakespeare.'

'D'you mean like Edgar Wallace?'

Sergeant Bagshaw considered this.

'Well, more like Shakespeare,' he said, wishing to get his values as accurate as possible.

'I told you so,' said Mr. Morris. 'We keep telling you. Like Shakespeare.'

'Look here, Bagshaw,' said the Inspector, 'where do you *get* all this?'

'I'll tell you. It was this way. I had occasion to speak to a gentleman—had to ask him his name. He said, "Thackeray". I said, "Thackeray, eh?" thinking of Charlie Thackeray, *you* remember, the forger. North Midland Bank Case. He said, "Know the name, what?" and I said, "I should think I do, sir"—well, considering everything. He says, "Some writer, eh?" and I says, "That's right, sir. What that Charlie Thackeray couldn't do with a pen—"and he says, "Charlie? To hell with Charlie. It's William." So I says, "Beg your pardon, sir, I ought to know, seeing as it was me—"and he says, "Bet you a fiver, Sergeant, it's William Makepeace Thackeray. *You*'re thinking of Charlie Dickens." Well, then it all came out, as you might say, and it transpired that this William Makepeace Thackeray was a northor like Shakespeare. What they call a classic.' He nodded at the Inspector. 'That's the way it was.'

'That's right,' said Mr. Morris, twiddling his hat. 'A classic.'

'Ah! Meaning it might be an *alias?*'

'A nom de pop,' translated Mr. Morris.

'That's right,' said the Sergeant.

'Might be,' said the Inspector judicially, 'and then again, might not be. He said it was his wife's watch, is that right, Morris?'

'Something o' that sort. I wasn't listening *too* 'ard.'

The Inspector turned back to Bagshaw.

'Is this William Makepeace Thackeray married?'

'I told you, 'e's dead.'

'He's lucky,' said Mr. Morris to the world.

'Like Shakespeare. Right off the map.'

'Ah! ... Well let's have a description of him.'

Mr. Morris looked expectantly at Sergeant Bagshaw, and waited for a description of William Makepeace Thackeray.

'*You*, Morris, you fool!' shouted the Inspector. 'What was this man like?'

'Who's a fool?' said Mr. Morris, annoyed.

'You are.'

'Oh, am I? Well, 'ow did I know you weren't asking about this other feller?'

'What does it matter about this other feller if he's dead?'

'Well, what does it matter about him whether he's married or not?'

'Who said it did?'

'You did.'

'No, I didn't.'

'You asked *him*,' said Mr. Morris, indicating the Sergeant, 'and *he*'ll bear me out, you asked *him* if this William Makepeace Thackeray was married or not. So naturally *I* thought—"

'Well, I didn't know he was dead then, did I?'

'Yes, you did. I'd just told you he was a classic. We'd both told you. 'Ow could he be a classic if—'

'Now, now, Morris,' said Sergeant Bagshaw pacifically. 'What was 'e like?'

Mr. Morris turned to him.

'I don't mind telling *you*,' said Mr. Morris with dignity, 'because you and I are educated men as knows what a classic is, and don't go calling each other names. Speaking as one college man to another, he was a short, stout feller with a little fair moustache.'

'Ah!' said Inspector Marigold coldly ...

Five minutes later Mr. Morris was in the open again, breathing an air unpolluted by policemen.

'Hips and Thigh-bones!' cried Mr. Morris to High Heaven. 'And *that*'s what has to catch our murderers for us! Why, they couldn't catch the measles in a Measle 'Ospital.'

III

Now all is set for the Inquest on Jane Latour. Now to the little courtroom in Merrion Place the fashionable world comes streaming. Hither come the Leaders of Society; the Young Eligible Set, the Young Married Set, the Young Divorced Set. Hither comes the Marquis of Puddlehinton on behalf of his Sunday paper. Hither comes the ex-President of Canova's solicitor, just in case.

Mr. Ponsonby Wicks, the Coroner, opens the proceedings. He touches lightly upon a number of matters which have interested him during the last few weeks: the inefficiency of the League of Nations, the rising spirit of unrest among the working classes, the growing licence allowed to novelists and other so-called artists, the necessity for removing children's tonsils as soon as they become available. 'It is for you', said Mr. Ponsonby Wicks to the Jury, 'to decide how this poor lady met her death,' and went on to denounce the corruption in American politics. 'You will not', said Mr. Wicks, 'shrink from the responsibility,' and spoke coldly of the Trade Agreement with Russia ...

The Jury retired and viewed what Dr. Willoughby Hatch had left of the body ...

Mr. George Parracot gave evidence. He was wearing the Old Felsbridgian tie and (though these were not seen) the Old Felsbridgian braces. He was, so it appeared at first, a bachelor, living at Auburn Lodge near the Brompton Road. He had been having a holiday at Eastbourne, and the house was empty. On the day in question he had left Eastbourne by an early train on his way through London to Cromer, and had looked in at Auburn Lodge in order to collect one or two things.

'What sort of things?' asked Mr. Wicks, feeling that all this would go better as a duologue.

'Oh, well, as a matter of fact,' said George carelessly, 'just one or two things. Brilliantine —and face cream—and—er—'

'Face cream?' said Mr. Wicks, frowning.

'Er—yes,' said George guiltily, realizing suddenly what he had said, 'as a matter of fact, yes.'

'Do you use face cream?'

Everybody looked at Mr. Parracot's face, which was now bright-red.

'Er—as a matter of fact, yes,' said Mr. Parracot doggedly.

'Why?' asked the Coroner, and the Young Eligible Set wondered if this was a new one which they hadn't heard about.

'For the face,' said George, after giving the matter careful thought.

Inspector Marigold whispered in the Coroner's ear.

'Arsting if 'e can't arrest 'im at once,' said the cheaper seats to each other hopefully.

'Ah!' said Mr. Ponsonby Wicks. And then to George: 'You are married, Mr. Parracot?'

'Well, yes,' admitted George reluctantly. 'Yes, as a matter of fact, yes.'

'And Mrs. Parracot was with you on your holiday, and called in at Auburn Lodge with you?'

'Well—er—yes,' admitted George, still more reluctantly.

'Then kindly say so. There's no need to be ashamed of it, Mr. Parracot, not even in these days.'

Everybody laughed; the Young Eligible Set loudly, the Young Divorced Set defiantly, the Young Married Set self-consciously.

'Go on, Mr. Parracot, please.'

Mr. Parracot went on. The cheaper seats were now distinctly hostile to him, and wondered if it would be safe to take the children to Cromer this year. The stalls looked at him admiringly. Every one knew that that fellow Parracot was well known to Scotland Yard as a drug-trafficker, and now it seemed that he was mixed up in the White Slave Traffic too. Some lad ...

Old Girl gave evidence. The cheaper seats felt sorry for Old Girl, married to a murderer. The stalls also felt sorry for Old Girl. I mean to say, darling, positively *nude* about the face, and simply *too* dairymaid altogether.

'You were not personally acquainted with the deceased, Mrs. Parracot?' asked the Coroner, and the stalls laughed at the idea of Toto knowing Laura ...

Inspector Marigold gave evidence. The cheaper seats whispered to each other that this was one of the Big Five, but, when challenged, were uncertain who the other four were. The stalls looked at him with mixed feelings. He had the reputation of being a difficult man to bribe, and the less affluent of them had found this to be true. Also he had no sense of humour, and when the famous Baby's Bottle Party had overflowed into Merrion Place, and started playing Postman's Knock at three o'clock in the morning, he had been extremely stolid about it. But those of them who were running Night Clubs realized that Inspector Marigold had a human side which he did not allow the ordinary public, or his superiors, to suspect ...

Dr. Willoughby Hatch was called, and the Court sat up hopefully. Dr. Hatch gave, fortunately without being too technical, the result of his researches into the more sequestered organs of the deceased, Mr. Ponsonby Wicks drawing him out with a well-placed question whenever the interests of Justice or the press-value of the organ seemed to demand it. Coming, a little reluctantly, to the external injuries, the Court learnt that these were caused by a blow on the head from a narrow sharp instrument of some nature.

'Not', said Mr. Wicks, surprised, 'by a heavy, blunt instrument?'
'No,' said Hatch.

Mr. Wicks hid his disappointment as well as he could, and got down to business. 'Now, Dr. Willoughby Hatch,' he said, 'have you formed any opinion as to the physical characteristics of the assailant?'

'I have,' said Hatch.

There was a tense silence. Everybody looked at Mr. Parracot, and wondered how one would describe him. Inspector Marigold whispered in the Coroner's ear.

'Well,' said the Coroner on a different note, 'we need not go into that. All we are concerned with to-day is the cause of death. We will keep to that if you please, Dr. Hatch. What can you tell us of the personal habits of the deceased?' ...

And now Mr. Ponsonby Wicks is about to sum up. He looks through his notes, and sees that he has said nothing yet about Birth Control, Reparations, or the Sunday opening of Cinemas. He sums up ...

The Jury retires to consider its verdict. The stalls chatter, and those of them who have not yet caught the eye of the Marquis of Puddlehinton hasten to do so, in order that my lord's Sunday readers shall not be defrauded. The cheaper seats look at Mr. Parracot hopefully, with their mouths open.

The Jury delivers its verdict. To the relief of Inspector Marigold, who is now looking for a short, stout fellow with a fair moustache, and does not want to have George on his hands again, it announces that the deceased was murdered by some person or persons unknown. Everybody scowls at Mr. Parracot, who fingers his tie. The Court empties slowly ...

INQUEST ON JANE LATOUR
SENSATIONAL EVIDENCE

cry the posters.

Chapter Fourteen

Affray at Bassetts

I

The gentleman who had brought back a Rabelaisian robustness to the English novel loosened the cord of his pyjamas and sipped his early morning tea. It was good to be at Ferries again—without Fanny. Ferries (without Fanny) in the Garden of England, with the smell of hops, or something, drifting in through the open windows, was his true home. Here a man could write—God, how he could write! Already the slow loveliness of the place was inspiring him. Thoughts, flashing thoughts, which clothed themselves even as they lit up his brain in beautiful words, paraded for his approval, too quick for pen to record them. If only his secretary—Miss Fairbrother—had been here, alert to take them down in shorthand, just so, and only so, he might have kept pace with them ...

But then if his secretary—Miss Fairbrother —Nancy—were here at this moment, in this room, would they—

Obviously not ...

(Not shorthand.)

Nancy ...

A new set of thoughts flashed into his mind, and were made comfortable there. Robust thoughts. Rabelaisian ... Nancy ...

No. Idiot. *Julia.*

Julia! That was why he felt so gay, so eager, so young this morning. After breakfast he was going to write to Julia.

He rose. He looked at himself in the Queen Anne mirror, and found that once again it had no alternative to offer him. He shaved. He went into the sunlit bathroom and turned on both taps. Through the open casement July came in with banners, and he decided not to weigh himself.

After breakfast he wrote to Julia.

'Julia, my dear, something tells me that it is your birthday to-morrow, which means that once again you are a year younger and a year more beautiful; for so it is, divinely, that you live among us poor mortals, for whom birthdays are ever-hastening, ever-lessening, milestones to the grave. To-day you are twenty-five, is it not? To-morrow, when this reaches you, you will be twenty-four. In the little token which I send you for a reminder of our friendship, I have set out these twenty-four years as one sets out candles for a child around its birthday-cake—'

('Perhaps I *had* better count them again,' said Mr. Fenton. He counted again the little diamonds round the face of the watch. Twenty-four.)

'—birthday-cake, for it is as a beautiful and innocent child that I shall always think of you.'

('An awkward approach', said Mr. Fenton, 'to the suggestion that she should spend the week-end with me. Also the English is a little careless, and leaves it uncertain which of us is the beautiful and innocent child.')

'—birthday-cake, and above them I have placed a "J"—'

('No,' said Mr. Fenton. 'Hardly necessary. She will naturally assume that "J" stands for Julia, and I really cannot keep on calling her attention to the diamonds.')

'—birthday-cake, and if I am wrong, and you are only twenty-three—'

('I mustn't overdo this,' said Mr. Fenton. 'Actually, I suppose she is forty, and looks thirty-two.')

'—birthday-cake, and sometimes when you—'

('Damn,' said Mr. Fenton.)

'—birthday-cake.'

July still called insistently to him. He dropped his pen, and wandered into the garden for inspiration. He walked among his roses, he blew cigarette-smoke at the greenfly, he picked a bud for his button-hole. No inspiration came ... Birthday-cake ... Curse ... He went back to his room, tore the damned thing up, and began again.

'Dearest Julia, All my love comes with this trifle which I have designed for you for your birthday. It is your month, the most beautiful of the year, as it should be, and I have come down here to welcome it. Walking in my garden just now I wondered what it lacked of perfection, and the answer came at once—" Julia". If it could but have Julia for a little! Would you not drive down on Sunday morning and have lunch, and what else you will, with me? I am alone; we could talk; I could show you my garden. "You foolish man," I can hear you saying, "I have ten engagements for Sunday already!" Of course you have, but you will never sort them out properly, so let them go, Julia. You will? Thank you, my dear. And now give just a glance again at Julia's new watch, and say to yourself: "He is counting the hours until I come, from now on he is counting the hours"—and Come!'

Mr. Fenton read this through and was moderately pleased with it. Remained the signature.

What?

At their last meeting she had greeted him 'Hallo, Funny-face', but one could hardly sign a well-phrased letter of this sort 'Funny-face'.

Archibald? But nobody called him Archibald.

Archie, then? She had never called him Archie; she had never called him anything distinctive (unless Funny-face was distinctive); the occasional 'Darlings' which she had thrown at him, he shared with a hundred others. If he signed it Archie, would it define him in her mind? Probably not. And the address meant nothing to her.

Archibald Fenton, it must be. It lacked intimacy, but, after all, it was his signature, and in a sense made the letter more valuable.

Come! Archibald Fenton.

Mr. Fenton thought, and perhaps may be excused for thinking, that really, you know, *'Come! Archibald Fenton'* ought to be good enough for anybody.

II

Miss Emily Gathers, aged fifty-four, popped a small piece of barley-sugar into her mouth and returned the jar to its shelf. George Alfred Hickley, aged four, went out, clinging to a larger piece. 'Shut the door, Georgie, there's a good boy,' called out Miss Gathers. George Alfred Hickley shut it. He had always meant to do this, so that he could open it again and make the bell ring. 'No, Georgie, no!' said Miss Gathers firmly after the third ring, and George Alfred Hickley, thinking that perhaps she was right, left the door open, and came out into the sun again, with the air of a man who was having, one way and another, a good pennyworth. But there was still some small change to come. A car was rushing up, was stopping; a man was getting out, was taking a parcel into the shop. George Alfred Hickley sucked his barley-sugar and waited.

'Hallo, Tommy,' said Mr. Fenton genially.

George Alfred Hickley said nothing.

'Barley-sugar, eh?' said Mr. Fenton, and getting no reply added, 'Well, well,' and patted George Alfred Hickley's head in a kindly manner. Then, feeling that he had entered into the life of the village enough for one morning, he passed through the door, and closed it behind him. George Alfred Hickley opened it, so that Miss Gathers should know that somebody was coming …

'Why, bless my soul,' said Miss Gathers, hastily swallowing, 'if it isn't Mr. Fenton! Well, you *are* a stranger, Mr. Fenton.'

'Good-morning,' said Archibald gaily, for it was indeed a beautiful morning, and Julia was getting nearer every minute. 'Registered, please.'

He handed over his parcel, and the Postmistress became professional …

'Quite a Gathering of the Clans,' she said archly, as she wrote.

'I beg your pardon?'

'Your brother is at Bassetts again, isn't he, Mr. Fenton?'

'Oh!' said Archibald coldly.

'*And* your sister, I understand.'

'My sister?'

'Miss Naomi. She was in here telephoning. Quite romantic. Her friend spraining her ankle, I mean, and then finding that her brother was quite close.'

Miss Gathers held a sensible view of her responsibilities as a postmistress. She was the last person to betray a trust; but if she accidentally overheard a telephone conversation or glanced at a post card, or when, as was inevitable, she was taken into the confidence of a telegram, she looked at the matter all round in a broadminded way. For example: when Mrs. Trevor from the Round House went up to the nursing home in London (and not a moment too soon), and the telegram came: '*Diana Mary arrived safely this morning all well'*, and when, five years later, Diana Mary came in with her nurse and asked for a pennyworth of bulls'-eyes, one couldn't refuse to serve the child on the grounds that one had heard of her existence officially, and under the pledge of secrecy. Pursuing this line of reasoning to its logical conclusion, one realized that if Miss Naomi Fenton, or anybody else, telephoned to Mrs. Bassett, or anybody else, and if Mrs. Bassett, or whoever it might be, was one's intimate friend (as she was) and quite certain to reveal every detail of the conversation at their next meeting, whenever this should happen to take place, then for practical purposes, and looking at the matter all round in a broadminded way, this could not be regarded as knowledge which had come to one in an official capacity, but as knowledge which would naturally come to one as a friend of Mrs. Bassett's, and of course if it had been two strangers telephoning it would have been different.

'Quite romantic,' said Miss Gathers again. 'But I expect you've heard all about it from them by now. That will be eightpence exactly, Mr. Fenton.'

Mr. Fenton had not heard anything about it. He had not even seen the original telegram *'Gloria Naomi arrived safely this morning all well'* which should have told him that he had a little sister. He was interested.

'No, I hadn't heard,' he said. 'When was this?'

'Yesterday. About lunch-time.'

'And she's staying there?'

'So I understand, Mr. Fenton. So,' said Miss Gathers, anticipating a little, 'Mrs. Bassett informs me.'

'I must go over and see them,' said Archibald firmly.

'Well, I'm sure that would give them great pleasure, Mr. Fenton.'

Archibald was not so sure. Indeed, he hoped it would give them no pleasure at all. Sister! Ha! And this was the moral Derek! He would go over this afternoon and see them ... and watch the moral Derek trying to carry it off. *Sister!*

'Thanks,' said Archibald, receiving his change. 'Well, good-morning, Miss—er—' What was the damned woman's name?

'Good-morning, Mr. Fenton.'

As Mr. Fenton came out, his electric motor-horn, which had been silent too long, gave a sudden welcoming cry. Removing George Alfred Hickley at the very peak of endeavour from the off side running-board, Mr. Fenton climbed into the car and drove off. What seemed to be the greater part of George Alfred Hickley's barley-sugar went with him.

III

It was summer afternoon at Bassetts, but rain was coming. 'P'raps not Friday, p'raps not Sat'day, but 'tis coming.' Farmer Bassett felt it in his bones, and in the autocracy over which he ruled the authority of his bones was acknowledged. To the last man, woman and child his subjects were in the fields, making hay while the sun still shone.

Jenny, an opened book on her lap, sat alone in the cool of the little parlour, delightfully postponing sleep. She felt restful, at ease, well cared for. Derek would be coming back to her soon, but she was in no hurry for him. When he came back, they would have to talk things over again, make some new plan together. That would be fun, making plans with Derek; but the lazy content which enveloped her, the consciousness of being wholly and perfectly herself, was a happiness which no other could share, or by his presence intensify. She was Jenny. Jenny was good, Jenny was beautiful, Jenny was clever. Now Jenny was going to sleep …

There was a sudden knock on the door, sudden and alarming to one who seemed to have the quiet afternoon so completely to herself. Jenny was on to her feet, her heart ridiculously beating.

She tried to say that it was a friend of Mrs. Bassett's, a tradesman, a passerby in quest of something, but absurd little fears were creeping into her mind, and growing there, and taking wellrecognized shapes: Tramps at Lonely Farms, Policemen Effecting Arrests: Law and Violence now equally her enemies. Jenny, Jenny, pull yourself together! This is childish, and you are so brave.

'I know!' she thought suddenly, and, holding her breath, she tiptoed into the passage and past the slender barrier of the door, and so up the stairs to her room. From behind the curtains she peeped at the unknown.

Not a Tramp, not a Policeman. Just a man from a car, well dressed, short, stout, reassuring.

'I'm an idiot,' laughed Jenny to herself, 'but I shan't be an idiot again'; and to make sure that she should not be an idiot again, she took from its drawer Watson's Wonderful Combination Watchdog-and-Water-pistol and the two pink garters. With Watson in his place she went downstairs light-heartedly, almost wishing now for adventure.

She opened the door.

'Oh, good-afternoon,' said Mr. Archibald Fenton, and registered an immediate impression that Derek was doing himself well.

'Good-afternoon,' said Jenny. 'Did you—Mrs. Bassett—everybody's down in the fields, getting the hay in. Did you—'

'Ah! Forgive me, but have I the pleasure of speaking to Miss Naomi Fenton?'

'Er—yes,' said Jenny.

It was not her fault that she did not recognize him. She had never seen him; and the many impressions in the papers of the famous Archibald Fenton, showing him to be a slender, good-looking young man of twenty-three, as indeed he had been for a few moments, and in a favouring light, twenty years ago, had not prepared her for the present authorized edition, as to which Nancy had never let fall any more enlightening word than 'catastrophic'.

'But, darling, what do you mean, catastrophic?' Jenny had asked.

'Well, wait till you see it, the whole thing's a disaster, that's all.'

Now she was seeing it.

'I heard in the village that you were paying your brother a visit,' said Archibald, enjoying himself extremely, 'and I ventured to call.'

'Oh! Oh, how nice of you. Won't you come in?'

'May I? Thank you so much.'

He followed her into the little parlour, and looked round him complacently, feeling sure of its secrets.

'I'm afraid Derek's out. He had to go into Tunbridge Wells. Do sit down, won't you? And smoke.'

'Thank you. Won't you—' He held out his case. She shook her head.

'So Derek's in Tunbridge Wells,' said Archibald, lighting a cigarette. 'And you're all alone. Poor little girl.'

'Why?' said Jenny.

Archibald had called a good many people 'Poor little girl', but never been asked 'Why?' before.

'I was sympathizing,' he said stiffly.

'Yes, but why? I don't mind being alone, do you?'

'It depends whose company I am missing. Just at the moment, my dear Naomi, I am very happy not to be alone.'

Jenny began to feel a little bewildered.

'Who are you, please?' she asked. 'Are you a friend of Derek's?'

'You might say so, yes. I have known him a very long time.'

'Oh!'

'He has often talked to me about you.'

'Oh!' said Jenny again.

'His little sister Naomi. You've no idea how proud he is of his little sister Naomi.'

'Oh!' said Jenny for the third time.

He had never taken his eyes off her. There was a look in his eyes, amused, appreciative, possessive, which she hated. He seemed to be sharing some secret with her. What did it mean? Did he know that she was a fraud?

'Even when little Naomi was a child,' the voice went on, 'he used to tell me of the amusing things she said. They were not very funny,' admitted Archibald, 'but then the things which children say never *are* very funny, are they? But Derek used to assure me that if I could have heard the dear little mite saying them—dear little Naomi—' He broke off and puffed at his cigarette, still keeping his amused eyes on her.

How much did he know? Perhaps—sudden brilliant thought—he knew nothing. Perhaps there had been, or was still, a real Naomi Fenton of whom Derek had spoken, a sister who had died or been married.

'You haven't told me your name, have you?' she said, trying to smile brightly. 'Perhaps Derek has talked to me about *you*.'

'I'm sure he has,' said Archibald blandly.

'Oh?'

She seemed so innocent that for a moment his complacence was disturbed.

'Look here,' he said a little anxiously, 'I'm not making a mistake, am I? You *are* Derek Fenton's sister?'

'Y-yes,' said Jenny.

'Good. So you're Archibald Fenton's sister too, of course?'

Jenny nodded.

'Then,' said Archibald, getting up, 'I really must have one.'

He came over to her chair, and Jenny jumped to her feet. 'What do you want?'

'A kiss,' he said gaily. 'Just a kiss. Because you see, Naomi darling, I am your long-lost brother Archibald.'

'Oh!' cried Jenny. 'How awful!' She stared at him.

She thought: No wonder Derek hates him. No wonder Nancy says what she does about him. What am I going to do? Why doesn't Derek come back? Who shall I say I am? I think he's hideous. Fancy if he *had* kissed me! What *are* we going to do? He's not a bit like Derek. The funny thing is I did rather like *A Flock of Sheep.* I think I'll say nothing.

'Well?' said Archibald, still smiling, and coming a little closer.

Jenny went back a step and said breathlessly: 'Your brother will be here directly. Won't you sit down and wait for him? He will tell you anything you want to know.'

'*Our* brother, isn't it, Naomi?'

'*He* will tell you why I—who I—how it is—'

'Oh, but I think I know how it is, don't I?' smiled Archibald.

Jenny gasped.

'Do you mean you know who I am?'

'Of course I do, my dear child.'

Let's have the worst, thought Jenny.

'Who?'

'Not', said Archibald, 'Derek's—sister.'

Instinctively she moved away from him, and in moving knocked her leg against the corner of the chair. Ah! How silly to have forgotten! The faithful Watson! Now she was quite cool again.

'Please go away,' she said firmly.

Archibald shook an indulgent head.

'Not till I have had that kiss.'

'Please go away at *once*.'

'Oh, come, my dear, don't be silly. What's a kiss more or less to a girl like you?'

Jenny stooped for a moment and stood up again.

'If you don't go at once, I shall fire,' she said. Almost unconsciously she spoke in the voice of one who had had to do this

169

sort of thing a good deal lately, and Archibald, recognizing the note, moved hastily back.

'Please go,' said Jenny.

The famous novelist recovered his poise.

'You've been going to the pictures a good deal, haven't you?' he laughed. 'What is it? A water-pistol?'

He was so nearly right that Jenny lowered her protector hastily lest all its secrets should be revealed. This was enough for Archibald, who jumped hurriedly for his kiss. A more active man might have reached her, but he was a stout mover, and Jenny's arm came up just in time. There was a flash which seemed to fill the room with sound. As instinctively he closed his eyes to it, something stung him sharply on the temple. Vaguely he felt for the place with his hand. The hand came away wet and horribly, horribly red. Vaguely he looked at the hand, as if trying to read its message. Then, suddenly realizing it, he dropped to the floor, and lay there ...

It had all happened so quickly, it was all so utterly realistic, that Jenny could only stand there stupidly, looking at the pistol in her hand, as if to make sure that it was indeed the toy which Mr. Sandroyd had sold to her, and not some monstrous changeling. Perhaps Mrs. Bassett kept a real pistol in that drawer, she thought. Perhaps I'm going mad. Perhaps it's all a dream. Then she thought: I'm being a little fool, he just fell down.

'Please get up,' she said, 'it's quite all right.'

Mr. Fenton did not move.

'It *is* a water-pistol really, only I filled it with red ink. That was what frightened you, I expect.'

Mr. Fenton said nothing.

'That and the bang. It bangs too. That's really why it's so good. I bought it at Tunbridge Wells.'

Even so, Mr. Fenton did not move.

'*Really* you aren't hurt,' pleaded Jenny. 'It's only because I used red ink. I bought a bottle in the village.'

Even so, Mr. Fenton remained silent.

'Oh, dear! Perhaps he has bumped his head.'

And suddenly she began to pray that he *had* bumped his head; for an apprehension slowly filled her mind of all the vague tales she had heard of people being frightened to death; tales told her in childhood of men pretending to be ghosts, and of mock-executions; and she remembered Aunt Caroline's warning to her once when she had jumped out at Cook: 'Never try to frighten anybody, Jenny. At the best it only causes justifiable annoyance, and at the worst it may have very serious effects.' Which was this?

'Oh, God,' prayed Jenny, 'let it be a justifiable annoyance, and *not* a very serious effect.'

Before any decision could be taken in the matter, the door opened, and Derek was there.

IV

When Derek had dropped his newspapers into the car and gone up into the High Street, his intention had been to buy two or three of the better-class milliner's shops for Jenny; for he knew that so charming a girl could not live charmingly for long on nothing more embellishing than one knapsack and a loan of Mrs. Bassett's wedding-dress. But on looking into his notecase, and finding that he had only thirty shillings with him, he realized that the dangers of choosing a wrong shape or an unfashionable shade were so outstanding that it would be kinder to Jenny to limit himself on this occasion to a box of chocolates, a basket of cherries and a flask of eau-de-Cologne. Having then no more than five and sixpence over, he rejected a passing thought about champagne, being in any case fairly sure that this was either the hour when you could buy a bottle but were not allowed to take it away, or the hour when you could take it away but were not allowed to buy it. Champagne, he felt, might have helped them to come to a wise decision on some of the important problems which would face them to-night; or perhaps not; but anyhow it would have been pleasant ...

How brave Jenny was ...

How beautiful ...

How sweet ...

How entirely idiotic.

To-night they must really go into the matter seriously, and decide what was to be done ...

He came into the parlour, one half of his mind still with Inspector Marigold in London, the other half on this new difficulty of opening a door without dropping one of his six newspapers and three parcels; and almost before he could straighten himself, Jenny was adding to the confusion in his arms.

'Oh, *Derek*,' cried Jenny, 'I've killed somebody!'

'Not *again?*' said Derek, surprised. 'Here, wait till I get these things out of the way.'

'He says he's your *brother!*'

'Oh, well, that's all right.'

He put the parcels on the table, Jenny moved out of the way ... and there was Archibald.

'Good lord,' said Derek, 'so you have.'

Jenny, holding her breath, watched him as he knelt by the body.

'Is he dead?' she ventured at last.

'No,' said Derek. 'But he's much too fat.'

Jenny gave a deep sigh of relief.

'What happened?' he asked.

She explained it all ...

'I see. Well, now you know why I like him so much.'

He was angry. She loved him for being angry.

'It must have been rather funny, though,' said Derek, beginning to laugh.

Now he was amused. She loved him for being amused.

'Has he fainted?' she asked.

'Yes. When he comes round, he'll say, "Where am I?" What does one do? Their knees have to be higher than their head, don't they? Or is it lower? At present the only part of him which is quite insistently higher than anything else—'

'Aunt Caroline used to faint sometimes.'

'Ah! What happened then?'

'Well, we used to loosen her stays.'

Derek regarded his brother's outline thoughtfully.

'Would you say he was wearing stays?' he asked.

'Well, I think you ought to loosen his collar.'

'That's a good idea. And, while doing it, we could throw away his tie.' He removed the tie and held it up to Jenny. 'There's a wastepaper-basket just behind you. Do you mind?'

Obediently she dropped it in the basket without quite knowing why. But she supposed that Derek disliked it for some reason; and indeed its colours, red and yellow stripes, assorted ill with the rest of Archibald, and were not wholly at ease among themselves.

'Club colours of the Royal Society of Literature,' explained Derek carelessly over his shoulder.

'Oh, I see.'

'We won't take his watch,' he went on, still busy at the body, 'because it wouldn't be fair, but we must think seriously about his eye-glass. How do you feel about that?'

'Oughtn't we to do something to revive him? With water or something?'

'Yes. Now wait a moment.'

He began to wonder what would happen when his brother came back to life. How were they going to behave, the three of them? Were they all going to talk together at the tops of their voices, arguing, recriminating, losing their tempers? Or were they all going to be perfect ladies and gentlemen, pretending that nothing had happened? Or were they—

'Yes. That's the way. Now listen.'

'Yes, Derek?'

'Fly up to the bathroom. You'll find a baby sponge there, which I use for cleaning tennis-shoes. Rinse it out a bit and bring it down, wet.'

'Yes, Derek.' She turned to fly.

'Wait. In the little cupboard there's a roll of bandage—or was. Bring it down.'

'Yes, Derek.'

'Wait. There's a small bowl in my room, or perhaps it's in the bathroom, or anyhow there must be a small bowl somewhere. Is there any red ink left in your bottle?' She nodded. 'Well, fill the bowl with water, and put some red ink in to give it a little local colour, and bring bowl, sponge and bandage down here. Quick!'

She was very quick ...

'Good girl. Now then, take all those parcels—they're yours—and the papers—Oh, and here's your letter—and go up to your room, and read and enjoy yourself, and leave everything else to me.'

He opened the door for her.

'Are you sure—'

'Quick! Fly!'

She flew. He hurried back to the body.

V

When Archibald came to himself, he was lying on the sofa, his head heavily bandaged. At the table by his side was a bowl of what had once been water, but now was dyed ominously red.

'Where am I?' said Mr. Archibald Fenton.

'With friends,' said Derek soothingly. 'How are you feeling now, old boy?'

Archibald put his hand to his head and knew that it was not a dream.

'She shot me,' he said weakly.

'That's right. You were making advances to her.'

'I wasn't.'

'Well, making something.'

'All I—I just said—Anyway, she had no business to shoot me.'

'She didn't know what else to do. It was all so sudden.'

'You can't go shooting people like that,' said Archibald sulkily. 'She might have killed me.'

'I'll tell her. She thought you were making advances to her, that's how it was.'

'Well, I wasn't.'

'I'll tell her.'

'She said she was my sister, and naturally I asked her for a kiss. And then she shot me. I say, am I—'

Derek gave him a surprised look.

'How do you mean she said she was your sister?' he interrupted.

'How do you mean, how do I mean she—I'm telling you. Oh, gosh, I feel sick. She said she was my sister. Our sister. Naturally—'

'Who did? Miss Benton?'

'Miss who?'

'Benton.'

'Who's Benton? I'm talking about this girl who calls herself Naomi Fenton.'

'Naomi Benton, that's right.'

'No, *Fenton!* I tell you she said you were her brother.'

'Not me. Benton. You've got it muddled.'

'I tell you—'

'Don't talk too much, old boy. Not with a head-wound. It's dangerous.'

'I said "Then you're Archibald Fenton's sister too," and she said "Yes," and I said "Well, I'm Archibald Fenton," and she said "Oh!" and I said "Well, if I'm your brother—"'

'You're not *her* brother, old boy, you're mine. It will all come back to you soon. You're Archibald Fenton.'

'Look here—'

'So you couldn't be Miss Benton's brother. Cousin, yes. Brother, no. But I'll explain about that when you're stronger. How are you feeling now?'

'You fool, I never thought I—I say, am I badly hurt?' He saw the bowl suddenly. 'I say—'

Derek patted his shoulder reassuringly.

'Nasty scalp-wound, that's all. Miss Benton has tied it up for you. She knows all about that sort of thing. She's a nurse.'

'Oh, is that what she calls herself?'

'Yes.'

'And what,' said Archibald sarcastically, 'is this so-called Miss Fenton who now calls herself Nurse Benton doing here?'

'You mean what is this so-called Nurse Benton who you thought called herself Miss Fenton doing here?'

'What's she doing here?' shouted Archibald.

'Steady, old boy. Not with a head-wound. Miss Benton particularly warned me—'

'Who is she? What's she doing here?'

'But why shouldn't she be here? You remember Molly Bassett, don't you? The red-haired one who married John Benton from Five Ashes? Well, John Benton has a sister, and this sister—'

'Oh!'

'Exactly. And what happens?' said Derek reproachfully. 'You make advances to her.'

Archibald was silent, thinking.

'Don't think too hard,' said Derek anxiously, 'because of what I said just now about head-wounds.'

'I don't care who she is,' announced Archibald. 'She said she was your sister.'

'Not mine. Benton's.'

'*Yours*, damn you!'

'I knew a man, an accountant by profession, who had a nasty head-accident in Piccadilly, and when he came round, and they asked him how it had happened, he said that his sister had pushed him off the rocking-horse. It seems that in these cases one's memory often goes back to the last time one has fallen on one's head, and naturally—'

'Oh, damn you, shut up.'

'Right. Take it easy, that's the way. Do you mind if I smoke?'

'I don't care *what* you do.'

'That's right. Just lie there quietly, and don't bother about me.'

Archibald Fenton lay there quietly, but he was not taking it easy. He was thinking. *Could* he have got it muddled? The whole business had been so sudden, so surprising, so confusing that it was difficult to be certain of anything. And then with a nasty head-wound like this—and feeling rather sick—

'Ah!' said Archibald triumphantly. Now it had all come back to him.

'What?'

'That woman at the post office said she was your sister!'

Derek shook his head.

'I have no relations in the post office,' he said simply. 'I have', he added, hoping to strike some chord of memory, 'a brother in Bloomsbury. A novelist.'

'You fool, I don't mean she said *she* was your sister, I mean she said Miss Fenton was your sister.'

'It is true', admitted Derek, 'that, if I had a sister, she would be Miss Fenton. Undoubtedly. But I haven't. *We* haven't. Don't you remember how you used to say to me with tears in your eyes: "Oh, if only I had a little sister!" and I used to say: "But you've always got *me*, Hippo," and *you* used to say—'

'My God!' said Archibald Fenton.

'Well, not quite that, but something like it.'

'I've had enough of this. I'm going.' He took his legs off the sofa, and tried to stand up.

'Steady,' said his brother, hurrying to his help. 'Just sit like that for a moment. That's right.'

'I say,' said Archibald, a little frightened suddenly, 'I say, how bad am I? I feel pretty rotten. Oughtn't I to see a doctor?'

'Honestly, if you go to bed as soon as you get home, and keep that bandage on till tomorrow, you'll be all right. You can let your housekeeper have a look at it in the morning. Miss Benton has taken every precaution, I assure you.'

'If she'd taken the elementary precaution of keeping her finger off the trigger—'

'I thought I'd explained that. You see, you made advances to her—'

'Ordinary people don't get shot just because they ask a pretty girl who says she's their sister to give them a kiss.'

'Ah, but then you're not an ordinary person, my dear Archie. But listen. That's what I want to talk to you about. You don't want to tell your housekeeper that you tried to assault a complete stranger, and got shot for it—'

'I tell you I didn't. I mean I didn't try—'

'And Miss Benton naturally doesn't want to get into trouble for shooting you. So what about all of us agreeing that you had a nasty motor accident on the way here to see me, and—and so on?' He made a circle in the air with his pipe to indicate the subsequent course of the story.

'She ought to be prosecuted.'

'Yes, but the Jury might think that you ought to have been shot.'

Mr. Fenton considered. Nobody took a more broad-minded view of publicity than he, and he had often thought that to be mixed up in a murder which one hadn't committed might be extremely good for trade, if one's publishers handled the affair properly; but this was not so good. In a sense not dignified. And only Heaven knew what lies Derek and this girl would tell in the witness-box.

'Oh, all right,' he said.

'Good. I'm sure you're wise. And now, how about getting home? Shall I drive you? You're a bit shaky still, I expect. It would hardly be safe—'

'Oh—thanks,' said Mr. Fenton grudgingly.

'Come on, then. And I'll bring your car over in the morning. Put your arm round my shoulder.'

Lovingly the two brothers walked to the door, and out. Tenderly Derek helped the wounded man into the car.

'All right? Good.' He climbed in and started the engine. 'Now then,' he said, as he rocked into the mainroad, 'we must think of an accident for you. What sort of accident would you like?'

Chapter Fifteen

Mixed Emotions in Kent

I

Jenny thought, going up to her room: How lovely to have Derek to leave everything to. I'm glad that horrid man isn't dead. Of course there's no reason why brothers should be alike, really. And then she remembered something which her fourth governess had told her, which was that every seven years you became a completely different person, all your skin and everything was different; so that, as Derek was at least ten years younger than his brother, it really meant that they had had quite different fathers and mothers, so that there was no danger that when Derek got older, he would get at all like Archibald Fenton, because in a kind of way they really belonged to different families. Besides, look at Nelson and Shakespeare and Joan of Arc, who can't have been a bit like their relations, and look at Aunt Caroline and Aunt Jane, well you couldn't have more unlike people than Aunt Caroline and Aunt Jane, and they were sisters—well, that really did show ...

She sat down on her bed, dropping her parcels around her; and then, remembering, but without any conscious effort of memory, Aunt Caroline's disapproval of this as being in some way slovenly, and in any case bad for the bed, she took the papers over to the little table in the window, and sat down there. Should she read the papers first, or Nancy's letter?

Before she could decide, she found herself thinking again: Fatness. Of course, fatness is quite different from character. Fatness does go in families. And looking at Nelson and Here-ward the Wake and Garibaldi isn't really any good, unless you know for certain that their brothers weren't fat. And then she thought suddenly that of course *all* fatness can't be descended, because somebody must have started it some time, and perhaps Archibald Fenton was the one who was starting it in the Fenton family. Which would be quite all right, because then it needn't have anything to do with Derek at all ...

Absurdly happy now, she felt that no luxury of happiness must be missing. Little idiot so nearly to have forgotten! She flashed across to the bed and tore open the parcels. Oh, *Derek!* Then, holding Nancy's letter in the left hand, and feeling absently for cherries with the right, she got into touch again with London ...

But at first she didn't seem to be quite in touch. Who were the 'two new exhibits' who had joined the 'menagerie'? Who was Bertha Holloway? 'Did you see her that time you came?' Which time? Jenny wrinkled her forehead, and went on reading, but now a little doubtfully. What had happened to Nancy? 'The Jenny the police are looking for is not her illegitimate daughter.' Well, of course she wasn't. How could Nancy possibly—She took another cherry, and read again: 'The Jenny the police are looking for.' Then the police *were* looking for her. She thought: I'm glad to know that. I'm glad Nancy told me that. That's really what I wanted to know. That and the clothes. She looked down the page and saw the word 'georgette'. Ah! She read on very quickly, in case Nancy had minded about the clothes ... Nancy hadn't ... She read very slowly ...

Now she understood. How clever of Nancy to have written like that. A thought leapt into her mind, and was followed in a flash by another, and the two thoughts, as it were, faced each other challengingly, and then turned their backs on each other and slunk away, refusing the combat.

How lovely if Nancy and she—
Derek and Nancy ... and she.

Jenny sighed and stood up, and went round the table so as to lean out of the window; and she leant out of the window, her chin in her hands, and thought: How everything changes. Where shall I be when autumn comes? I wish I could die now, while everything is so beautiful.

I suppose he'll never see that green georgette now. It's funny how nothing is ever the same as anything else, but only better or worse. I wonder where I shall be in ten years' time. I think dark people are prettier, *really.* Then she came away from the window, and suddenly a headline from one of the papers screamed at her 'WHERE IS JENNY?' Little idiot, she thought, why, I'd forgotten all about the papers. She snatched eagerly at one of them, and began to read ...

Oh, dear!

Oh, Derek!

Oh, how awful!

Now she read Nancy's letter again; and, reading it now, she could translate it into all that Nancy had not said. But Nancy's letter was written on Tuesday evening. It was old news by now. She went back to the papers and read them slowly ...

'Renton Frers in shoes.' Now who *could* have known that? Because she'd always got her shoes at Winthrops, until the other day, when she had found herself looking in at Renton's window and remembering what that girl at Norah's had said. About being the best place for shoes. Of course they would know at home, but then, why send a letter-card—

Silly! Why, of course it was Nancy, who had the shoes in her flat now. But *why?* Oh, I see, said Jenny, nodding to herself, it's so as Uncle Hubert shouldn't be anxious. How funny that Nancy and she should both think of that at the same time.

No, not funny. Weren't they Gloria and Acetylene, and didn't they always think of things at the same time? Like that day when they were driving the French out of the Peninsula, and they both thought of sending a message by the other to Wellington, saying that the Portuguese weren't feeling very well on the right, and could he reinforce them strongly ...

She used to leave a twig about, and Nancy used to leave her tammy. Or any sort of cap. A cherry-stalk would make a good twig. Jenny put another cherry in her mouth, and thought: I don't believe we ever used cherry-stalks. I wonder why not. Nancy made a paper cap once ... and we had that pistol-cap ... and ...

Jenny stopped a cherry half-way to her mouth, and stared down at the table. On the outside of the *Daily Mail* somebody had drawn a cap—in just the way Nancy always used to draw a cap when she was signing a document secretly so that only Wellington knew. Could I have drawn it myself, wondered Jenny, without knowing? She looked at the table, shook the papers and looked beneath them, but there was no pencil there which she might have picked up unthinking. Then Derek must have drawn it.

It was funny that Derek and Nancy should draw caps in exactly the same way. Perhaps they did a lot of things in exactly the same way. Perhaps they were sort of made for each other. I suppose, she thought, dark people *are* prettier, I mean *really*.

She got up and looked at herself in the wardrobe glass.

She thought: Of course my hair is awful like this. It isn't fair. I mean (and she smiled at her reflection, because she was making a kind of joke) it isn't *fair* anybody seeing me like this. I'm quite different really. Even the photographs in the papers look more like me—She felt suddenly that she must look at all the photographs again, because she wasn't so very hideous in some of them, and it was sort of helping her to escape if she looked at the photographs again, to make quite sure that she had disguised herself properly ...

Another cap! And in the same paper, and on the 'Where is Jenny?' page! It *must* mean something! Eagerly she rustled through the other pages ... and there in the margin among the advertisements she found the message.

MTASK2 2RTLEOTF6EELITHONS5BEYOROO
45EULICD33LEITMO5QANW6EAACHWMFYAP

Nancy! Nancy!

Now how did one uncipher it? She hardly dared to begin. If she began and then couldn't do it! If she tried to remember and found she had forgotten! She walked up and down the room saying to herself: 'I can do it, I know I can do it. As soon as I begin to think, I know I shall remember it. There's nothing to be afraid of, because I haven't begun yet.' But dared she begin? If she looked in her mind and found nothing there! Voices and the noise of a starting car came through the window. She peeped out. There they go, she thought. He's alive, and Derek's driving him home, so it's all right. Now if only I can do this—Oh, Nancy! Oh, darling! *You* remembered, so surely *I* can! I'm not thinking yet, I'm not trying to think. I'm just going to have one of those chocolates first ... and I've got a clean handkerchief still, so I'll just try the *eau-de-Cologne* ... Lovely ... Now where's a pencil (I'm not thinking yet), I know I saw one—oh, there it is, and paper and everything. Now then. Now I'm going to begin to think. Oh, please let me do it. Now then ...

AM AT CASTLE HOTEL WITH MONEY
FOR YOU ALICE PITMAN

II

Derek and Archibald had little to say to each other on the way to Ferries. Derek was wondering what was to be done about Jenny. Archibald was telling himself for the hundredth time that all relations were a curse.

This business about brothers. All wrong. Look at the animals. Mother-love, yes. The tiger defending her cubs—charming. Love between the sexes, by all means. Two turtle-doves on a spring day, two—well, two anything on a spring day. Nobody could object to love between the sexes. It was natural ... so long as one didn't clutter it up with ecclesiastical tradition. But whoever heard of two rabbits from the same litter being expected to keep in touch with each other through all the exigences of a rabbit's career, or two frogs assuming a friendliness which they did not feel, simply because they had been eggs in the same spawn. Ridiculous.

'Let brotherly love continue.' But why should it ever have begun? He hadn't chosen Derek; he hadn't wanted him. From their very first meeting Derek had had an offensive way of looking at him, and as soon as the kid had had any eyebrows to raise, it had started raising them. And now that one of them was a famous man and the other one wasn't, what happened? Derek still went on raising ironical eyebrows ...

Cousins, brothers-in-law, aunts—God, what a crowd. All trying to borrow money or asking him to use his influence. At least there was this to be said for Derek: he had never tried to borrow money ...

The thought flashed into Archibald's mind and was hurried out again, that really the most offensive thing about Derek was that he had never tried to borrow money ...

'Here we are,' said his brother suddenly, 'actually turning into carriage-sweep, and still no story for your housekeeper. What do we say?'

'I expect I shall think of something,' said Archibald stiffly.

'Well, but—'

'I must really remind you, my dear Derek, that for twenty years I have been earning my living by making up stories, and I am quite capable of making up one for Mrs. Pridgeon now.'

'You don't want a collaborator?'

'Frankly, no.'

'Right. Well, what is the story?'

'As I say, I expect I shall think of something.'

'Just as you like, Hippo. But don't look to me for corroborative detail on the spur of the moment, if you leave me in the dark like this.'

'I don't see—'

'I haven't your quickness of invention, and it makes all the difference to me to know beforehand whether we are talking about a bicycle accident or about something with a traction-engine in it. When Mrs. Pridgeon—'

'There is really no need for you to see Mrs. Pridgeon.'

'Not when you ring for drinks?'

'Oh! ... Do you want a drink?'

'Obviously not now. No.'

'You can have one if you like,' said Archibald grudgingly.

'No thanks, I'm a teetotaller.'

'If you think I'm going back on what we agreed—'

'That's just the trouble, we haven't agreed.'

'We agreed to pretend that I had had an accident, and we agreed not to say anything about the deliberate attempt at murder—'

'No, I don't think we had better say anything about that.'

'Well, I have given my word not to, and that's really all that concerns you. There's no need for you to hang about in order to see if I keep my word.'

'Right. Then all I say to anybody is that you were driving over to see me, and had a bit of a smash, and that we tied you up, and helped you home?'

'Exactly.'

'Good. Then I have a free hand as to how much I smash up your car?'

'What's that?' said Archibald.

'Quite rightly in the case of a head-wound, you are exerting your brain as little as possible. But you do see, don't you, that if one has a bit of a smash when driving a car, both the driver and the car have the bit of a smash.'

'Oh!' said Archibald.

'I'm not worrying about the wind-screen, because of course that must go anyhow. That's all right, I can do that with a niblick. And dents in the mudguard, obviously. But when we get down to the finer details—'

'I'm damned if I'm going to let you smash up my car.'

'Entirely for you to say, Hippo. Only do let's have a story that hangs together. Like', he added kindly, *'Lovely Lady'* or any of your major works.'

Archibald grunted. The car stopped.

'Well, here we are,' said Derek. 'Do I come in and help you with the story?'

'All you've got to do is to leave my car alone. Do you understand?'

'Perfectly. I won't even clean it.'

His brother was silent for a moment, and then said, as if grudging the information: 'I was standing in the road when I was knocked down by another car.'

'What were you standing in the road for?'

'Anything you like,' said Archibald impatiently. 'What the devil does it matter? The engine was missing, and I'd got down to look at it.'

'Would you do that just outside the house you were going to stop at? You know, this is what *The New Statesman* complained about when it said that Mr. Fenton seemed to have no idea of probability.'

'Hell, how can I think with a head like this?'

'Then let me suggest that the gate into Bassetts was shut, and you had got down to open it.'

'Oh ... All right ... Anything you like.'

'Thank you. Then that will be all to-day. Good-bye.'

As he drove away Derek's thoughts were back again with Jenny. Only once did Archibald come into his mind; and that was when he wondered vaguely, and in no particular connexion, whether weddings were ever so quiet that brothers didn't get invited to them.

III

He stopped the car and called up to her bedroom.

'Naomi!'

Her head came out of the window.

'Derek!'

'I say, have you had any tea?'

'Mrs. Bassett left it all ready, I've got the kettle on.'

'Good. I'll just put all these cars away and join you.'

'Was he all right?'

'Perfectly. I left him sipping a whisky and soda, and telling his housekeeper how he won the battle of Waterloo.'

'Why did you—'

'I know what you're going to say. Why didn't I drive him down in his own car?'

'Well, I wondered.'

'The answer is that I didn't want to walk back all by myself. *And* I wanted my tea. Do you really think you were prettier before you cut your hair?'

'Before I—? Oh! Oh, but it's cut so frightfully. It looks awful.'

'If you could see it from down here, you wouldn't think so. Are you alone in the house?'

'Yes. Why?'

'Jenny.'

'Yes.'

'Just Jenny, Jenny, Jenny. I'm practising. In a little while I shall have to think of you seriously as Jenny. It's much the best name we've had so far.'

'Oh, Derek.'

'Now I'd better go back to Naomi again, I suppose, in case we get overheard. It's very confusing. Well, Naomi, did you read the papers?'

She nodded.

'Exciting, aren't they?'

She nodded again, smiling mysteriously.

'What does that mean?'

'One of them's *very* exciting.'

'Oh? They all seemed to hold the attention quite comfortably. Well—' he switched on the engine—'let's have tea. Farewell, Miss Jenny Windell. If I had been trained in a circus, I should now drive these two cars off simultaneously, a foot on either running-board. As it is, I shall take the safer, if less spectacular course, of driving them one by one. Make the tea, there's a good sister.'

Jenny went downstairs and made the tea. She carried it into the apple orchard, thinking as she went: I might have been in London now. If I hadn't hidden behind the curtains, I might have been pouring out tea for Uncle Hubert. She looked back through a lifetime of growth, of experience, of knowledge, to the child who had knelt behind the curtains two days ago. When she had arranged the table, she went upstairs and gazed earnestly at herself in the glass. Why did he like her hair so much? She thought: I shall never know what I really look like. I suppose I *am* pretty in a way.

With his first cup Derek said: 'Well, what's the news? I mean the very exciting news.'

'I've heard from Nancy! I mean again.'

'Again? But how does she know you're here?'

'I don't know. It was in the paper. Look!'

Derek looked, and naturally asked: 'Meaning what?'

'Am at Castle Hotel with money for you Alice Pitman,' translated Jenny.

'But however—You're sure Alice Pitman is Nancy Fair-brother?'

'Must be, mustn't she?'

'You would know, Miss Windell-Fenton-Harris. But how could she write in *my* paper?'

'You didn't stop and talk to anybody—or anything?'

'No. Except the hairdresser. You like my hair like this? Good. Oh, but wait a moment. I bumped into somebody when I was asking for your letter. She must have heard me ... and then ... still I don't see—Oh well, never mind.'

'*Is* there a Castle Hotel at Tunbridge Wells?'

'Yes. I suppose we'd better collect her, and then she can tell us all about it.'

Jenny said: 'Oh, I never thanked you for all those lovely things. Oh, *thank* you! It was lovely of you.'

'I meant to get a lot of other things, and then I hadn't any money.'

'I do want—well, one or two things. And now Nancy's got some money for me, so could we perhaps—I mean I haven't even got a hairbrush.'

He looked across at her and said: 'What do you want a hairbrush for? I thought I told you—'

'Oh, but one *must!*'

'All right, you shall have a hair-brush.'

'You see I *have* got some money now, I mean when I see Nancy, because of my watch. Why are you frowning so?'

The frown went as Derek began to laugh.

'You *are* a couple, you two. You realize that the police know all about your watch, and are looking for the young woman who pawned it?'

'I expect she's disguised all right,' said Jenny confidently.

'Alice Pitman.'

'Yes. But she really would be Alice Pitman. She's wonderful like that.'

'And you think the police will never find her?'

'Nancy? Of course they won't,' said Jenny scornfully. Was this not the girl who had baffled Napoleon himself on more than one occasion?

Derek laughed again, and said: 'Shall we go and help with the haymaking after tea?'

'Oh, do let's.'

'I'm thinking of that fellow Parracot. If the police are really after him—but we shan't know that till to-morrow. I mean the inquest. I'll ring up Miss Pitman to-night, and tell her to expect me to-morrow morning, and we'll come back with the papers, and when we've read them, we'll decide what to do. Which gives us the rest of the day to ourselves. So let's make hay while we can, because by to-morrow we may all be in prison.'

'Yes, Derek,' said Jenny happily. There was a prison at Maidstone, and she seemed to remember that, in touching upon this aspect of life there, her third governess had mentioned casually that the Maidstone prison was a mixed one.

IV

Miss Pitman went into the book-shop in the High Street, and asked one of the assistants for a nice book.

'Yes, madam. Any particular sort of book?'

'A nice one,' said Miss Pitman patiently.

'Certainly, madam.' He looked round the crowded shelves in a bewildered sort of way. 'Have you any particular—'

'Is this nice?' asked Miss Pitman, picking up *The A.B.C. of Horsemanship.*

'That's very good,' said the assistant, brightening. 'But I have another very good book just come in, if you are interested in the Horse—'

'Not specially,' said Miss Pitman. 'I like a *nice* horse,' she added.

'Now this is really the latest text-book on the care and management of Horses—

Miss Pitman fluttered the pages, and said 'It doesn't look very exciting. Are all your books about horses?'

'But I understood you to say, madam—'

'Haven't you anything not about a Horse at all?'

'Certainly, madam.' He handed her a book with a flourish. 'Archibald Fenton's masterpiece.'

Nancy opened *A Flock of Sheep* at page 576 and read the top paragraph.

'Is this nice?' she asked.

'Oh, very, madam. That is his last published book. His new book is not out until next week, but if you haven't read that one, you should certainly read it first, because many of the characters—'

'Haven't you anything smaller?'

'Smaller?'

'I really want something small to read at dinner,' said Miss Pitman earnestly. 'Propped up against the cruet. You see, I'm all alone in a big hotel, and one gets so tired of reading the wine-list. Have you any book which you could prop up—'

'We have the small cheap editions, naturally, madam.' He pointed to a row of shelves. 'Perhaps you would care to choose something for yourself—'

'Oh, thank you! Then I can tell the size, can't I?'

She chose a detective story which she had read happily when it first came out, but since forgotten, and went back to her hotel. 'Of course,' said Nancy to herself, as she came in sight of the

Tank again, 'Miss Pitman is not really such a fool as that, but a girl must amuse herself somehow.'

She dined, as she said, alone. The headwaiter handed her the wine-list, opened, but not very hopefully, at the champagnes. Miss Pitman studied the champagnes carefully; asked if Perrier Jouet 1923 was nice; hesitated long and earnestly between that and Bollinger 1921; and finally chose water. 'Really,' thought Nancy, 'the woman's being a perfect idiot. I shall lose all control of her directly.'

She was finishing the caramel pudding and the second chapter when the message came.

'Miss Pitman?'

'Yes?'

'Mr. Derek Fenton would like to speak to you on the telephone.'

'Uncle Derek!' said Miss Pitman joyfully, and hurried out. 'So *that's* who he was,' she thought. 'Fenton's brother.'

'Hallo!'

'Miss Alice Pitman?' (*Better be careful, thought Derek, in case Miss Gathers is listening.*)

'Speaking.' (*Better be careful, thought Nancy, in case the girl is listening.*)

'This is Derek Fenton.'

'Oh, is that Uncle Derek?' (*Bother, thought Nancy. I haven't really given my mind to this. Now I'm Archibald's illegitimate daughter.*)

'Er—yes.' (*I seem to be collecting relations, thought Derek. This may be awkward.*)

'How *did* you know I was here?'

'Naomi told me.' (*Now, will she get on to that or won't she?*)

'Who?'

'Na-om-i.'

'Naomi? Is *she* with you? How lovely!'

'Staying with me for a few days.' *(You angel!)*

'I say, you didn't really mind my calling you Uncle Derek? You sounded a bit as if you did. Naomi and I call you that for a joke sometimes.' (*Good. Now I'm legitimate again.*)

'Delighted and honoured to be your uncle, Miss Pitman. And, after all, I suppose I *am* too much of the elder brother to Naomi.'

'Oh, she only does it for a joke. She's very fond of her brother really.'

'Good.' (*She's just like lightning, this girl.*)

'How *is* Naomi?'

'Splendid. And are you all right again?'

'Yes, thank you.' (*Again?*)

'Naomi told me about your ankle. Rotten luck.'

'Wasn't it rotten?' (*The man's drivelling.*)

'Is it all right again now?'

'Well, I have to be careful.' (*And I certainly am being.*)

'Well, look here, what I rang up for was—could you come over to-morrow morning and spend the day with us? I'd call for you at ten o'clock. Would that be all right?'

'Lovely.'

'That's splendid. Ten o'clock then?'

'Thank you so much. Good-bye—*Uncle* Derek.'

' Good-bye—Alice. '

'Give my love to your sister. Tell her I'm longing to see her again.'

'I will. Good-bye.'

'Good-bye.'

They hung up their receivers.

Derek thought: So that's Nancy. What a girl! The vexed question of who writes Archibald's books for him is now explained.

Nancy thought: Well done, Jenny darling. I knew you'd do it. The man seems quite intelligent. This must be celebrated in some way.

She went back to the dining-room, and ordered a *crème de menthe* with her coffee.

'It *is* good for the digestion, isn't it?' she asked the head waiter. 'I mean, quite medicinal?'

The head waiter assured her that it was.

V

A similar conversation, but with reference this time to a double brandy, was taking place in the best bedroom of Ferries.

'Not if it was me, I wouldn't,' said Mrs. Pridgeon.

'Why, my dear Mrs. Pridgeon, brandy is the first thing that a doctor orders in the case of shock. As a matter of fact, it's the only way of getting it when the pubs are closed.'

'Just as you say, Mr. Fenton. And sees that they drink a whole bottleful of Burgundy first, I dare say.' She held the bottle up to the light to make sure that Mr. Fenton had obeyed the doctor's orders.

'Oh, come, there's no harm in Burgundy.'

'That's what we'll know to-morrow, one way or the other. Anything else you'll be wanting?'

'No, thanks.'

'Well, don't sit up reading too long. You want to give your head a rest, *I* should have said.'

Archibald screamed to himself, 'For God's sake go,' and said aloud, 'It shall have it.'

'Then I'll leave you.'

'Good night, Mrs. Pridgeon.'

'Good night.'

Mr. Fenton was left alone with Plato. Six months ago he had been invited, by somebody who preferred that somebody else should do his writing for him, to contribute to a symposium entitled *Books Which Have Influenced Me*. Having mentioned

The Republic as the principal one of these, Mr. Archibald Fenton had now got into the habit of taking it to bed with him (when alone) with the intention, one night, of seeing if it could justify the distinction which he had given it. Now, propped on pillows, with the last rays of the setting sun lighting up the bandage round his head, heroically he began to read:

'I[b] went down yesterday to the Peiraeus[c] with Glaucon the son of Ariston, to pay my devotions[d] to the Goddess[e] ...'

Grand stuff!

If only his publisher could have seen him ...

FRIDAY

Chapter Sixteen

Close-up of Miss Julia Treherne

I

It was Miss Julia Treherne's birthday. She was thirty-nine. She sat up in bed, a tray by her side, letters and parcels, some opened, some unopened, on her lap. She looked adorable.

She felt lazy this morning, being thirty-nine, and proposed to stay in bed until it was time to get ready for a luncheon engagement. Getting ready was always a protracted, if fascinating, business. Half an hour in the bathroom; half an hour in front of the mirror; half an hour deciding upon, and putting herself into, the privileged costume. Luncheon was at one-thirty. She need not get up until half-past eleven. It was only just ten. O blessèd bed!

She was thirty-nine, and owed it to her toilet-table that nobody believed it. For it is one of the disadvantages of the New Cosmetic Era that the search for youth, however successful, never fails to suggest a corresponding need for search. In her natural purity, as seen only by her husband and her maid, Miss Treherne looked no more than thirty. Made-up for the early twenties, to which, from her professional record, she could not possibly belong, she immediately suggested the middle forties. But the bones of her face were so good that nothing could hide its beauty.

There was a tap at the door. She picked up a hand-mirror from the bed, pushed at her hair and called: 'Oh, Henry darling, come in.'

Her husband came in.

'Hallo, sweetheart, just off?' said Julia, pitching her voice to reach the upper circle, and giving in this way an air of increased spaciousness to her bedroom. 'Did you get your scrambled eggs as you liked them this morning?'

'Yes, splendid, thank you.'

'Because I can easily talk about them again.'

'Thank you for talking about them once. It was marvellous of you to remember.'

'Well, darling, if I'm not a good wife, what am I?'

'An angel.'

'No, there you're wrong, sweetheart. Angels are definitely not good wives. They lack just that something. Or so', said Julia, fluttering her eyelashes, 'I have been told.' The eyelashes which she would flutter at Our Theatrical Correspondent over the luncheon-table would be longer and of a different colour, but she would flutter them as skilfully.

'Enjoying your birthday?'

'Look!' She held up the back of a hand to him, and waggled the fingers.

'Like it?'

'Adore it. Thank you, my sweetheart. Come and kiss me.'

'Yes, I think I will.'

Five minutes passed, and Julia said: 'One of our longer kisses. Won't you be late?' She picked up the mirror to see what was left of her.

'Probably. When do I see you again? Come up and lunch with me in the City somewhere. Do. Why not?'

'Sorry, darling. I'm lunching with Bertie.'

Once again that curious tightening of the mouth was visible, which was the instinctive reaction in so many husbands when Bertie's name was mentioned.

'Must you?' he asked.

'Afraid so. It's a date.'

'What I meant was—'

'I know what you meant, darling.'

'Oh, all right,' said Henry with a shrug. 'We'll have supper somewhere after the show if you like.'

'You know you hate it.'

'As a habit. Not on special occasions.'

'Darling, I've promised to have supper with O.D.'

'That swine?'

'That one.'

'I wish you wouldn't.'

'Darling, as long as I know that he's a swine, it's all right, isn't it?'

'What's he after?'

'Shakespeare at the moment. And a very long way after, I suspect, unless I keep an eye on him.'

'Why choose your birthday of all days?'

'Good Heavens,' cried Julia, throwing up her arms to them, 'if I mayn't begin to arrange to play Juliet for the first time on my thirty-ninth birthday, when may I begin?'

'Oh, I see ... You've got lovely arms.'

'I know. So had Juliet. "Arms, take your last embrace!" Oh, no, that was Romeo. Damn, I've upset the milk. Darling, take the tray away before it leaks, and then take yourself away. And we'll have an early dinner together if you like, but I know you hate that.'

'No, let's. Somewhere near the theatre. I'll be back by six. Good-bye, darling.'

His arms took their last embrace, Julia said: 'Oh, Henry, not again,' and felt for the mirror. Henry went out.

There were three parcels yet unopened. One was a book. John. Not really a birthday present, because he'd promised it to her anyhow. The next—oh, dear! The Ermyntrude child again.

Real name: Gladys Walker. Age: nineteen. For nine years Gladys had had a passion for Miss Treherne, and on every birthday she sent the beloved one something of her own making. It was time, thought Julia, that she married some good, strong man and went to live in India.

The third parcel was registered. Now whoever's this, wondered Julia. This is rather exciting. Endover. Never heard of it. Who writes like that? Somebody.

She cut the string and discovered a letter and a box. Should she open the box and see what somebody had sent her, or should she read the letter and see who the somebody was? She lit a cigarette, picked up the mirror and looked at herself again. Was that a spot coming on her chin? Curse all spots. No, nothing. She dropped the mirror on the bed and opened the letter.

Archibald Fenton. Well! She read the letter. Well! (What *was* she doing on Sunday?) She opened the box. *Well!*

She looked at the watch with 'J' in little diamonds for 'Julia', and began to think how sweet it was, and how nice of him—(he *was* the tall thin one, wasn't he?)—and of course he oughtn't to do a thing like that really, and she tried to disentangle him in her mind from all the other hundred men who might have given her watches with little diamonds on them, but hadn't. She found this difficult, because to Julia all men, save her husband, were the same; just men; who said amusing things and complimentary things and paid the waiter and were called 'Darling'; and if they had characters of their own, as she supposed they had, and souls, and aspirations, somehow she had never found time to explore them, nor they the impulse to reveal them. Perhaps it was because one didn't at lunch, or at supper, or when dancing, or in a dressing-room, or at cocktail-parties, and these seemed to be the only times which she had. It was easy to know about women, to know one woman at a glance from another, but a dozen men trying to make a good impression were the same man, with nothing but their faces for remembrance.

All the time that she was thinking this, and playing with the watch, another part of her mind was wondering what it was which had happened before like this. Where had she seen a watch like this? Who else had given her a watch like this? To whom else had Archibald Fenton given a watch like this? Surely somehow, somewhere ...

'My God!' said Julia, and picked up the mirror, and looked at herself to see how surprised she was. 'Clara!'

'Yes, madam?' said Clara, putting a head hastily in at the door.

'Have you got last night's paper in the kitchen? And the morning ones, too. Bring them all. Hurry!'

Three minutes to study the papers, two minutes to make her plans. She was always a quick worker.

'Bertie, is that you?'

'Hallo!'

'Julia. Listen. I want you to be at Scotland Yard at—I must be quick, that's all—at half-past eleven, and wait for me.'

'At *where*?'

'Scotland Yard. S for Scotland, Y for Yard.'

'I say, are you being arrested?'

'Keep the jokes for afterwards, Bertie. This is business. Now listen. Have two cameramen ready. Miss Julia Treherne entering Scotland Yard. Got it?'

'May I ask what it's all about?'

'I'll tell you later. What time do the evening papers go to press?'

'All day.'

'Of course. Silly of me. Oh, well, that's all right.'

'You can't give me an idea of what's on?'

'Well, listen. This is utterly private until I say. Bertie, it's the Auburn Lodge murder!'

'Thank God for all his mercies! I'd been wondering if we couldn't get you into that. My dear, we can work this—'

'No, but listen. I'm not absolutely certain if it's—'

'You aren't Jenny, are you?'

'Idiot, Jenny's eighteen.'

'That's what made me ask.'

'Sweet of you, angel. Now is that all right? I'll see you when I come out, and tell you if we can use it.'

'You're sure you *will* come out? They haven't got anything on you?'

'Good Heavens, no, *I*'m all right. I'm giving important evidence—'

'My dear, this is too marvellous. You'll be a witness at the trial—'

'*Listen*, Bertie. Not a word till I tell you. I may be wrong about it all, but I don't think I am. Now we don't want a mistake. Is there a main entrance to Scotland Yard, or are there a whole lot of little entrances, or only one or what? And how far can you drive in? I shall come in a taxi, and—'

'None of that. I'll call for you.'

'Oh, but—'

'I'll arrange for the photographers now, and decide where to put them —I rather see you making inquiries of a policeman outside the gates—'

'That's good, Bertie. Get a *big* policeman if you can. A big, fair one.'

'I expect we shall have to take what's provided. And then I'll come and fetch you, and explain the words and business to you on the way. Eleven-fifteen. That all right?'

'Well, I shall have to hurry. My God, I *shall* have to hurry.'

She hooked up the receiver, took one look at herself in the hand-mirror to see if she had altered, and jumped out of bed.

II

'Now,' said Inspector Marigold, curling his moustaches symmetrically with both hands, and gazing at the wall in front of him, 'let's see where we are. I'm going to run through what's in my mind, and if there's anything that isn't quite straightforward, you say so. Right?'

'Right,' said Sergeant Bagshaw.

'Right. Now then. The murderer is a short, stout feller of sedentary occupation. We know that because Hatch tells us so. Right?'

'Right,' said Sergeant Bagshaw.

'Right. The man who pawned Jenny's watch was also a short, stout feller, but whether of sedentary occupation or not has not yet transpired. Right?'

'Right,' said Sergeant Bagshaw.

'Right. For working purposes we may assume that there's not going to be two short, stout fellers mixed up in the same case. Right?'

'Right,' said Sergeant Bagshaw.

'Now follow me closely, Bagshaw. I therefore deduce that the murderer is a short, stout feller with a fair moustache, because the short, stout feller who pawned Jenny's watch had a fair moustache, and we have established, owing to there not being two short, stout fellers in the case, that he is the same short, stout feller as the other one. Right?'

'Right,' said Sergeant Bagshaw.

'Now then. The man who pawns Jenny's watch gives his name as William Makepeace Thackeray, thus using the name of a well-known literary classic. The natural deduction is that he himself is a literary man, as being conversant with the literary works of the said William Makepeace Thackeray. Right?'

'Wait a moment there,' said Sergeant Bagshaw, holding up a large hand. 'What about me? *I* knew about Thackeray and I'm not a literary man.'

'*You* knew about him from information received in the course of duty. That's different.'

'Ar, that's different,' agreed Bagshaw.

'Very well then. On the one hand we see that the man who pawned Jenny's watch is of literary habits, on the other hand we see that the man who murdered Jane Latour is of sedentary habits. Putting two and two together, we deduce that the murderer is a short, stout feller with a fair moustache of the sedentary occupation of literary work. Right?'

'Right,' said Sergeant Bagshaw.

'Right. We get further proof of this, if further proof were necessary, by reason of the fact that the murderer may be presumed to move in the same circles as his victim, who was an actress, and as such likely to move in the same circles as a short, stout feller of literary habits. Right?'

'Right,' said Sergeant Bagshaw.

'Right. We pass on. Leaving aside the question for further consideration whether the girl Jenny is victim or accomplice, we have the fact that two communications have transpired which may be assumed as coming directly or indirectly from the murderer, one, by letter-card from the neighbourhood of Bloomsbury, the other, by female voice, from the neighbourhood of Tunbridge Wells. Furthermore, we have been informed by Doctor Hatch that the murderer was undoubtedly left-handed. So,' said Inspector Marigold to Sergeant Bagshaw, 'summing the whole matter up, we come to this conclusion. What we want is a short, stout, left-handed author of fair moustache and literary occupation, who lives in Bloomsbury and has a place in the Tunbridge Wells district where he could take a girl. See what I mean?'

'That's right,' said Sergeant Bagshaw.

'Well,' said the Inspector, after an interval of silent moustache-curling, 'now we've got to find him.'

'That's right,' said Sergeant Bagshaw again.

Vague pictures formed themselves in the Sergeant's mind. He saw himself, disguised down to the boots as a literary man, moving in the literary circles of Bloomsbury, and keeping his eyes open for stoutness, and his ears alert for mention of William Makepeace Thackeray. The prospect did not please him; for, being unaware that the two main schools of fiction were the Beer School and the Gin School, he saw himself condemned to a long course of the barley-water and health-biscuits with which, for some reason, he had always associated literature. One day, p'raps in the British Museum Refreshment Room, he would meet a short, stout feller with a fair moustache, and they would get talking about Thackeray together, and then he would ask the feller to have a barley-water with him, and order two small b-w's, and the feller would pick his glass up with the *left* hand, and then at last, he'd KNOW.

But it was a dreary prospect for an ordinary human being. Sergeant Bagshaw blew out his cheeks in a sigh, and thought wistfully of the Edmonton murderer, who had taken him round gallantly to one Spring Meeting after another, before giving himself up, in sheer embarrassment, at Epsom.

'Show her in,' said the Inspector down the telephone. The Sergeant came out of his nightmare and looked up.

'Sent round from Scotland Yard,' explained the Inspector. 'Julia Treherne, the actress. Something to tell us. Friend of the Latour woman probably.'

Julia made a beautiful but extravagant entry. The cameramen were down below waiting for her to come out.

'Miss Treherne?' said the Inspector, rising. 'Pray take a seat. Er—your husband?'

'Lord, no,' laughed Julia. 'This is Bertie Klink.'

'Oh—er—?'

'Come to take care of me. D'you mind?'

'You're quite safe *here*, Miss Treherne,' said Marigold with a gallant bow.

'I'm never safe with a really handsome man, Inspector. Two really handsome men,' she corrected herself, giving Sergeant Bagshaw a gracious smile.

The Inspector, feeling a little annoyed at the inclusion of Bagshaw, and wishing to dissociate himself from his inferior, said: 'Let me see, Miss Treherne, the last time I had the pleasure of seeing you on the stage was in *The Bing Boys*, I think.'

Miss Treherne's smile faded into coldness as she said: 'Bertie, explain the difference between me and George Robey to the gentleman.'

Bertie explained. The Inspector coughed officially, and asked Miss Treherne if she would be kind enough to state her business.

Julia stated nothing. Very slowly she opened her bag; took from it a box; opened the box and produced something in tissue paper; removed the paper and placed a little diamond-studded watch in front of the Inspector. 'Remind me at lunch to tell you a funny story about a small child at the Zoo,' she said in a stage whisper to Bertie. 'I've just remembered it.'

Inspector Marigold had no time in which to wonder why the Zoo. He stared at the watch; then turned it over and stared at the back of it.

'Where did you get this, madam?' he asked.

'A friend sent it to me to-day. It's my birthday.'

'Miss Treherne's thirtieth birthday,' explained Bertie.

'May I have the name of the friend?'

'Archibald Fenton,' said Julia with something of an air, for even among the many famous people she knew, Archibald Fenton was not least.

'Occupation?'

'I beg your pardon?'

'What is Mr. Fenton's occupation?'

'How do you mean?' said Julia, rather bewildered.

'What does he do for a living?'

Julia raised her eyebrows at Bertie, who said, with the careful articulation due to a deaf foreigner: 'He writes.'

'He wrote *The Sign of the Cross* and *Huckleberry Finn*,' explained Julia.

'And *The Bride of Lammermoor,*' added Bertie.

'But *not,*' said Julia, 'the poem beginning "There are fairies at the bottom of the garden".'

The Inspector and the Sergeant exchanged nods. Then the Inspector, caressing his moustache with trembling fingers, said: 'Should I be correct, madam, in saying that Mr. Fenton is a short, stout gentleman?'

'Oh, *no!*'

'*Not*, madam?' said the Inspector, amazed.

'Well, how would *you* describe him, Bertie?' asked Julia, wondering if she could possibly have got them muddled.

'Near enough,' said Bertie. 'Short and fat.'

'Ah!' The Inspector was triumphant.

'*Then who's the tall, thin one?*' whispered Julia, frantically.

Bertie, misunderstanding her, said behind the back of his hand: 'One's an Inspector and the other's a Sergeant.'

'Oh, never mind,' said Julia impatiently.

'And should I be right in saying, Madam, that he had a fair moustache?'

Now she remembered him.

'Oh, that one! Yes, that's right, a fair moustache.'

'And left-handed?'

Julia wasn't so sure of that. All she could say for certain was that he shook hands with the right. 'Well, you know what I mean, Bertie, I've never seen him throw or play tennis or anything like that.'

'And now, madam, if you could tell me a little more about the circumstances of the gift. Was it presented to you personally or—'

'Oh no, by post.'

'Did a letter accompany it?'

'Of course.'

'May I see it?' asked the Inspector, holding out his hand.

'I'm afraid not,' said Julia, shaking her head, but smiling sweetly at him. 'It's rather private, you know.'

'I'm afraid I must insist, madam.'

'What nonsense! I've never heard such nonsense. Bertie, have you ever heard such nonsense?'

'I don't think Mr.—'

'Klink. You know Bertie Klink? Bertie, I thought all the police knew you.'

'I don't think Mr. Klink's opinion is going to help us. May I see that letter, madam?'

With a shrug of her shoulders Julia opened her bag, took out Archibald's letter, and pushed it down the front of her dress. 'It's going to be *very* uncomfortable down there all through lunch,' she said reproachfully. 'I shall probably crinkle every time I swallow, and people will think that I have some most irregular disease. Bertie, you'll have to explain to them.'

The Inspector stood up. So did Bertie.

'Bertie,' said Julia delightedly, 'he's going to assault me.' The Inspector sat down again. So did Bertie.

'I must warn you, madam,' said Marigold sternly, 'that your conduct is calculated to defeat the ends of justice—'

'What nonsense!'

'It is essential that I should know from where that letter was written.'

'Well, my dear man, why didn't you say so? Now I've got to—do you mind all looking at the ceiling while Bertie counts ten? It's really gone down much farther than I meant.'

At 'seven' Julia said: 'Ferries, Endover, Tunbridge Wells', and the two policemen exchanged triumphant nods.

'Have you any idea, Miss Treherne, how this watch came into his possession?'

'Well, I suppose he saw it in a pawnbroker's, and thought the "J" would do for "Julia". It's Jenny's, isn't it?'

'But he's in the country?'

'Oh! Well, perhaps—' She stopped powdering her face, and turned to him excitedly. 'I say, you don't think—'

The Inspector said to Bagshaw: 'Ring up Mr. Watterson's house and get somebody to come over and identify it.' Bagshaw went out.

'Bertie! Have I been made love to by a murderer?'

'Looks like it. Have you ever been photographed with him?'

'No.'

'A pity,' said Bertie sadly.

The Inspector stood up.

'Well, thank you, madam. I shall have to keep this, you understand?'

'Well, of course, if it's Jenny's.'

'Thank you. Good-day.'

'Good-bye. And give my love to that nice—I mean say good-bye to that—'

'Come on,' said Bertie, clutching her arm.

They went out. As they came to the entrance into the street Bertie whispered to her, and stopped to do up his shoe-lace. Julia went out alone with an air ...

MISS JULIA TREHERNE LEAVING MERRION PLACE POLICE STATION

Chapter Seventeen

Transformation of Jenny

I

Nancy sat in the lounge of her hotel, reading the latest allocution from Smilax Beauty Preparations, entitled: How I Keep my Face Clean and Free from Blemish—by Julia Treherne. In this respect she was having the advantage of Miss Treherne.

'I don't mind what I'm supposed to say about it,' Julia had explained to Bertie, 'as long as I needn't read it, and haven't got to use the stuff.'

'Well, of course not,' said Bertie. 'Give it to Clara.'

So this was done; and Nancy struggled on, unaware that she was reading: *How I Keep my Face Fairly Clean and Free in one or two places from Blemish—by Clara Watkins.*

Derek came down the hill from the top of the common, in his pocket a list of things which Jenny wanted. This included certain Smilax beauty preparations. Jenny's face was absolutely clean and entirely free from blemish, but naturally she wished to keep it so.

He parked his car opposite the hotel, and went in. He shook hands with Nancy.

'Ah!' he said. 'It *was* you.'

'You mean at the post office?'

'Yes. I want to hear all about that.'

'I want to hear all about everything.'

'You shall. Are you ready?'

'Yes.'

'Come on, then.'

They went outside together.

'Now then,' said Derek, when they were sitting in the car, 'we can talk safely. First of all, you *are* Nancy Fairbrother, aren't you?'

'Undoubtedly.'

'So am I. I mean I'm quite genuine too. With all these detectives about, one has to be careful. Now, Jenny wants a lot of things. Here's the list. Just look at it, and tell me what you feel about it.'

Nancy glanced at the list and said: 'How do you mean feel? There's nothing difficult.'

'Well, have you got enough of Jenny's money?'

'Lord, yes.'

'Good. And do you want me to come with you and carry the parcels, or would you rather be on your own?'

Nancy looked at the list again.

'I think Jenny—I think I shall be quicker alone. Besides, if you're there, I shall be saying "Jenny" by accident.'

'That would be fatal. We should be arrested at once. Well, I'll walk up to the High Street with you, and leave you to it. What do you want, about half an hour?'

'Three-quarters.'

'Good Heavens, are you sure you've got enough money?'

'Quite. I may be an hour.'

'Then I shall get my hair cut again.'

As they walked up to the shops Nancy said: 'You realize that I don't even know yet why Jenny ran away, or what she saw or anything?'

'You shall hear it all as we go back.' He was silent for a little, and then said: 'I like your Jenny, you know.'

'So do I, you know,' said Nancy.

So she heard all about it on the way back to Bassetts, and the story was finished just as they came in at the gate. Then she and Jenny were in each other's arms.

'Oh, Jenny! Oh, darling!'

'Oh, darling! Oh, Nancy!'

Derek decided to leave them to it. After all the terrible adventures which they had been through, they would have much to say to each other. They said it.

'Darling, your hair!'

'I know! Isn't it awful?'

'Did you do it yourself?'

'Well, I had to. Nancy, did you get my things?'

'I rather like it. Turn round and let's have a look.'

'Oh, *darling*!'

'Sort of wind-swept.'

'Well, I did wonder about that. I mean getting a proper windswept when I went back. Did you get my things?'

'Rather. I don't think it's bad, that skirt. Turn round again.'

'Oh, but it *is* short.'

'Jenny darling, you do look funny in my clothes. I can't tell you how odd it is.'

'Darling,' gurgles Jenny. 'If you could *see* Miss Pitman! What *have* you got underneath? Did you get *all* the things?'

'Of course. Yes, it is a bit short. You ought to have had the other.'

'Oh, but I couldn't! Did you get the dress?'

'Out in the car. Yes, I do like the hair, Jenny.'

'Oh, darling! But, darling, could you *get* a washing-silk in green? I mean in Tunbridge Wells? How wonderful of you.'

'Not in green. I simply couldn't, darling. And of course with your Derek getting his hair cut over and over again, and looking at his watch every five seconds, and comparing it with the nearest policeman's—'

'Nancy! He had his hair cut yesterday!'

'I know. It's getting a mania with the man. So you see, Jenny darling, I had to take what I could get. It's white, and—'

'Oh, Nancy!' said Jenny tragically.

'Yes, but listen, darling. It's got a green belt, and a little turn-down green collar, and little green buttons all down the front which give a most unsettling effect. Really sweet, Jenny.'

'Oh, how lovely! You angel! Is it in the car?'

'And I got some green sandals—quite cheap—six and eleven—'

'Did you really?' cried Jenny, seeing them.

'And it has an absurd little pocket over the chest, so I got a little green handkerchief to put in—two in fact—one to dangle—'

The thought of the little green handkerchief to dangle was too much for Jenny. She took a sudden heroic decision.

'Nancy darling,' she said, 'I wish you hadn't got to be Miss Pitman. Couldn't we *both* change now, and you could wear your own things, and I could wear the washing-silk, and you could take off the spectacles and all the *layers* you must have underneath, and be Nancy again. I hate to think of Derek not really seeing you.'

'Shall I?' said Nancy eagerly. Wavering.

'Come on, darling, let's get the things out of the car, and take them up! You got the stockings, didn't you?'

'Jenny?'

'Yes?' said Jenny nervously, knowing what was coming.

'Look me in the face.'

'Yes.'

'Hand on heart.'

Jenny put a hand on her beating heart and held it still.

'Now then, say it.'

A little girl again in Nancy's nursery, Jenny said meekly:

'Cross my heart, and let me die,
If ever I tell my friend a lie.
Cross my knees and waggle my toes—
When *I* know anything, Nancy knows.'

'Well?' said Nancy.

Two large eyes looked out pleadingly from Jenny's burning face.

'All right, darling, I think I know.'

'Oh, Nancy!'

'Come on and let's get the things. What larks.'

Clutching the precious parcels they went up to Jenny's bedroom. For an hour they stayed there ... and along the remotest backwaters of Bassetts Farm the ripple of their chattering voices played unceasingly.

II

'Derek, this is Nancy,' said Jenny proudly.

Derek looked at Nancy, and then said: 'Who's the other one?'

'Jenny,' said Nancy.

Derek looked at them both as they stood there, hand in hand, and nodded to himself.

'Right. It's a bit confusing just at first. Now then—oh, by the way, Miss Fairbrother, we have a good deal to settle, and saying "Miss Fairbrother" won't make us any quicker, if you see what I mean.'

'Quite, Mr. Fenton.'

'No, no, that's what you say to Archibald. My name's Derek.'

'I'll make a note of it, Derek.'

'Good. Let's take a cushion or two outside where nobody can hear us.'

They made themselves comfortable at the far end of the orchard. Jenny thought: I wish we could just sit here, me in this dress, and not bother about *doing* anything.

'Now, then,' said Derek, 'what are we going to do? I've been reading about the inquest. They aren't arresting Parracot, so we haven't got *him* on our hands yet. Nancy, you're the latest from London—who does the average Man about Town, West-end Clubman or Man in the Street suspect?'

'The Man in the Train—'

'That'll do. Well?'

'Jenny. He told me he knew it for a fact.' She gave a quick impression of the Man in the Train knowing it for a fact. Derek laughed. Jenny, feeling completely right and envious of nobody in the new washing-silk, smiled happily to herself to think that this was her friend who had made Derek laugh.

'Yes, but now what about the watch? Or is that going to make it still worse for Jenny? I mean, will people think that just because a woman—of course you aren't a bit alike really—'

'Oh, but I didn't pawn it.'

'Nancy!' cried Jenny. 'Then where did all that money I've been spending—Darling, you haven't been—'

'No, I mean, Mr. Fenton pawned it for me.'

'Archibald?'

'Yes. So you see, as soon as he saw the papers, he'd write to Scotland Yard, and tell them it was me. So the pawnbroker wouldn't come into it at all, and I couldn't be mistaken for Jenny.'

'But Archibald is here!'

'I know. At Ferries. That's how I could get away.'

'But, my dear girl, we don't get papers down here.'

'Oh!' said Nancy, astonished. 'Why not? Are you afraid', she asked earnestly, 'that the locomotives will frighten the cows, or is education not spreading as much as one thought?'

'When I say we don't get papers, I mean that we don't buy them in the village shop as we buy cigarettes and nutmeg-graters. There *is* a way of getting a paper delivered, which I haven't quite mastered yet, but anyhow it takes a little time to get it into motion. How long has Archibald been down?'

'Wednesday evening.'

'Did he come suddenly?'

'Very.'

'Then he hasn't the slightest chance of seeing a paper until next Monday. Unless of course he goes into Tunbridge Wells or somewhere.'

'He wouldn't do that. He's working very hard.'

'Well,' said Derek, 'not so hard but he's found time to pay us a call.'

'Jenny!' cried Nancy. 'Did you see him?'

'Not only saw him, but shot him,' said Derek.

'Darling!'

(There was an interval while the story of Archibald's visit was told to a delighted Nancy.)

'So that was that. Well now, how do we stand? The pawnbroker comes in very strongly now with a description of Archibald. Is it on all the hoardings of London? What a glorious thought!'

The little sleeveless washing-silk with the green belt and little turn-down green collar and the green buttons down the front and the green handkerchief peeping out of the absurd little pocket felt very, very good to Jenny, so good that she was sorry suddenly for all the poor people who were not wearing such a darling dress; and as these undoubtedly included Mr. Archibald Fenton (who, indeed, would have been ill-suited by it), she felt sorry for Mr. Fenton, and the more so because at any moment he might be wrongfully hanged.

'Derek,' she said shyly.

'Yes?'

'I think I'm going to give myself up.'

'I'm dashed if you do.'

'Darling,' said Nancy, 'wait till—Derek, *when* did you say the village would be reading all about last Thursday's weather?'

'You misunderstand me. What I said was that Archibald would be reading next *Monday's* paper on Monday.'

'Well, then, wait till Monday, and I'll give myself up too.'

'And so will I,' said Derek. 'Accessory after the crime. We all will.'

'But we can't let poor Mr. Fenton—'

'How would it be', said Nancy, 'if I went to Ferries this afternoon to spy out the land?'

'Just how does one spy out land? Spy out a bit here to show us.'

Nancy went through the exaggerated movements of a bloodhound looking for its collar-stud.

'Yes. Well, you *could* do that, of course. And then we could do something helpful afterwards.'

Nancy waved him into silence.

'*Having* done that,' she said, 'or not, as the case may be, I then ring the bell and ask for Mr. Fenton. I say that I'm spending my holiday in Tunbridge Wells, and came over to see if I could do anything for him. That's all quite natural, and he'd want to know my address anyway. He is delighted to see me, gives me three autograph albums to return, and asks me how to spell "disassociated".'

'Can you?'

'No. But he wouldn't know that. Then we get talking, and I find out how much he guesses, and if he's read the papers, and so on.'

Derek looked inquiringly at Jenny.

'What do you think? Not bad, is it?'

'Oh!'

'What's the matter?'

'I've just remembered. We've still got his car.'

'Oh, Lord, yes, we've got to get that back somehow.'

'Well, why couldn't you drive me down in it?' suggested Nancy.

'Good idea!' said Derek eagerly. 'And then we leave you and the car, and Jenny and I walk back and collect mine, and drive down again, and—'

'Wouldn't your brother recognize his car, and wonder how Nancy came in it from Tunbridge Wells?' said a lazy voice.

Derek broke off and stared at Jenny. Then he turned to Nancy with a look of patient suffering.

'*Stupid* idea,' he said, shaking a reproachful head at her. '*Why* do you make these idiotic suggestions, Miss Fairbrother?'

'Sorry. I'll try again. How would it be if I ran both ways?'

'It would be hot,' said Derek simply. 'But', he added, 'we could lend you a bicycle.'

Nancy turned on him a look of patient suffering which bettered his own.

'And suppose your hawk-eyed relations recognized it, and saw at once that it had started from Ipswich?'

'They wouldn't. This is an anonymous bicycle.'

'Any particular sex? Or is there a pair of trousers which goes with it?'

'There's a—'

'It would be better the other way round,' said Jenny thoughtfully.

'You mean facing the back-wheel, darling?'

'Thus,' said Derek, 'giving the false impression that one was travelling *to* Tunbridge Wells—'

'*From* Ipswich. Ingenious,' said Nancy, 'but tiring.'

Jenny, smiling lazily at the foolish pair, said:

'The best way would be for us to take Nancy down in *Derek's* car, hide it somewhere, and walk back here for the other. Then when we got to Ferries again, it explains why we're there—to return Mr. Fenton's car—'

'Listen to this, Miss Fairbrother. This is the real thing.'

'And we can walk in, and be introduced properly to Mr. Fenton's secretary.'

Nancy blinked rapidly at Derek, and said brightly to Jenny: 'Your brother, Mr. Fenton? Really? So you have a brother? I thought you only had a mother.' And then to Derek: 'Isn't it amusing, Mr. Fenton, that I am also a brother, a Fairbrother, and you are a dark brother, ha-ha, very amusing, I often say things like that to your brother and then he uses them in his novels, no, he doesn't pay me, but I'm allowed to see the press cuttings.'

This was the sort of thing that Nancy did so well; spontaneous, unaffected: as it seemed inevitable, when you had touched the right button and set her off. Derek laughed whole-heartedly; Jenny smiled a little wistfully.

'Well, anyhow,' said Derek at last, 'let's do that. Starting about three. Agreed?'

'Agreed,' said everybody.

Lying there in the half-shade of the apple-orchard they drifted lazily into their own thoughts.

Derek thought: She's heavenly, this girl. We must see a lot of her when we're married ...

Nancy thought: He's up to the ears, this man. I shall be chief bridesmaid ...

And Jenny thought: They're lovely together. They just suit each other.

She felt glad and proud about this, not sorry; because the day was beautiful, and, whatever might happen in the future, this one hour was assured to her, when she and Derek would walk back from Ferries together, she bareheaded and in her new washing-silk.

Chapter Eighteen

Portrait of the Artist

I

Mr. Fenton stared at a patch of sunlight on the wall and began to think about Chapter Five ...

Chapter Five ...

To-morrow he would be getting ready for Julia. On Sunday Julia would be here, and there would be no time for anything but Julia. Yesterday, apart from getting shot, he had done nothing. Supposing Julia stayed the night, then he would do nothing (nothing, that is, literary) on Monday. Certainly, then, he must work to-day.

Chapter Five ...

The curse of being a writer was that one was never comfortable when not writing, and the curse of being a successful writer was that one was offered so many delightful alternatives to writing. Another perfect day, and a perfect garden in which to enjoy it ... who cared what happened to Eustace Frere?

Chapter Five ...

The real curse of writing was that one was always looking forward to some particular scene in the book and having to hold oneself in check until one came to it. In Chapter Seven Eustace Frere was to sail for America (whence Archibald

Fenton had lately returned), and never was a visit to America so eagerly anticipated by the man chiefly responsible for it. Mr. Fenton had had America docketed in his mind for months. Thus:

CHAP. 8:	*The First Day Out*
CHAP. 9:	*The Second Day Out*
CHAP. 10:	*The Third Day Out*—(it was one of those long books)—
CHAP. 11:	*Mid-Atlantic*
CHAP. 12:	*Landfall*
CHAP. 13:	*'Ilion like a mist rose into Towers'*
CHAP. 14:	*Settling Down*
CHAP. 15:	*'You're Welcome'* ...

Once away from Southampton the book would swing him along from chapter to chapter. Frere, travelling on his cuff-links, would naturally be among the third-class passengers; but from his lordly upper deck Archibald had watched them sunning themselves, and had felt himself made free of their lives too. Even now, on the sunlit wall in front of him, he saw Eustace and the little sempstress, Stella, emerging, heads bent, from the hatchway into the morning, and sitting with their backs up against a bollard ... bollard? ... bollard, but Miss Fairbrother had better just make sure ... wondering what the new world had in store for them ...

Meanwhile—Chapter Five ...

Of course it was idiotic to try and work in the afternoon. After lunch. After steak-and-kidney pie. After one of Mrs. Pridgeon's steak-and-kidney pies. And a tankard of beer and one's own new potatoes. Yet, after wasting the morning, what could he do but try? It was that damned girl's fault for shooting him. For not shooting him. How could anybody have worked in the morning when he was in complete uncertainty as to whether he had been shot in the head or he hadn't?

'Well, how's the head?' Mrs. Pridgeon had asked, when bringing him his morning tea. 'Kept you awake all night, I expect?'

'No, no, I got a little sleep, thank you,' said Archibald.

'Better let me dress it again. You probably got a bit of gravel in it or something.'

'It's all right, thanks. It was washed very carefully.'

'Sometimes a bit of gravel or something gets left in. Anything like that left in sets up mortification, and before you know where you are—'

'Quite. But this was attended to by a hospital nurse.'

'Oh well, you know best. Only you want to be careful not to leave a bit of anything in. Same as when I got a bit of glass left in me elbow, bit of broken ginger-beer bottle the doctor said it was when he got it out. What's happened once can happen again, I always say, and if there's anything like a bit of broken ginger-beer bottle left in, it's much better out. I've got your marmalade for you this morning.'

'Oh, good. Then I'll be getting up.'

Archibald was not anxious that Mrs. Pridgeon should examine his head. The bullet, he was beginning to think, could only have grazed the scalp. He had pressed his fingers, lightly at first, then more heavily, on what he supposed was the actual wound, and felt no serious pain. Probably in Mrs. Pridgeon's opinion, a piece of sticking-plaster was all that was now wanted. Archibald preferred a bandage. Any man about to be visited by, and make love to, a charming woman would prefer a bandage. Archibald, having seen his bandage in the mirror, had every intention of keeping his bandage on until Sunday ... and then bravely making light of it.

He got out of bed and looked at it once more. Curiously effective, anything round the head. All the same he might just have a glance at the place. He could tie it up again afterwards just as effectively ... perhaps more effectively.

He began unwinding, gingerly. However slight the wound, there would be a nasty moment at the end, when the bandage stuck ... Careful ...

Nothing stuck. There was no nasty moment. Odd.

He looked at the bandage in his hand. Signs of blood, but nothing more. A very clean wound. He felt the wound; it didn't seem to be there. He examined it in the glass ... in several glasses held at several angles ... it didn't seem to be there. And yet there was blood. Most odd.

The oddity of it pursued him through his dressing, his breakfast, his first struggles with Chapter Five. A moment's escape sent his hand to a tray of pencils in front of him; now he could begin. But he did not begin. He found himself staring at a bottle marked RED INK.

Mechanically he unwound the bandage from his head; stared at the blood-marks; stared at the bottle. Mechanically he took the cork from the bottle, and poured a little more blood on to the bandage. A detective would have seen at a glance that it was the same blood.

'My God,' said Archibald coldly.

Well, who could work after that? And then, to spoil the morning completely, came the telephone call.

'Is that Mr. Archibald Fenton's house?'

'Yes.'

'Can I speak to Mr. Fenton?'

'Speaking.'

'Oh.' Silence. A dimly heard whispering. Then: 'Will you be in about four o'clock this afternoon, Mr. Fenton?'

'I expect so. Why?'

'That's all, thanks.'

'Who is it?'

No answer. End of telephone call. Who? Why?

II

Mrs. Pridgeon came in, said 'Oh, he's working,' went out, knocked and came in again.

'Yes?'

'There's a lady come to see you. Calls herself Miss Fairbrother. What shall I do with her? I've got her in the hall.'

'Miss Fairbrother?' repeated Archibald, surprised.

'Sounded like. Shall I ask her again?'

'No, that's right, it's my secretary. Show her in.'

Mrs. Pridgeon came out to Nancy, said 'In there' with a jerk of the head and returned to the kitchen. Nancy went in and found the author hard at it.

'Hallo, Miss Fairbrother,' said Archibald's back, 'sit down, I shan't be a moment.' He wrote 'CHAPTER FIVE' slowly and thoughtfully, underlined it twice, and turned to her.

'Oh, good afternoon, Mr. Fenton. I just—Oh, good gracious, have you hurt yourself?'

'What? Oh! Oh no, it's nothing.'

'But, Mr. Fenton!'

'It's nothing, really. I very stupidly got knocked down by a car—'

'Oh, but how awful!'

'Well, it was my own fault really. I—er—

Various romantic ways of being knocked down by a car offered themselves in rehearsal for Sunday, but were firmly rejected. One mustn't get carried away.

'I believe', said Nancy, looking at him with awe, 'you were saving somebody's life!'

Of course if the girl insisted—'Well, hardly that,' he said with a shrug. 'Even if I hadn't been there, I don't suppose—Well, never mind that. What are *you* doing in this part of the world? I thought I told you to take a holiday?' He smiled genially, paternally.

'Well, I am, you see, only I'm in Tunbridge Wells, you see, so I thought I'd come over in the 'bus to see if you wanted anything, and take back any letters you had for me.'

'Well, that's very charming of you. As it happens, there *was* something—I'd made a special note in my mind—What was it? Oh, yes—what's a bollard?'

'A what?'

'A bollard.'

'Isn't it something you do to a tree?'

'No,' said Archibald, 'it isn't anything you do to a tree.'

'Oh, *bollard*!' said Nancy. 'How silly of me! Weren't they followers of Wyclif?'

Archibald said that the ones he meant weren't so much followers of Wyclif as things you hitched a rope to on a pier, and what he really wanted to know was whether they were also things you hitched a rope to on a liner, and if so, whether you could lean against them. Miss Fairbrother, frowning to herself a good deal, said she was almost certain you could.

'Yes, you're not really being very helpful about bollards, Miss Fairbrother.'

'I'm sorry, Mr. Fenton, I'm afraid my brain all seems to go when I get away from London. I'll find out for you, of course.'

'That's very kind of you.'

'Oh, Mr. Fenton, I wanted to say how very kind it was of *you*—about the watch, I mean. It *was* kind—and *such* a lot. I don't know *what* Joyce will say.'

'Oh, you got that all right? Good. Joyce does understand that I sold it, not pawned it? Probably', said Archibald, 'it's in somebody else's possession by now. A good watch like that soon gets snapped up.'

'Oh, that's quite all right, thank you. Oh, there's one thing I meant to ask you. Did you do anything before you left London about having *The Times* sent on to you? Or shall I write to have it stopped while you're away? I thought perhaps if you didn't get any papers down here, you might like—'

'Yes.' Archibald considered. 'You might do that. Write to the newsagent and tell them to send it here until further instructions. Oh, by the way, you didn't telephone to me this morning? Asking if I'd be in this afternoon?'

'No,' said Nancy, wondering.

'I had a mysterious message. Probably some reporter or other—'

'Somebody wanting to know about the new book.'

'Yes. Look here, you'd better stand by. I may want to turn him on to you, if—'

'Quite, Mr. Fenton,' said Nancy sedately, the complete secretary again. Miss Fairbrother, obviously, was the right person to be enthusiastic about the new book.

'Good.' He got up. 'You've never seen Ferries, have you? Come and have a look at it.'

They went out and had a look at it. Nancy, not on duty for the moment, was a charming little thing. He liked showing her Ferries.

III

It was not a reporter.

At five minutes to four Mr. Fenton returned to the house, leaving Miss Fairbrother in the garden. 'This fellow will be here in a moment,' he said. 'I'll send for you if I want you. And then we'll have tea.'

'Oh, but I—' What about Derek and Jenny, wondered Nancy. He would hardly want to give them tea too, with that ridiculous bandage round his head.

'That's all right,' said Archibald, and was gone ... Five minutes later Inspector Marigold arrived.

'Two gentlemen to see you,' announced Mrs. Pridgeon. 'Says they've rung up and it's very important. Here you are.'

Here they were. Reporters? Reporters didn't come in couples, as a rule. Still, one couldn't afford to take risks. Archibald rose courteously, motioned them with an old-world gesture to a sofa, and asked what he could do for them.

The visitors remained standing. Inspector Marigold glanced swiftly round the room with the air of one whom nothing escapes. If Jenny had been there, he would probably have seen her; but she wasn't. However, he noticed that Mr. Fenton was wearing a bandage round his head. Suspicious.

'Yes?' said Archibald.

'Mr. Archibald Fenton, the author?'

'Yes,' said the author modestly.

The Inspector handed over his card. Sergeant Bagshaw looked stolidly out of the window. His Hyde Park days were over, and the two pigeons on the stable roof who were rendering themselves liable to summary arrest roused no emotion in him ...

Definitely not reporters.

'Well,' said Archibald, with a note of reserve in his voice, 'and what can I do for you, Inspector?'

'You've had an accident, sir,' said Marigold, deducing from the bandage that this must be so.

'Well?'

'May I ask how it happened?'

'No,' said Archibald, 'you mayn't.'

'You don't wish to make a statement on the subject?'

'No,' said Archibald, very naturally, 'I don't.'

'Ah!' said the Inspector. His suspicions were now certainties. Evidently there had been more of a struggle at Auburn Lodge than he had supposed. He looked across at the Sergeant, who brought out his notebook, and thumbed over the pages.

'But I will tell you this, Inspector. I'm a very busy man.' To indicate the nature and volume of his business Archibald gave a meaningful glance at the words 'CHAPTER FIVE' on his desk, and added kindly: 'If you are collecting for the Police Orphanage, my secretary will attend to it.'

'No,' said Marigold, with all the sarcasm he could get into his voice, but he was not very good at it, 'we are *not* collecting for the Police Orphanage.'

'Then', said Archibald, 'what *are* you collecting for?'

He was beginning to enjoy this. After all, he was Archibald Fenton. He knew the Home Secretary, the Public Prosecutor, the Editor of the *Sunday Sentinel*, three Judges of the High Court, five Police Court magistrates and, as it seemed to him sometimes at the Club, the whole of the Bar. He met them frequently. He had also met, but not so frequently, one of the Princes. An ordinary man, faced suddenly with an Inspector who was *not* collecting for the Police Orphanage, would have been vaguely apprehensive, wondering if he had run over some silent old lady at the crossroads last week, or left the bath-tap running. Even if his conscience was clear on these and all other matters, he would still wonder if they had found out about his Income Tax. But Archibald Fenton was not an ordinary man. He was *the* Archibald Fenton, whom only reviewers frightened. Inspector Marigold meant nothing to him. He was much more concerned with Sergeant Bagshaw, who, from the way he was licking his pencil, looked as if he might be the Literary Critic of the *Police Gazette*.

'I am not', said Marigold with extraordinary dignity, 'collecting for *any* charity.'

'Then why', asked Archibald reproachfully, 'are we talking about them?'

The Inspector had no idea. All this came, he felt, from being mixed up with literary people. He decided to get down to what he thought of as brass tacks.

'Have you ever seen *this* before?' he said.

Archibald took Jenny's watch from him, and stared at it.

'Where did you get this?' he asked sharply.

'Never mind that, sir, I'm asking you have you seen it before?'

'Never mind that,' said Archibald, 'I'm asking you where did you get it?'

The Inspector wanted to say 'I asked you first,' but thought it would be undignified.

'That watch', he said, 'was handed to me this morning by Miss Julia Treherne, who informed me that you had sent it to her.'

It is annoying to send a birthday present to a lady, and find that she has immediately handed it to a rival in the police force. Archibald was annoyed.

'If Miss Treherne says I gave it to her, I did.'

'Ah! You notice that there is a "J" on it in diamonds?'

'As I put it there, naturally I notice it.'

'You put it there?'

'Had it put.'

'And what, may I ask, does "J" stand for?'

'It was meant to stand for Julia. Apparently Miss Treherne thought it stood for James.'

'Would it surprise you to hear that "J" stands for Jenny?'

'Not at all. It could stand for almost anything beginning with J.'

'And that this is Jenny's watch?'

'I gathered that it was yours.'

'That it has been identified as Jenny's?'

'Indeed? And who is Jenny?'

It was the question which the whole of England had been asking two days ago, but now it seemed to the Inspector an unnecessary one. 'Jenny Windell, of course,' he said sharply.

'And who is Jenny Windell?'

'Come, come, Mr. Fenton, don't play with me.'

'My dear Inspector, do we look as if we were playing to-gether? I appeal to your literary friend. Am I', he said to Sergeant Bagshaw, 'playing with the Inspector? And if so, what? On the contrary, I am trying to work, and being continually interrupted.' He turned to his manuscript and drew another line under CHAPTER FIVE.

'Now I warn you, Mr. Fenton. This will only get you into trouble.'

Archibald Fenton gave a sigh of exasperation.

'Can you begin from the very beginning and tell me what you're talking about? All we have arrived at so far is this: You deny that you are collecting for the Police Orphanage Bazaar, and yet you tell me that Miss Treherne has just given you a diamond-studded watch for it. As one man of letters to another,' he said, turning to Sergeant Bagshaw, 'I ask you, does not this call for explanation?'

The Inspector knew what it called for, and what in any other country it would get. Denied the natural expression of a policeman's feelings, he said in a cold official voice:

'On the 29th *ult*. the woman Jane Latour was found murdered in the drawing-room of Auburn Lodge. Incontro-vertible evidence proves that her niece Jenny Windell was present at the scene of the crime. This young woman has since completely disappeared. On the 30th *ult*. a watch belonging to the said Jenny Windell is pawned, and subsequently re-purchased, by a man giving the assumed name of William Makepeace Thackeray, and answering to your own description. On the 1st *inst*. this watch is sent to Miss Julia Treherne, admittedly by yourself. I am now asking you if you wish to give any explanation of these facts.'

Archibald's immediate explanation was an amazed 'Good lord!'

So that was what it was all about! He had seen the papers on the Wednesday before he came away, and knew that the Latour

235

had been found dead. He remembered now that there had been some talk of a Jenny who was missing. And it was his secretary, Nancy Fairbrother, now sunning herself in his rose-garden, who had given him the missing Jenny's watch, with an entirely made-up tale of a little sister Joyce! Good lord!

'Well,' said Mr. Fenton ...

'It was really like this,' said Mr. Fenton ...

'What actually happened—'

'Don't be in a hurry, sir,' said Marigold. 'And', he added kindly, 'if you like to explain at the same time how you hurt your head, then we shall know *all* about it.'

Mr. Fenton was not an Old Felsbridgian; and though, as a boy, he had passed through Eton on a bicycle, he was not, strictly speaking, an Old Etonian. But he had been at Harrow for a few terms, and even if the school motto, *Stet fortuna domus*, had never been a real inspiration in his life, he did realize that there were some things which no decent man could do. He could not give away a charming little thing who was just going to have tea with him.

'Are you seriously suspecting me of murdering Jane Latour?' he asked, with as careless a laugh as he could manage.

'That I shall know, sir, when I have heard your explanation.'

'Well, I'm not sure that you're going to get one.'

'It's only fair to warn you, Mr. Fenton, that there is a great deal of evidence pointing in your direction already, and that your refusal to give a reasonable explanation—'

'You mean you're going to arrest me?'

'Well, sir, as things are, you're practically asking for it?'

'Got the handcuffs?' sneered Archibald.

An accidental clink came from the direction of Sergeant Bagshaw, as he put his notebook back in his pocket. The Sergeant gazed stolidly out of the window at the pigeons. Still at it.

Archibald thought quickly. He did not tell himself that an innocent man could not be hanged in England, because he had every reason to believe that he could; but he did tell himself that an innocent Archibald Fenton, who knew the Editor of the *Sunday Sentinel*, the Home Secretary, the Public Prosecutor, three Judges, five Police Court magistrates and practically the whole of the Bar could not possibly be hanged. He also told himself that his new novel was coming out next Tuesday ...

After all, one must do something for one's new novel. In the old days he had given it a cocktail party, to which had been invited such literary friends of his as might conceivably review it, together with such fashionable acquaintance of his as might conceivably make the invitation attractive. Himself and the latest Lovely had held the book rigidly between them, in the manner of two members of a jury taking the oath, and the press photographer, who had accidentally found himself there, nobody quite knew how, had said: 'Now keep it cheerful, Mr. Fender, we don't write a new book *every* day,' and, Mr. Fender keeping it cheerful, the *maître d'hôtel* of the moment had christened it (to use again that strangely inappropriate word) with a gin and vermouth, most of which was trickling up Mr. Fenton's (or Fender's) sleeve as the camera clicked. Archibald had liked these parties, for he felt that some such spontaneous expression of gaiety was natural on these occasions. But now the thing was becoming ridiculous. The dignity of letters was in danger when authors of whom one had never heard gave christening parties for books of which one never wanted to hear, and got more publicity in the illustrated papers than one did oneself, simply because they had scraped acquaintance with still more members of the peerage.

So there was to be no party for the new book; no fuss; simply the bare announcement in the papers: 'Mr. Fenton was much the least concerned man in London yesterday when his long anticipated new novel was at last published. I found him sitting quietly in his library, reading the *Odes* of Horace ...' and so on, with, of course, a photograph of Mr. Fenton doing this. Perhaps now it would be 'walking in his garden at Ferries, his country seat in the heart of the Hop district, and apparently much more concerned over the shaping of a new rose-bed than over the sensational success of his new book'. That was all. Unless …

Arrested for murder!

What an advertisement!

'Well,' said Inspector Marigold, 'are we going to have that explanation, or aren't we?'

'No,' said Archibald firmly. 'I shall say nothing until I have seen my solicitors.'

With an air of great dignity he put his wrists together, and held them out to Sergeant Bagshaw. The clinking noise this time was louder.

Chapter Nineteen

Six meet at Ferries

I

As they drove back to Ferries in Archibald's car Jenny was singing. From time to time Derek's hand left the wheel and found hers, and said to hers 'I love you, I love you, I love you', and went back to the wheel again; because this was a strange car, and the one terrifying thought in the world now was that there might be an accident in which Jenny, just found, was lost to him. But Jenny thought of nothing. She was enfolded in a dream of happiness, and hardly knew that she was singing.

'There's Nancy,' said Derek. 'May I have my hand, darling? I want to stop.'

Nancy was waiting for them outside the gates. She came up to the car eagerly.

'I say! The police are here!'

'Good lord! Have you seen them?'

'Saw them come. I talked to your brother. He didn't know anything about anything. All quite innocent. Then we went round the garden and did the Ruth Draper business, and somebody telephoned to say they would be there at four, so he went in so as to be ready for them, and I spied round the bushes and it was the police.'

'D'you hear that, Jenny?'

'Did I?' said Jenny vaguely.

'How long ago was this?'

'About ten minutes ago. He's probably just being arrested, and clapping a white tablet to his mouth, and the Inspector is leaping forward and saying "Not that way, sir," and Mr. Fenton is saying "You fool, it's a soda-mint," because he always carries them about with him, and—'

'Quite so. Hadn't you better get in?'

'I'm all right here,' said Nancy, standing on the running-board. 'Hallo, darling.'

Jenny smiled vaguely and went on singing.

'I don't mind telling you,' said Derek, 'that just at the moment I'm not afraid of twenty policemen.'

'Actually there are two.'

'Good, then I'm eighteen in hand. Now we'll just go in as if we were paying an ordinary call, and see what the position is. We shall have to do a whole lot of explaining some time or other, but don't let's be in a hurry. The great thing is to see how the conversation goes, and come in at the right moment.'

They came in at the right moment. The arrest had just been effected. This was how the conversation went.

'Hallo!'

'My God, you again!'

'Excuse me, sir; excuse me, ladies. Now then, sir, if you're ready.' Inspector Marigold's party, Archibald in the middle, began to move towards the door.

'Are you being arrested, Hippo?'

'I'm afraid, sir, I cannot allow any conversation with the prisoner—'

'Oh come, if an intelligent man sees his only brother knocked on the head and hauled off in chains by two obvious policemen, the least he can do is to say "Are you being arrested?" Anything less would be—'

'I cannot allow that statement to pass, sir.'

'Which one?'

'That the prisoner has been knocked on the head by the police. The prisoner himself will tell you—'

Sergeant Bagshaw hurriedly got his notebook out again, in case the prisoner made a statement.

'What the devil are you doing here anyhow?' said the prisoner.

'Brought your car back. And now that we're all together—'

'Now then, sir, *if* you please.'

'Look here, you can't seriously mean to arrest Archibald Fenton? Not old Hippo?'

'*Alias* Hippo,' wrote Sergeant Bagshaw in his notebook.

'I should advise you, sir, not to interfere with the police in the execution of their duty.'

'But he's absolutely innocent. As innocent as a—'

'New-born babe,' prompted Nancy.

'As innocent as a—well, as a matter of fact I was going to say a "babe unborn". I don't know that there's much in it.'

'Babe unborn,' said Nancy. 'Much better. Sorry.'

'Thank you. As innocent, Inspector, as a babe unborn. And you know how innocent *they* are. I tell you, the whole thing's ridiculous.'

'Oh, shut up!' commanded Archibald, seeing his advertisement slipping away from him.

'Indeed, sir? And may I ask of *what* he is so innocent?'

'Yes,' admitted Derek thoughtfully, 'that's a nasty one.'

'And how you know what he's being charged with?'

'Don't rub it in. I see your point.'

'The fact is,' said Nancy, 'I happen to— Ow!'

'Look at it this way, Inspector,' said Derek, removing a warning heel from Nancy's instep. 'I don't know if you have any brothers—or you, sir,' he added courteously to Bagshaw—'but if you have, you will realize the impossibility to a brother of—'

'Yes,' said Inspector Marigold, curling his moustache at the three of them, 'I think perhaps I *should* like to know a little more about you all. Sit down, please, ladies.' He turned to Archibald. 'If you would like to sit down, sir—'

'Mayn't he take his cuffs off?'

'Certainly not,' said Archibald with dignity. 'It would be most irregular.'

'Now, sir.'

'May I sit down too?' asked Derek, and, taking the Inspector's permission for granted, sat down on the sofa between Jenny and Nancy.

'Name, please?'

'Derek Peabody Fenton.'

'Peabody?' said Nancy, surprised.

'Yes. Why not?'

'Oh, I don't know.'

'Profession?'

'What's the matter with Peabody?'

'Oh, nothing. It just seemed rather funny.'

'Profession?'

'Well, it's really more of a business. I'm in the wine-trade.'

Nancy's quick look behind his back at Jenny said 'Oh, is that what he is?' and Jenny's answering look made it clear that he had nothing to do with the bottles but only with the grapes. 'More a gentleman-fruit-farmer, sort of,' said Jenny proudly, and Nancy allowed that that made all the difference and that, when you were as nice as Derek, it really wouldn't have mattered if you were the man who licked the labels.

'And you, madam?'

'Nancy Slade Fairbrother.'

'Slade?' said Derek, surprised.

'Yes. Why not?'

'Oh, I don't know.'

'Married or single?'

'What's the matter with Slade?'

'Oh, nothing. It just seemed rather funny.'

'Married or single?'

'Single.'

'Any occupation?'

'Secretary to Mr. Archibald Fenton, the author.'

'Ah!' said the Inspector meaningly. Now the whole case was getting linked up.

'Mr. Fenton and I', explained Nancy, unlinking it, 'were together in his house at Bloomsbury throughout the whole of Tuesday morning. He was dictating to me Chapter Four of his new novel *Parallel.*'

'One "r", two "l's",' said Derek behind his hand to Sergeant Bagshaw.

'Three,' said Nancy.

'Three,' corrected Derek. 'A little one at the end.'

'You can make a statement later if you wish, Miss Fairbrother,' said the Inspector coldly. 'Now, madam. You?'

'Jane Windell.'

'Married or single?'

'Single.'

'But about to be married,' explained Derek.

'Jenny!' cried Nancy. 'Darling! *Really*, darling?'

Jenny nodded happily.

'Oh, Derek!' cried Nancy.

'I know, isn't it marvellous?'

'Oh, I *am* glad. When did you—'

'Please, *please!*' said Inspector Marigold.

'Really,' said Archibald, disgusted to find himself no longer in the foreground, 'this is almost too crude.'

'Sir!' implored the Sergeant in a loud aside.

'Occupation, if any?'

'Inspector, how can you ask,' said Derek reproachfully, 'when I've just told you we're engaged?'

'Sir!'

'Well, well, what is it?'

'Windell! Jane Windell! *Jenny* Windell!'

'*What?*'

'I say, look here,' said Archibald, 'we can't have this sort of thing.'

'Are you Jenny Windell?'

'Yes.'

'Ah!' The Inspector drew a deep breath. Unaided he had tracked her down.

'Really,' said Archibald, 'these hysterical females will call themselves anything. Psychoanalysts—'

'Just a moment, sir. Now then, Miss Windell. Carry your mind back to the morning of the 29th *ult.*'

'He means where were you on Tuesday, darling.'

'Were you in the company of the prisoner—'

'No,' said Archibald.

'I have already told you that Mr. Archibald Fenton was with *me*,' said Nancy. 'Dictating the fourth chapter of his new novel *Parallel.*'

'One "r" and *three* "l's",' whispered Derek to Sergeant Bagshaw. 'We got that wrong last time.'

'Never mind that,' said Archibald, feeling that it was time he asserted himself. 'Never mind where I *was*; the point is, where am I now? I have been arrested at a very inconvenient moment when my new book *Waterfall* is just coming out. I have—'

'*Waterfall?*' said Sergeant Bagshaw, scratching his head. 'I've got it down *Parallel.*'

'Oh, my dear Sergeant,' said Archibald, clinking his handcuffs irritably, 'do use your intelligence. My new novel which is being published on Tuesday at eight-and-sixpence is called *Waterfall*. The one which I am now writing, and shall not finish until next year—'

'Now please, please, *please!*' implored the Inspector. 'Let us get things in order. Miss Windell, I am asking you—'

'All I am saying is that, having been arrested in this summary manner, I naturally wish to get in touch with my solicitors. Sitting here and listening to the life-story of a young woman who may or may not be Jenny Windell, who I have very grave— *whom* I have very grave reasons to suspect of not being Jenny Windell, of, in fact, going about the country—'

'Come to think of it,' said Marigold thoughtfully, 'you aren't much like the photographs in the papers, miss.'

'How right you are, Inspector,' said Derek. 'But then, how rarely photographs in the papers do one complete justice. Now take your own case. I pictured you—it is the famous Inspector Marigold, isn't it?'

The Inspector curled his moustache, and inclined his head.

'Exactly. But who would have known from those photographs of you that the handsomest man in the police-force—'

'*Have* I been arrested, or have I not?' shouted Archibald. 'That's all I want to know. If I have, then my natural desire to get in touch with my solicitors—'

'Shall I ring them up, Mr. Fenton?' said Nancy.

'No. Ring up the Home Secretary. He'll be at the Club. He always goes there for tea. Tell him that Mr. Archibald Fenton—'

'Well, Mr. Fenton,' said Marigold hastily, 'I did ask you to explain about the watch. Even now, if you care to give me an explanation, I shall be only too glad—'

'Jenny's watch? Why, of course, *I* gave him that.'

'*You*, miss? What did you say your name was?'

'Nancy Fairbrother. I—'

'Nancy *Slade* Fairbrother,' corrected Derek. 'Do let us stick to the facts.'

'I gave it to her,' said Jenny, 'so as she could sell it.'

'And Mr. Fenton very kindly offered to sell it for me. And—'

'Is that right, sir?'

'I have already told you', said Archibald with dignity, 'that I have nothing to say until I have seen my solicitors. Hardcastle and Hardcastle. In any case I have no intention of sheltering myself behind these two ladies. As it is, I ask myself what the police-force of this country is coming to. In America an arrest like this would have been conducted with a simple formal dignity. Having been photographed in his handcuffs for the principal daily papers, the accused would have made a short statement for publication—'

'Haven't you got a camera here, Hippo? We'll take one now.'

'No, no, sir, I can't allow that.'

'Indeed?' said Archibald coldly. 'Are you presuming to tell my brother which of the family he may photograph? There's a camera on the shelf over there, Miss Fairbrother. If you wouldn't mind getting it—'

'Here, give me that key,' demanded Inspector Marigold of the Sergeant. The Sergeant gave it to him.

'What are you going to do? Go away! No, look here, you mustn't do that!'

'No violence, please. There!' The handcuffs came off.

'That', said Archibald bitterly, feeling in his pocket for his cigarette-case, 'constitutes an assault.'

'Forcibly depriving a gentleman of his cuffs,' nodded Derek.

'You cannot have it both ways. You cannot go on handcuffing and unhandcuffing a man just at the whim of the moment. If I was legally arrested before, then I have now been illegally de-arrested. If on the other hand—take a note of this, Miss Fairbrother—if on the other hand—'

'Which hand would that be, Mr. Fenton?'

'If I was legally de-arrested, then it follows—'

'Sir, sir!'

'What is it now, Bagshaw?'

'He's lighting his cigarette with the left hand!'

The Inspector gazed, open-mouthed.

'If', said Archibald, blowing out the match, 'I was legally—'

Legally or illegally Mr. Archibald Fenton was then arrested again.

II

Jenny was in the living-room with Nancy, telling her all about it; Archibald was in the rose-garden with Sergeant Bagshaw, taking exercise; Derek was in the dining-room with Inspector Marigold, giving him a drink.

'This is very charming of you, Inspector,' said Derek. 'Say when. Oh, come, it's a warm day. Soda or plain? Quite right, we mustn't spoil the colour. Well, now—'

'Your health, sir.'

'Thank you, Inspector, that's very—'

'Course you do see, sir, I got my duty to do.'

'Absolutely. Have another.'

'Well, sir—That's enough, sir, thank you.'

'What? Oh, sorry.'

'P'raps I was a bit hasty that second time—Your health again, sir.'

'That's very kind of you. I think I'll join you.'

'That's the way, sir. No, no more for me—oh, well, thank you, sir.'

'Your very good health, Inspector.'

'Thank you, sir. What I was saying. Short, stout, left-handed man of sedentary occupation. Now, sir, is that your brother, or isn't it? I ask you, man to man.'

'Undoubtedly. How does this whisky strike you? It's pre-war.'

'First-rate, sir. Capital. What I was—'

'Just a spot more.'

'What I was saying. Dr. Willoughby Hatch's diagnosis of the murderer is of a short, stout, left-handed man of sedentary occupation. No, sir, you shouldn't have done that.'

'Between ourselves, Inspector, I always regard a really good whisky like this as more medicinal than anything else.'

'Well, sir, there *is* that to it. What I was saying. Dr. Hatch tells me I'm looking for a short sedentary feller of stout occupation. And that's the man I see. But is he left-handed? Who knows? And then, right in front of my nose, as cool as brass, out comes his match-box, and—well, p'raps I lost my head a little. Who wouldn't?'

'Who indeed?'

'Mind you, I don't say I've made up my mind, but what I do say is I can't afford to take risks. That's why I'm listening to you now in this informal way, because I can see you're a gentleman who understands how these things have to be done.'

'That's very gratifying.' Derek looked cautiously round the room, and then said in a lowered voice: 'Quite between ourselves, Inspector, do you believe *everything* which Dr. Hatch tells you?'

'Well, sir, that's one way of putting it. I see what you mean, sir, without going so far as to—Well, let's put it this way. Supposing I didn't believe everything a certain gentleman says? Supposing sometimes I found myself thinking "Ho! And who told *you* I should like to know, Dr. God Almighty Hatch?" Well, I shouldn't say it, that's all. Not even to you, sir. Your very good health, Mr. Fenton.'

'You know,' said Derek, absent-mindedly tilting the bottle, 'I sometimes feel that if Dr. Hatch said that a short, stout, left-handed man had committed a murder, the really sensible thing to do would be to look for a tall, thin, right-handed man who had committed suicide.'

'Ha-ha-ha! That's good, sir. That's very good. Witty. Your health, sir. I see what you mean, and I know you understand my position, sir. And you understand what I mean when I just put it like that. Witty. Well, p'raps I will, sir, it's thirsty work, keeping a guard on yourself so as you don't say more than you ought to.'

'Exactly. Well now, Inspector, I want to tell you just what happened at Auburn Lodge which a certain medical friend of ours didn't happen to notice.'

'That's good, sir, I like that way of putting it.'

'It's a story which Miss Jenny Windell—a charming girl, Inspector?'

'Very natty. Her health, sir. Well, just up to the—thank you, sir.'

'As you know, Miss Windell was born and brought up at Auburn Lodge, and all those happy childhood memories which mean so much to us, and have such an influence on our lives—'

'That's right, sir. I remember a buck-rabbit I had in nineteen-owe-one—'

'All her happy memories were bound up in this house, Auburn Lodge, now let furnished to these strangers to her, the Parracots.'

'That's right, sir. Handsome woman, Mrs. Parracot. Nineteen-owe-two it would be.'

'Miss Windell had in her possession—after all, it was her house—a latch-key to Auburn Lodge, and last Tuesday morning she had a sudden urgent desire to re-visit, just for a brief moment, the home of her youth. We can understand that, can't we, Marigold? We don't blame her, Marigold?'

'We don't, sir. Very natural. I remember this buck-rabbit o' mine—'

'After all, what harm in it? She knew that the Parracots were away, that the house was standing empty. It may be—she hasn't actually told me this yet—but it may be that she wished to look again upon some of the photographs of her family, standing in silver frames upon the grand piano, which meant so little to these strangers, the Parracots, and so much to her. That I think,

Marigold, would be a natural, almost a laudable wish? A pretty thought, Marigold?'

'Very laudable, Mr. Fenton. Very pretty. And borne out by the facts of the case. I made a particular note of those photos. All solid silver. A fine show.'

'And then, in the drawing-room of Auburn Lodge, she finds the dead body of her aunt.'

'Is that so, sir? *Found* her there. Dr. Hatch said—Quite so, sir.' The Inspector chuckled, watched his glass being re-filled, and gave the toast: 'Dr. God Almighty Hatch!'

'Apparently Miss Latour had slipped on the polished boards—'

'Well, they certainly were that, sir. I nearly—'

'—and struck her head against a curious brass ornament.'

The Inspector struggled out of his glass.

'Is this Miss Windell's story, sir?'

'Yes.'

'Well, sir, I'm bound to tell you—'

'Wait a moment, my dear Marigold. Without thinking what she was doing, Miss Windell picked up this brass ornament, wiped it, and restored it to its place upon the grand piano.'

'Stop there, sir,' said Marigold, holding up his hand. He closed his eyes. Derek watched him anxiously, wondering if he had decided to go to sleep, and appalled at the thought of having to begin all over again, when, and if, he woke up.

'A piece of brass,' said the Inspector slowly, still with his eyes shut, 'representing as it might be the effigy of a castle. Am I right, sir?' He opened his eyes, and waited expectantly.

'Are you right?' cried Derek. 'My dear Marigold, you're a marvel. Nothing escapes you. You must have another.'

'No, no, sir.'

'Yes, yes, I insist.'

'Well, sir, if you—thank you. Your health, sir, *and* the lady's. Yes, I remember that castle. In brass it was. Ornamental.'

'Conway Castle.'

'Is that so, sir? Well, I didn't notice that. But I'll tell you what I did think was funny, Mr. Fenton.'

'What was that, Inspector?'

'Why, being on the piano at all. Because, rightly speaking, it was what they call a door-stop, what people use to keep doors open with when serving food and coming in and out.'

'Marigold,' said Derek, gazing at him with awe, 'this is almost unbelievable. This must be celebrated. I know! You must have a drink with me.'

'I couldn't do that, sir. I never as you might say drink, not to say drink, at this time of day. Not till after supper's always been my rule.'

'I don't care. You must break your rule for once.'

'Well, thank you, sir. That's enough, sir. Thank you.'

'You've solved the problem, Marigold.'

'Is that so, sir?'

'You see how the pieces of the jig-saw fit themselves together?'

'Your very good health, sir. And the lady's.'

'Thank you, Marigold. You are a good man.'

'What you were saying, sir, about the pieces of the jig-saw—'

'Exactly. The Parracots, knowing this ornament for what it was, a door-stop, kept it on the floor. Miss Windell, whose childish memories are of a castle, instinctively picks it up, and puts it back on the piano where she had always seen it. Isn't that what happened?'

'Looks uncommonly like it, sir. Yes, that's about how I should figure it out. All the same, sir, you know as well as I do that she had no business to touch it.'

'Absolutely right, Marigold. But—a young girl like that, a—what was it you called her?—a charming young girl like that—'

'That's right, sir, very natty.'

'You and I are experienced men of the world—'

'Well, sir, we're certainly—'

'You're younger than I am, of course—'

'Well, I wouldn't say that, sir.'

'Nonsense, you're not a day more than thirty.'

The Inspector curled his moustaches and said: 'What would you say if I told you that I shouldn't see forty again?'

'You don't mean that?'

'It's true, sir.'

'Then you must have another drink. I haven't liked to press you before, but if you say you're forty, then you're just at the age when one really begins to want it. How's that?'

'Thank you, sir, that's plenty.'

'Well now, you know women, Marigold. It isn't many that do, but—'

'Well, sir,' said Marigold complacently, 'I won't say—'

'And the first thing you'll tell me, as a man of real experience, is that women are impulsive. Aren't I right?'

'That you are, sir.'

'Then do you blame Miss Windell that she acted on a sudden feminine impulse? I don't like these manly women, Marigold.'

'No more do I, Mr. Fenton. A man's a man and a woman's a woman, just as God made them. This buck-rabbit o' mine—'

'Do you blame her that, hearing the Parracots arriving and knowing that she had no business to be there, she fled? Do you blame her that she wandered about the country in a dazed manner for two days before I found her? Do you blame her that, when at last she realized what had happened, she decided to come to my brother for advice, knowing that he was an intimate friend of the Home Secretary, the Public Prosecutor *and* the Chief Commissioner of Scotland Yard?'

'Is that so, sir?' said the Inspector thoughtfully.

'You do blame her, Marigold? Well, perhaps you are right. Dr. Willoughby Hatch would certainly blame her. Your Sergeant, excellent man as he is, but, if I am any judge, entirely ignorant of women and wholly lacking in imagination, your Sergeant would blame her.'

'Bagshaw's a fool, sir.'

'Hallo, there's still some in the bottle. Just a spot more——'

'Well, I oughtn't to really, sir—— Thank you. Your brother seems to know a good many people, Mr. Fenton.'

'Archie? But, good lord, everybody knows Archie Fenton. I tell you, Marigold, we're in the wrong job. These popular novelists——'

'Course it's easy to me now to see how the whole thing happened.'

'As soon as you put your finger on that point about the doorstop, you'd got it. Very quick that, Marigold. Very subtle.'

'Course I shall have to ask the ladies a question or two. Just for corroboration.'

'Of course. I say, we haven't quite finished it, after all.' He turned the bottle upside-down.

'Thank you, sir. I shan't worry them, Mr. Fenton.'

'That's very nice of you, Inspector. I was sure of it.'

'Well—good health, sir.'

'Good luck.'

Inspector Marigold wrung out his moustache, curled it back into shape, and marched to the door. Derek looked at the empty bottle, and then at the open door through which the Inspector was walking so straightly. The echoes of a perfectly articulated 'corroboration' were still ringing in his ears. Once again he marvelled at the efficiency of the London Police Force.

Chapter Twenty

Hussar says Good-bye

IT was naturally a disappointment to Archibald to learn that he was a free man again; but he agreed, gracefully enough, that he could not insist on being charged with a murder at which he had not been present, and which, in fact, had not been committed. Indeed, he became quite genial, and suggested that the police officers should have a drink before leaving for London.

'It's very kind of you, sir,' said the Inspector firmly, 'but it's against orders to drink while on duty. I won't say but what if Sergeant Bagshaw was to slip off to the kitchen for a glass of beer while I was looking the other way—no, thank you, sir, nothing for me.'

So Sergeant Bagshaw slipped gratefully off, and Archibald Fenton, much touched by the Inspector's sense of duty, and no less by the humanity which softened it, wondered if he would care to be photographed under the Elizabethan window, which was a feature of some historic interest. Whereupon Mr. Fenton and Inspector Marigold were so photographed; and, some days later, when it transpired that it was not generally known that the clearing up of what had been termed the Auburn Lodge Mystery was in large measure due to the activities of the famous author of *A Flock of Sheep*, whose new book *Waterfall* was so much in demand, and who had taken an active interest in what had at first promised to be a sensational case—when all this came out, it was discovered that, by a happy accident, a photograph of Inspector Marigold and Mr. Fenton in consultation at the latter's country seat, Ferries, was available for publication. Which was very gratifying to all concerned.

By and by Sergeant Bagshaw came round the corner drying his moustache, and the Police climbed into its car and drove off. 'This', thought Marigold, 'will make a sensation in the papers to-morrow, and be one in the eye for G. A. Hatch.' But it was not so. For at that very moment Miss Innocent Home (*née* Winkelstein), the famous film star, was stepping down the gangway and calling over her shoulder to her manager: 'Say, what's this darned burg anyway?' and her manager, who had previously assured her that it was *not* London, was now explaining that it was actually called Southampton. But in a little while she would be in London; and in readiness for her the route from Waterloo to the Carlton Hotel had been sanded, and lined with policemen. And fighting madly for a glimpse of her, were a hundred thousand women who had seen Innocent Home on the screen, but much preferred Ronald Colman, and a hundred thousand women who had never heard of her, but wanted to see what the other women were looking at, and ten thousand men who would otherwise have been distributed among the more exciting street accidents of the moment. Was it any wonder that the Press, with its fingers on the public pulse, should decide that, in comparison with Innocent Home's front page and shouting streamers, Jenny's claim on the attention was now met by six lines among the Bankruptcy notices beneath the modest heading 'Miss Jane Latour'?

And so Derek and Jenny, Archibald and Nancy were left alone at the front door. Then Jenny did a very brave thing. Knowing that this was going to be her brother-in-law, she turned to Archibald and said meekly: 'May I have that kiss now?' So Archibald, looking a little pink, kissed her, and somehow, in the embrace, his bandage fell off, and they all moved casually away and left it there. Really, thought Archibald, she's rather a nice little thing, though I must say I prefer Miss Fairbrother; and just for a moment he wondered whether it mightn't be a good idea to have a double wedding, he marrying Nancy, and Jenny, Derek. Then he remembered that he was married already, and had six children. So, instead, he suggested that they should all stay to tea and dinner, and he would drive Miss Fairbrother back after dinner to her hotel. Derek, who wanted to be alone with Jenny, was a little gloomy about this; but he brightened up when Archibald said that, if they could possibly find something to do, he did rather want to work after tea, and perhaps Miss Fairbrother would be kind enough to take some dictation, as he suddenly felt in the mood. And at dinner Archibald produced a Perrier Jouet 1923, which Nancy recognized at once as a good wine, and healths were drunk.

At last Jenny and Derek drove off together, but not until Derek had told his brother several times that he didn't want a whisky before he went, and Archibald had assured him several times that he had one bottle left of absolutely pre-war if only he could find it. They said loving good-byes to Nancy, and promised her that they would come to see her to-morrow; they interrupted Archibald's monologue in the cellar, and left him at the front door still muttering that it was a damn funny thing about that bottle; they waved once more as they turned the corner … and then they were out on the road together, hand in hand (since it was now Derek's car) with Hope and Inexperience for guides, and the world in front of them.

The night was very still. Jenny lay in bed with her eyes shut, and whispered:

'Hussar?'

'Hallo, Jenny.'

'Darling, I thought of getting married. You don't mind, do you, darling?'

'Well, that's very funny, because I was just thinking what a good idea it would be.'

'Darling, were you really? How lovely of you!'

'Who were you thinking of marrying, Jenny?'

'Well, I was wondering if you could think of anybody?'

'Do you mean a soldier, or something like that?'

'Oh, dear! Oh, *darling!*'

'As a matter of fact, Jenny, I don't think a soldier. Soldiers aren't what they were.'

'Just as you like, darling.'

'I thought more like somebody as it might be in the wine-trade.'

'Oh, Hussar, isn't it funny? I do just happen to know somebody in the wine-trade! Do you think that would be a good idea?'

'I think it would be a lovely idea, Jenny.'

'All right, then, I will. Thank you, darling.'

'Good-bye, Jenny.'

'Good-bye, darling, *darling* Hussar,' said Jenny, knowing that now it was really good-bye.

Then she curled up and went to sleep.

Also Available

In his classic autobiography A. A Milne, with his characteristic self-deprecating humour, recalls a blissfully happy childhood in the company of his brothers, and writes with touching affection about the father he adored.

From Westminster School he won a scholarship to Cambridge University where he edited the university magazine, before going out into the world, determined to be a writer. He was assistant editor at *Punch* and went on to enjoy great success with his novels, plays and stories. And of course he is best remembered for his children's novels and verses featuring Winnie-the-Pooh and Christopher Robin.

This is both an account of how a writer was formed and a charming period piece on literary life - Milne met countless famous authors including H. G. Wells, J.M Barrie and Rudyard Kipling.

OUT NOW

Also available

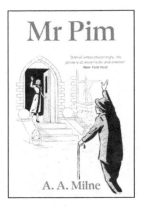

Gentle chaos sets in when the absent-minded Mr Pim calls in to see George Marden, bearing some innocent news...

George is a fine upstanding citizen and a stickler for doing the right thing. He has a devoted wife, Olivia, and is guardian to his somewhat flighty niece, Dinah.But his careful peace is broken when Mr Pim casually announces that he's recently seen an ex-convict from Australia, Telworthy.

The only thing is that the character sounds awfully like Olivia's first, and supposedly deceased, husband... and if he's really still alive, then Olivia is a bigamist.

OUT NOW

Preview

How well can you ever know another person?

Happily married, Reginald and Sylvia seem to lead a perfect, and perfectly quiet, life. They have more than enough money and their own country house. But when success overtakes them, and allure of London life pulls Reginald in, they find parts of themselves they never knew. Where does their happiness really lie?

Reminiscent of Evelyn Waugh, this wry, intimate examination of a relationship is a gem of 1930s literature.

OUT NOW

Preview

Chloe Marr is young, beautiful and so irresistible that countless people fall in love with her, and friends are hypnotized by her charm and warmth. Her origins are a mystery and, in London society, such mystique carries both allure and suspicion.

But when an untimely exodus pulls Chloe from the people around her, they soon realise nobody really knows the truth about anybody else...

A. A. Milne's ability to portray interwar society is second to none, and this classic novel of an elusive Mayfair delivers his signature humour and lightness of touch.

COMING SOON

Preview

A new collection of A. A. Milne's short stories and sketches for grown-ups. Collected in full for the first time, they are an epiphany, and show Milne's renowned charm, concision and whimsical flair in all their brilliance.

He paints memorable scenes, from a children's birthday party, to an accidental encounter with murder, and a case of blackmail – often with an unexpected twist. But he also deals in poignancy, from the girl who pulls the wool over her boyfriend's eyes, to a first dance and first disappointment or family reunion and domestic dissonance.

Beguiling and evocative, Milne's thought-provoking stories will make you see his works for children in a whole new light.

COMING SOON

Preview

The Rabbits, as they call themselves, are Archie Mannering, his sister Myra, Samuel Simpson, Thomas of the Admiralty, Dahlia Blair and the narrator, with occasional guests. Their conversation is almost entirely frivolous, their activity vacillates between immensely energetic and happily lazy, and their social mores are surprisingly progressive.

Originally published as sketches in *Punch*, the Rabbits' escapades are a charming portrait of middle-class antics on the brink of being shattered by World War I, and fail entirely to take themselves seriously.

So here they all are. Whatever their crimes, they assure you that they won't do it again – A. A. Milne

COMING SOON

About the Marvellous Milne Series

The Marvellous Milne series brings back to vivid life several of A.A. Milne's classic works for grownups.

Two collections – *The Complete Short Stories*, gathered together in full for the first time; and *The Rabbits* comic sketches, originally published in *Punch* and considered by many to be his most distinctive work – showcase Milne's talent as a short story writer.

Four carefully selected novels – *Four Days' Wonder*, *Mr Pim*, *Chloe Marr* and *Two People* – demonstrate his skill across comic genres, from the detective spoof to a timeless and gentle comedy of manners, considering everything from society's relationship with individuals, to intimate spousal relationships.

Alongside this showcase of Milne's talent is his classic memoirs *It's Too Late Now*, providing a detailed account of how his writing career was formed, as well as proving a charming period piece of the literary scene at the time.

The full series –
It's Too Late Now
Mr Pim
Two People
Four Days' Wonder
Chloe Marr
The Complete Short Stories
The Rabbits

About the author

A.A. Milne (Alan Alexander) was born in London in 1882 and educated at Westminster School and Trinity College, Cambridge. In 1902 he was Editor of *Granta*, the University magazine, and moved back to London the following year to enter journalism. By 1906 he was Assistant Editor of *Punch*, where he published a series of short stories which now form the collection 'The Rabbits'

At the beginning of the First World War he joined the Royal Warwickshire Regiment. While in the army in 1917 he started on a career writing plays and novels including *Mr. Pim Passes By, Two People, Four Days' Wonder* and an adaptation of Kenneth Grahame's *The Wind in the Willows – Toad of Toad Hall*. He married Dorothy de Selincourt in 1913 and in 1920 had a son, Christopher Robin.

By 1924 Milne was a highly successful playwright, and published the first of his four books for children, a set of poems called *When We Were Very Young*, which he wrote for his son. This was followed by the storybook *Winnie-the-Pooh* in 1926, more poems in *Now We Are Six* (1927) and further stories in *The House at Pooh Corner* (1928).

In addition to his now famous works, Milne wrote many novels, volumes of essays and light verse, works which attracted great success at the time. He continued to be a prolific writer until his death in 1956.

Note from the Publisher

To receive updates on further releases in the Marvellous Milnes series – plus special offers and news of other humorous fiction series to make you smile – sign up now to the Farrago mailing list at farragobooks.com/sign-up